WRONGLY

J. MICHAEL HUNTER

ACCUSED

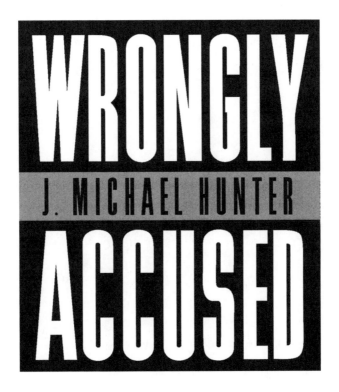

a novel

Covenant Communications, Inc.

Cover image © Digital Vision/Getty Images

Cover design copyrighted 2004 by Covenant Communications, Inc.

Published by Covenant Communications, Inc.
American Fork, Utah

Printed in Canada
First Printing: July 2004

10 09 08 07 06 05 04   10 9 8 7 6 5 4 3 2 1

ISBN 1-59156-493-X

To my wife LeAnn

Acknowledgements

I would like to express my appreciation to Jennifer James Spell, my sister-in-law, whose excellent editorial assistance made this a better story. I would also like to thank Jennifer, along with my wife LeAnn for their encouraging words. I express appreciation to Detective Heather Stringfellow of the Salt Lake City Police Department. Detective Stringfellow reviewed the manuscript for errors in police procedure as it pertained to police work in Salt Lake City. I tried to be as accurate as possible in these matters; any inaccuracies are solely the responsibility of the author who hopes that the reader will understand that this is a work of fiction rather than a documentary.

Finally, I would like to thank the wonderful people at Covenant, especially Catherine Langford for being an excellent editor, and Shauna Humphreys, Covenant's managing editor, for guiding me through this new experience and bringing this whole project together.

CHAPTER 1

Friday, December 12

Brad's roommate, Jess, woke him at 5:55 A.M. They'd overslept. Jess should have been at Salt Lake International no later than 6:00, since his flight to San Francisco was scheduled to leave at 7:00. With both of their alarm clocks flashing zeroes, there was no question that the electricity had gone off at least momentarily in the night.

"I'm going to miss my flight," Jess said as he rushed about the dorm room, trying to dress as he grabbed the last few personal items he needed to take home with him to California. "We shouldn't have stayed out so late last night."

Brad jumped out of bed and grabbed his discarded jeans from the floor. "Don't worry, Jess. You'll make it." He fitted one leg after another into his jeans and pulled them up. "But I don't see what staying out late has to do with our alarm clocks not going off."

"When I go to sleep on time," Jess said, "I wake up on time, with or without my alarm clock."

Brad looked at his cousin Jess through blurry eyes. Even in a rush, Jess managed to look like he had just stepped out of a Nordstrom ad. His blue oxford shirt and tan pants were wrinkle free and his belt matched his brown oxford shoes. Brad never looked that well pressed, even when he spent all morning trying.

As Brad pulled a shirt over his head, Jess started organizing his textbooks in a neat pile on his desk. Jess was definitely in panic mode. When things got stressful—like exams—Jess started organizing. Somehow, external order created internal peace for Jess. Brad was the opposite: the more stressed he became, the messier he got.

Maybe Jess's tidiness also came from not having a mother for the past two years. Maybe that's how Brad would be if he didn't have a mom to pick up after him, to wash and iron his clothes. He took his laundry home every week for his mother to wash. She expected it.

Brad sat on the edge of his bed and pulled on a dirty pair of socks, then his Reeboks. Jess was starting to make his bed. Brad grabbed his green parka from the floor and stood up. "Come on, Jess, you don't have time for that." Brad grabbed Jess's suitcase by the door.

Jess left his bed unmade, and grabbed his carry-on bag. He turned and looked one last time at the messy room before turning off the light and closing the door behind him.

* * *

The Wasatch Mountains were hiding behind a heavy blanket of fog, which had descended low into the Salt Lake Valley. The gray covering invoked an image in Brad's mind of someone closing the cap on a jar. When the air looked like this, Brad felt he was in that jar, struggling for air and almost suffocating. At times, winter in the Rocky Mountains was dreary, grim, and claustrophobic. He couldn't wait for the cloud cover to lift and reveal the beautiful mountain peaks mottled with snow.

Brad hadn't expected the heavy snow. Every few miles his heart raced as he drove past accident flares, red and blue twirling highway patrol lights, the distressed looks on the faces of accident victims. The tires of his BMW slid from time to time, and he always stiffened until he regained control. Yet he was determined to make an all-out effort to get Jess to the airport, even if it turned out to be a futile effort. He knew Jess would blame him if he missed his flight. It probably was Brad's fault that they had stayed out so late.

They had taken Brad's car to the restaurant where they'd gotten together with friends the night before. Jess had suggested it was time to leave a few times. Brad realized that he had done a lot of the talking, telling everyone how he hated pre-med and wanted to switch his major to journalism. Jess scoffed at the idea. Brad had tried to ignore Jess's negative comments at the time, but found himself bothered by them as the night went on. He had been offended by what Jess had said and was still feeling the irritation this morning. He told himself to drop the whole subject but found his mouth moving before the self-suggestion sunk in. "I don't know what you have against journalism, Jess. It could be an exciting profession."

Jess ignored the comment for a moment and stared out the passenger window. He seemed to be carefully considering his response. "I have nothing against journalism, Brad. I just don't think it's right for you. It's hard to make a living as a writer, and medicine just seems to be a more stable career. Besides, it's a family tradition. If you want to rebel against your dad, do it with something less critical to your future."

"Is that what you think this is about? Rebelling against Dad?"

"You're the one who keeps saying he's pushing you toward medicine. You seem a little angry about it sometimes."

Brad clenched the steering wheel. "Jess, this may come as a surprise to you, but money's not the most important thing in the world. Doing something I like is more important to me than making a lot of money."

"You say that now, Brad, but wait till you have a family to support. You might see things differently then, except by then it might be too late to do anything about it."

Brad glanced sideways at Jess. "You worry too much, Jess. That's your problem. You need to loosen up, have some fun. You spend too much time worrying about the future and not enough time having fun in the here and now." Brad realized he was overreacting. The frustration he had felt all semester at being trapped in a major he was not excited about, and his unwillingness to talk with Dad directly about how he felt about medicine, were now being directed at Jess. Brad's frustration increased with Jess's attitude, partially because Brad expected the same response from his dad. Of course, the response—negative or positive—would only come if Brad could muster the courage to tell his father about his desire to change majors.

"There's nothing wrong with setting goals and planning, Brad. Someday you'll grow up and realize that it's just part of real life."

Brad didn't want to think about the "real life" Jess was talking about. He had his whole life to think about real life. He thought about Jess's lab job. His father, Brad's Uncle Gordon, had a friend in the Pathology Department who gave Jess the job. Jess loved it, but Brad knew he was missing out on so many other things because he was always either working or studying. "We're just going to have to agree to disagree on this one, Jess."

"Hey, you're the one who brought this up, Brad. I'm just giving you my honest opinion."

They sat in uncomfortable silence for the remainder of the trip. Brad sighed with relief as they pulled into the airport terminal. On this morning it was a popular place; SUVs and trucks raced by, their drivers unmindful of the icy conditions, anxious to make a flight. Brad pulled up to the Delta loading zone, parked, popped the trunk, and jumped out to grab some of Jess's bags from the trunk.

Jess stepped out. "What're you doing, Brad?"

"I'm helping you catch your flight."

"You can't park here. It's a loading zone. Any cars left unattended will be towed."

"With conditions the way they are, I have plenty of time to get you settled inside and get out here before they even notice my car."

"You're always taking unnecessary chances, Brad."

"Unnecessary? I want to make sure you make your flight. That's necessary. Come on. We're wasting time out here arguing."

They ran in through the revolving doors and glanced at the departure board. The snow had worked in Jess's favor; all flights at Salt Lake International were delayed. Jess would catch his flight.

"Thanks, Brad. It will be good to be back in California for a while. I'm anxious to see Dad. I just hope the flight goes by fast for me. You know how I hate sitting too long."

Brad smiled, thinking of Jess's energy. He was always on the move. He would someday make a great doctor. Even though Jess and Brad had the same tall, athletic build and dark hair, they couldn't have been more different in temperament and interests.

"Too bad you don't have a laptop to play games," Brad said. "Whenever I travel with Dad, I keep busy by playing games on his laptop."

"Maybe I'll try to sleep," Jess said. "Maybe you should go back to the dorms and try doing the same thing."

"Oh no. I'm not going back to the dorms until after the holidays. I'm going straight home to Mom's cooking."

"Look, Brad, you'd better go. You're parked in the loading zone."

Brad grinned at Jess, the consummate worrier. "Okay, I'm going." Brad walked to the nearest exit, glancing at the clock over the door. It was 7:20 A.M. He stepped into the windblown morning. It was cold and thick; clinging flakes chilled his face. Brad hurried to his parked car just as an airport security officer was looking at his license plate and talking into a radio. Brad ran to the driver's side and opened the door.

"Hey, what's wrong with you?" the officer yelled. "Can't you read?"

"Sorry," Brad said with a smile.

"Yeah, yeah," the man returned. "Just move it out of here."

Maneuvering his BMW along the icy roads, Brad made his way from the airport to the traffic backed up on North Temple, passing several accidents. In the Avenues, he came upon a yellow VW Bug that had slid off the road into a bank of snow. The driver appeared to be in her early twenties and was pushing on the gas in an impatient effort to get back on the road, sending her wheels spinning. Brad pulled over and ran to the driver's side of the stranded car. The woman rolled down her window just enough to talk.

"Need some help?" he asked.

"Yes, please."

"I'll get behind you and push. Just a minute."

It was obvious she wasn't used to driving in the snow. He noticed she had an Arizona license plate.

"Okay, put it in second gear and push on the gas."

The driver stepped on the gas again, and Brad pushed with all his might to send the VW sliding back onto the road.

"Thanks," the woman shouted from her window as she waved and drove away.

After that, he enjoyed a relatively smooth drive to his parents' house on Salt Lake's east side, not far from the University of Utah. The day before, his mom had called asking for his dirty clothes, so Brad had stuffed a duffel bag with what he would need for the break and dropped it and the dirty clothes by the house before his last exam that day. Jess, who had been trying to study at the time, made some pointed remarks about how spoiled Brad was.

Brad was smiling when he pulled into the driveway because the Christmas vacation was beginning and—perhaps more importantly— he was looking forward to his mom's homemade pancakes. She would make them for him, he was sure of that. She would make anything he wanted. She would hug him, kiss him, and make him feel like she hadn't seen him for months, even though he lived a few miles from the house. When he and Jess had arrived back at the dorm late the night before, he had glanced at the caller ID and seen that one of his parents—most likely his mother—had called. She was probably just calling to try and get him to change his mind about bringing Jess by the house for dinner, even though he had told her that he and Jess were going out to eat with friends.

As he parked in the snow-packed driveway, Brad glanced at his dashboard clock and noted the time: 8:16 A.M It usually took only twenty minutes to drive from the airport. The weather and helping the woman in the Bug had slowed him more than he had expected.

Usually his father had the large driveway plowed by this hour, but he was obviously running as late as Brad. No tire tracks appeared in the snow from the garage to the street. However, there were a few sets of footprints going from the street to the kitchen door.

He looked at the four-car garage. He could open the door with his remote and park in the garage, but his BMW was covered with dirty snow. His dad didn't like the garage floor to get too wet and dirty, so he decided to leave the car and return later to brush it off before taking his place in the garage. He'd go in through what his family called the "friend's entrance," which was the kitchen door between the garage and the formal entrance at the front of the house.

As Brad stepped from the car into the deep snow, he felt some of it slip into his Reeboks, and a rush of cold wind blew snow into his eyes and mouth. Halfway to the kitchen door, he realized he'd left his parking lights on, so he flipped his parka hood over his head, ran back, turned the lights off, slammed the door shut, and then rushed to the kitchen door.

Before entering, Brad picked up a plastic bag containing a rolled *Salt Lake Tribune* and shook the melted snow off. Dad is definitely running late this morning, he thought. By now he should have already read the entire paper and worked the crossword puzzle. He grabbed the brass knob and pushed against the door. It was locked. On a hunch, Brad lifted the lid to the Winder Dairy box next to the door and saw the milk was still there. *What is their problem this morning? I guess Jess and I weren't the only ones who overslept.*

He pulled his key ring out of his pocket and unlocked the door before shoving the newspaper under his arm and grabbing the milk, then pushed the door open with his spare hand. The steady beeping of his parents' alarm system started, beginning a forty-five-second countdown to disarm the system.

He rushed to the pad and suddenly realized that he didn't remember the code. The security fob he used to carry on his key chain could bypass the code, but it was in his desk at the dorm. He had stopped carrying it because it made his keys bulky, and since his parents only set the alarm before they went to bed at night and turned it off when they awoke early in the morning, he had found he no longer needed it. His parents were not in the habit of setting the alarm when they were away during the day. How could this be happening?

"Dad! Mom!"

Frantically he began to punch numbers at random. It was useless, and he knew it, but what else could he do?

"Dad! Mom! The alarm is going. What's the number?"

The last feverish beeps of the alarm had been replaced by a deafening screech, indicating that the alarm was now being transmitted across phone lines to the security agent, who would call the police.

The kitchen was dark, and, in spite of the squeal of the alarm, Brad felt disappointment that the aroma of his mother's breakfast cooking hadn't greeted him. He turned on the light and saw everything as his mom always left it, but something was wrong. The alarm should have roused an immediate response from even the deepest sleepers. Where were they? Why hadn't they told him they'd be gone? Maybe his father had gone in to the office after all. But the unmarred driveway told him no one had left the house since the snow had started, which had been since before Jess woke him.

The piercing ring of the phone suddenly added to the commotion. Brad grabbed the handset from the kitchen counter and did his best to block out the sound of the irritating alarm.

"Hello?"

"This is Dan with security. We have registered an alarm at this residence. Could I have your password please?"

"Oh, it's okay. I'm Brad Armstrong. I live here. I set the alarm off when I came in the house this morning."

"Your password, please."

"I don't remember it," Brad responded, his heart sinking.

"I'm sorry, sir. We're going to have to call the police."

"Do what you have to, but I'm telling you—"

The man hung up.

Brad put the phone down and made his way from the kitchen to the front foyer. The Christmas tree, a huge spruce, stood proudly by the bay window in the front sitting room. The gifts he'd chosen for his parents were under the tree, wrapped in paper from the stores where he had purchased them. A multitude of other gifts surrounded the tree. Mom and Dad had overdone it again. Conrad, his best friend next door, would tell him how spoiled he was.

A thought entered his mind. Perhaps Mom and Dad had gone to Conrad's house. They were best friends with Conrad's parents, Darlene and Fred Henderson. Darlene was from Atlanta, Georgia, and she sometimes invited them over for one of her famous southern breakfasts. He could almost smell the eggs, bacon, sausage, and French toast. Dad had often commented that he couldn't understand how Fred managed to stay so thin with a wife who cooked like Darlene.

He decided to check upstairs for clues as to his parents' whereabouts before heading over to the Hendersons' house. The upstairs hallway was cold, and he shivered. Passing his room, he noticed the open door, which was odd because his mom always kept it closed. On his bed, he could see the military-style duffel bag he had packed the day before. Down the hall, his parents' door was also open.

He trudged to the door and peered into the semidarkness. He was surprised to see them in bed under the blankets, so he approached the bed. His parents were lying on their backs in the bed, their eyes staring vacantly at the ceiling.

"Mom! Dad!" he shouted and jumped toward the bed. He reached his dad first and shook him, screaming, "Wake up, Dad! Wake up!"

CHAPTER 2

At 9:25 A.M the snow had let up and the fog was lifting as Vanessa Chandler drove the unmarked Ford Taurus from her downtown office through the Avenues, a trendy section of town tucked between North Temple and the mountains east of the Utah capitol. Populated by college students and young professionals with an artistic bent, the streets were lined with apartment buildings and houses in a variety of Victorian styles.

As she climbed higher onto the terraces of the Wasatch Mountains, the homes climbed in size and exclusivity. Federal Heights, the country club section of Salt Lake City, was a wealthy residential enclave just north of the University of Utah. It obtained its name in 1862 when the federal government established a surveillance fort so troops could keep an eye on the Mormons.

The area reminded Van of the neighborhood where she grew up in Boston. It was classy. Its outward appearance evoked a feeling of security and serenity, but the perceived safety and tranquility of this upscale neighborhood had been shattered earlier that morning when two of its residents were found shot to death.

A half-dozen police cars, two ambulances, and numerous unmarked police vehicles blocked the street. She assumed she was the last on the scene, since she had come from interviewing a witness for another case. It was an atypical crime scene, at least for her. She commonly found herself in rundown bungalows and split-levels, not extravagant mansions. Built of tapestry brick, the house was a fine example of Colonial Revival architecture with Federal-style detailing.

As she made her way up the front walk, a uniformed police officer glanced at the badge hanging around her neck that identified her as

Detective Vanessa Chandler of Homicide. The officer lifted the yellow police tape that blocked the front walk so she could duck under. On her way to the steep front steps, she noticed a small ice-covered walk from the driveway to what she guessed was the kitchen. Before pushing on the already-open mahogany door, she stopped to admire its ornate carving and the elegant Christmas wreath of fragrant pine. She then stepped into the entry hall and was impressed with the beautiful walnut staircase rising to the second floor. The house was swarming with people and was stuffy with activity.

She recognized Arnold Manwaring from the medical examiner's office. And there were the "crime-scene boys," Perry Hunsaker taking photographs and Bart Hogan checking for prints. Bob Jones was questioning one of the patrol officers. Jones was a short man with a large scar on his face from a gunshot wound. The other detectives called him Scarface, which appalled Van until she discovered Jones wore the title with pride. He was the department's cynic, always ready with a sarcastic quip, but he was a good interviewer.

Detective Marty Carmichael, a tall, thin redhead, was following the crime-scene boys around the house. Marty was the department clown and always looked as if he didn't know what to do. Detective Dave Jensen, a handsome blond, was searching through bureau drawers in what looked like a study. Thornton, no doubt, had taken care of the details of the search warrant.

In an elegant sitting room off the foyer, Detective Douglas Thornton, Van's senior trainer, stood questioning people she assumed were witnesses. A short, plump woman stood out among the rest. She wore a bathrobe, had big curlers in her red hair, and waved her arms as she talked.

In contrast, Thornton looked at home in the gracious room decorated in Chippendale. Thornton was not tall—five eight or nine—but had the muscular frame of a bodybuilder, with veins bulging on his neck and forehead. He lifted weights at the gym at least three times a week. She studied his outfit. He was wearing a charcoal-and-cream tweed sport coat with dark charcoal slacks, tan shirt, and tan silk tie. Not once in the past five months since she started working under him as a rookie detective had she seen him dress down. He always looked like he was ready to go on a date.

She took in the elegant room. How she loved fine things. The floor was oak covered in an exquisite floral oriental rug of antique green and dusty wine. She caught glimpses of the wine color repeated in the subtle floral print of the satin draperies. An antique harpsichord stood to the right of the double glass doors. The Chippendale settee and chairs were charmingly arranged around the room. Five paintings, mostly portraits and religious subjects, adorned the cream-colored walls. An oversized Christmas tree stood in the corner surrounded by elegantly wrapped gifts. The tree's decorations were as exquisite as the room itself.

The room's centerpiece was the marble fireplace. She recognized the replica of the Christus statue by Danish sculptor Bertel Thorvaldsen on the mantel. They were Mormon, Van thought. She herself was Mormon, having converted to the faith several years earlier.

What a contrast this east-side mansion was to the west-side bungalow she had investigated the day before. She cringed as she thought of the orange and brown floral furniture from the early '70s. The shag green carpet was stained with a murdered man's blood. A couple of hungry, hissing felines prowled the scene.

The victim, a twenty-five-year-old drug dealer, left a wife and two-year-old daughter. The wife stood in the filthy kitchen with an angry face, her left arm bruised and dotted with needle marks. The child was crying, screaming really.

"Shut up!" the woman shouted to the toddler. "I'll slap your face if you don't shut up."

Van had tried to calm the woman. "Do you know who did this?" Van asked.

"Gang members. They killed him. His brother will kill them for this," the woman had replied.

There were no screaming babies in this upscale home; only quiet, dignified sniffles. Thornton glanced up at Van and smiled. He acted like everyone's best friend but had an underlying arrogance that rubbed her the wrong way. He sauntered over to her in the foyer in his usual haughty style, with the smell of his cologne preceding him.

"Van, I'm glad you finally made it," he said as he closed the glass doors behind him.

"What do we have here, Thornton?" she asked as she fished a notepad from the pocket of her blue wool overcoat.

He flipped through his notes. "Two murder victims—husband and wife. Both shot to death in their bed. The male victim is Allen Armstrong, a researcher at the U. He's worth millions. He's also an acquaintance of the governor."

"That explains why the whole force is out here today," she said.

"The female victim is Peggy Armstrong, a housewife who was involved in a lot of community projects and charities."

"Who found them?"

Thornton grabbed the silk handkerchief from his breast pocket and dabbed at the sweat running down his forehead from his thick, curly mane of blond hair. "That kid over there. Their son."

Van looked past Thornton through the glass doors. She had been so intrigued by the room's furniture that she had failed to take a good look at the people. She berated herself silently for not looking—a bad habit in police work. Her eyes quickly found the young man slouching on the settee, his long legs thrown out awkwardly in front of him. His broad shoulders sagged, and his dark eyes stared out blankly from under thick, dark eyebrows. He looked disheveled, and his T-shirt and jeans were stained with blood.

"What's his story?" Van asked.

"Says he came home this morning from taking his cousin to the airport and found his parents dead."

"Did he call 9-1-1?"

"No. He set off the alarm when he entered the house at 8:18 A.M The security office called the station at 8:20, and dispatch called a patrol in the area to check out the situation. Patrol got here around 8:30. The kid was hysterical. Patrol called for ambulances."

"The alarm was armed?" she asked, furiously taking notes.

"Yeah."

"Do we know how long they've been dead?"

"Manwaring says it could have happened within four hours from the time he took the bodies' temperatures at 9:05. The bodies were still warm."

"That's the best he can do?"

"That's the best he can do."

"So," Van said, "they died sometime between roughly 5:00 and 9:00 this morning."

"You got it."

"Were there any signs of a break-in?"

"None whatsoever."

"Really? And the kid set the alarm off when he entered?"

"Yeah. I know, it doesn't add up."

"What do you know about him?"

Thornton flipped through his notepad. "Bradley Allen Armstrong, age eighteen, born September 5, 1985, in Salt Lake City. He's Mormon. Was president of his teachers quorum, Eagle Scout, captain of the East High swim team."

"Did he tell you all that?"

"Next-door neighbors. The woman is Darlene Henderson," Thornton indicated with a nod of his head. "That's her husband, Fred Henderson. He says he's the kid's bishop. The heavyset guy is their son, Conrad Henderson. He says he's the kid's best friend."

Van caught the slight disdain in Thornton's voice. He'd come to Salt Lake from Denver and was constantly criticizing what he called the "predominant culture."

"Did the Hendersons hear or see anything?" Van asked.

"Nothing."

"Did the son live here with his parents?"

"No," Thornton said, glancing down at his notepad. "After he graduated from East High in the spring—in the top ten of his class no less—he worked at the country club as a lifeguard. He moved into the dorms at the U in August with his cousin, who was also just starting. Both are premed."

"Has anyone checked his story out with the cousin?"

"No answer at his uncle's house. They're his only relatives that we know of."

"Where do the uncle and cousin live?" Van asked.

"San Francisco. The kid says his cousin left this morning for Christmas break."

Tao Uluave from homicide clumped down the stairs carrying a gun in a plastic bag. His Polynesian features carried the self-satisfied look he always got when he found something important. He was known in the department for his search skills; if there was something to be found, he usually found it.

Thornton whistled as Uluave approached. "What do we have here?"

"A .22 caliber revolver," he responded. "Found it in a duffel bag on the kid's bed."

Van looked at Thornton. "You've got the search warrant, right?"

Thornton snickered. "Of course, but thanks for keeping us in line."

Van looked over at the young man. "What's his name again?"

"Brad," Thornton said

Positions in the room had changed, and Brad was now cradled in the stocky woman's arms. The bishop and Brad's friend stood behind them. Brad had the same fear-stunned look Van had once seen in the eyes of a frightened child. Eighteen? Yet he looked so much younger. He looked like a kid.

"Why don't you talk to him?" Thornton asked. "Work your magic on him. Maybe you'll get more out of him than we did."

Van was acclaimed in the detective division for her ability to put witnesses at ease. She managed to take on the role of a confidante in minutes. It was a great skill—more than a skill, really. It was a gift, and she prided herself on it.

"What's he like?" Van asked.

"Well, right now he's quiet, serious—seems to be in shock. I don't think he's always this way. I sense a cockiness in him. I don't know, living off his parents. He looks to be the type for the neighborhood."

Van glared at Thornton. "What type?"

"You ought to know the type. I mean, you're the type yourself."

"Still carrying that poor-boy chip, Thornton?"

"Don't get angry, Van. I was making an impartial observation."

"There's nothing impartial about your observations, Thornton." Van walked past the detective to the sitting room.

"Excuse me," Van said as she approached Brad and the Hendersons. "I'm Detective Vanessa Chandler. If you don't mind, I'd like to speak with Brad here alone."

Darlene turned to Brad. "It's all right," she said with a faint southern accent. "We'll be out in the foyer if you need us."

"Thanks," Brad said. "I'll be okay."

"Take it easy on him, Detective," Darlene urged in a whisper. "He's been through a lot this morning. He's a good boy."

"I'll be as gentle as possible, Mrs. Henderson," Van responded with a comforting smile.

The bishop and Conrad followed Darlene out. Thornton then closed the glass doors and remained with the others in the foyer. Van pulled off her coat and threw it on a nearby chair and sat next to Brad on the settee. "You have a beautiful home here, Brad."

"It's not my house," he said.

"I'm sorry. I mean your parents have a pleasant home here. Did your mom decorate it?"

"Yeah. She liked things like that," he said, and tears welled in his eyes. He swallowed hard. "Dad thinks it's too stuffy. He wanted something more lived-in. Mom let him decorate the study. It's comfortable. That's where I study." He stared at the floor as he spoke, glancing up at Van from time to time.

"But you live in the dorms with your cousin, right?"

"Yeah, but I come here a lot to study because it's quiet. I can concentrate better here. Besides, Mom's food's better than the cafeteria."

Van smiled. "I'll bet your mom was a good cook."

He glanced up. "Yeah."

"She also had good taste," Van said. "This Chippendale settee is lovely."

He glanced up. "You're really a detective?"

Van smiled. "Yes. Why?"

"Why do you know about antique furniture?"

"Design is kind of a hobby. I've taken a few classes."

"In college?"

She shook her head. "Community ed."

"You didn't attend college?"

"Yes, I did. And some law school."

"Some? You dropped out?"

"Yes."

"Why?"

"I dropped out of law school because I was bored. I was fascinated with the law, but not that aspect of it."

"What do you mean?

"Well, to tell you the truth, crime fascinates me."

"So why did you go to law school in the first place?"

"Because my father told me to. I always did what my father said because I wanted to make him happy. You know what I mean?"

"Yeah, I know exactly what you mean."

"How so?"

"I'm majoring in premed because Dad wants me to be a doctor."

"And you don't want to be a doctor?"

"No." He threw a glance at her. As Van looked into his dark eyes, she could see his fear was subsiding.

"What do you want to be?"

"A journalist."

"Why a journalist?"

"Because I love to write. Dad always told me it could be an avocation but not a vocation"

"Well, I think it's important to choose a career that will make you happy. After all, you're most likely going to spend the rest of your life doing it."

He looked up at her, appreciation in his eyes. "Thanks," he said.

"I appreciate your cooperation here, Brad. Under the circumstances, I know it's difficult."

"Yeah. It is. Bishop Henderson tried calling my parents' attorney. His secretary said he was out of town for the weekend and won't be back until late Sunday night."

"I'm just asking routine questions here, Brad. Are you saying you would like a lawyer present for this?"

"I don't know. I'm not sure why he suggested it. Unless . . ." He broke off. His eyes became glassy, and his expression changed as if he'd had a sudden horrible thought.

"Brad?"

Brad seemed to return to the moment. "I'm sure the bishop just thought a lawyer could help me with some of the details. I'm not thinking clearly right now. There wouldn't be any other reason I'd need a lawyer, would there?"

Van shrugged. "Like I said, I'm just asking routine questions here."

Brad looked at her intently. "I just want you to find out who killed my parents. I don't know anything about what happened here."

At that moment, looking into his eyes, his fear and confusion convinced her that he really didn't know anything about what had happened. "Okay," she said, and took out a notepad from her pocket. "Let's just review what you do know. I understand you set off the alarm system when you entered the house this morning."

"Yeah. I couldn't remember the code."

"I would think you would have used it regularly."

"I never used it. I have a key fob that turns the system off."

"I take it you didn't have your fob with you?"

"No. I took it off my key chain a while back because it made my keys so bulky. They usually only set the alarms at night."

"Did your parents have one of these security fobs?"

"Yeah, they each had one on their key chains."

"Did anyone else have a remote to your security system?"

"No. Just the three of us."

"Did anyone else have the security code to turn off the system from the keypad?"

"Not that I know of."

"What about neighbors and friends? Did your parents entrust anyone with the code in case of emergencies?"

"I don't think so. When we went on vacations, Dad left one of our security keys with the Hendersons next door so they could water the plants and check on things."

"Did your parents have a housekeeper?"

"A cleaning service comes every Wednesday. Mom was always here while they cleaned though. She didn't trust them in the house by themselves."

"Was there a reason for her distrust? I mean, did anything ever turn up missing?"

"Not that I know of. She just didn't like strangers in the house."

"Don't you find it strange, Brad, that the alarm system was armed when you came in? An intruder would have set the alarm off, right?"

"I guess. All the windows and doors are wired. I don't know how it was done, but I know that some burglars know electronics well."

"How do you know that?"

"I watch TV."

"Well, no forcible entry was found. It doesn't appear to be a break-in. Nothing appears to be disturbed."

"How would you know? Do you know what we have in our house?"

"No. Have you noticed anything missing?"

"I haven't had a chance to really look."

"Do you know anyone who would want to hurt your parents?"

"Yeah. Like I told the other detective, a man threatened my father last Friday night."

"Who?"

"I don't know. I'd never seen him before. I was in the study working on a final project when he rang the bell. Dad answered the door, and they stood in the foyer talking. Dad left the man in the foyer and came into the study. He got something out of his briefcase. I wasn't paying much attention, so I don't know what he got, but when he went back out in the foyer, the other man became upset. He started yelling and talking like he was mad at Dad."

"Could you hear what he was saying?"

"He said something like, 'This isn't enough. I need more. You got me into this, now you're going to get me out.'"

"What was he talking about?"

"I don't know. I went to the hall and saw him just as he was leaving."

"You didn't recognize him?"

"No."

"What did he look like?"

"He was big, dark, with bushy hair and a mustache."

"Anything else?"

"Yeah. He wore a sweat suit that was too small for him."

"What do you mean?"

"He looked like he'd squeezed into it. I thought maybe he got it at the Salvation Army or something. It was red and black. It looked old. Maybe he was a panhandler wanting money."

"But you think your dad knew him, right?"

"It sounded like he might. And he was pretty mad at Dad."

"Why?"

"I don't know. Hobos make their way up into this neighborhood sometimes, and Dad recruited them a lot for his work."

"What kind of work?"

"Dad is—was a pharmacologist at the university." Again Brad began to tear up but took a moment to get control. "He tested new drugs. He always said transients make good participants because they need the money and often need medical help."

"I understand you took your cousin to the airport this morning. What time was that?"

"We overslept. Jess was upset with me for keeping him out late last night. We didn't leave the dorm until sometime around 6:10 or 6:15."

"Why were you out so late last night?"

"We needed to loosen up, have fun. Well, you know. Exams were over. We went for pizza and root beer at the Wasatch Café. We started talking with friends and time flew by."

"What time did you come home?"

"Sometime between 1:30 and 2:00. The café's open all night during exams."

"So what time did you get to the airport this morning?"

"A little after 7:00, I think."

"It took you more than forty-five minutes?"

"Yeah, the roads hadn't been plowed, and there were a lot of accidents. We sat in a traffic jam for something like twenty minutes too."

"How long were you at the airport?"

"Only a few minutes. I was parked in the Delta loading zone and Jess didn't want me to get a ticket."

"So you left before he boarded?"

"Yeah."

"How long did it take you to get home?"

"About the same. I got here at 8:16."

"So your cousin can verify your whereabouts until around 7:15 or so, and you were alone for the next hour until the patrol arrived here at 8:30?"

"That's right."

"The roads must have been bad."

"They were. And I stopped to help this woman whose car was stuck."

"Did you happen to get her name?"

"No. We didn't really talk. I just pushed her car for her."

"What kind of car was it?"

"A yellow VW Bug."

"Old or new model?"

"New."

"I don't suppose you caught the license plate."

"Only that it was an Arizona plate and seemed to be custom-made. The letters formed a name."

"What was the name?"

"It wasn't an actual name, but a nickname. I think it had the word Bug in it."

"What was the location of this incident?"

"Second Avenue and maybe J or K Street. I'm not exactly sure which side street we were on."

"Do you think she had actually slid off the road or was trying to pull out of a parking spot?"

"The tire marks in the snow made me think she had slid."

"Brad, one of our detectives found a .22-caliber revolver in a duffel bag on what is apparently your bed. What can you tell me about that?"

She watched his response carefully, but it was not particularly remarkable. He simply answered her question. "About a month ago, Dad suggested we join the gun club and learn to handle a weapon. We went to a west-side pawnshop near the neighborhood where Dad grew up. Dad knew the owner. Dad purchased a Colt .45 automatic, and I bought a .22 caliber revolver. It was all done legally."

"Do you happen to have the name of the pawnshop?"

"Westside Pawn."

"Why was the gun in your duffel bag on the bed this morning?"

Brad looked up, concern showing in his expression. "Why are you asking so many questions about my gun?"

"We have to check everything out."

"Dad and I practiced shooting at the gun club a couple of weeks ago. Dad was paged; something had come up at the office. I stayed behind to continue the practice shooting. Afterward, I took the gun back to my dorm room. I planned on returning it to the house as soon as I could. Then exams hit. I got busy. Yesterday when I was packing the duffel bag, I stumbled across the .22 hidden on the top shelf of my dorm closet. I stuffed it in the duffel bag."

"You brought the duffel bag with you this morning?"

"No, I dropped it off yesterday."

* * *

Doug Thornton stood in front of the glass doors to the sitting room and watched with admiration as Van worked with Brad. She could pacify the most agitated of suspects with her soft voice. Her looks didn't hurt either.

She carried her short, athletic build with spunk, and her short brown hair bounced as she talked. But most of all, he loved her ocean-blue eyes, which were accentuated by her blue sweater. A dimple on each cheek reminded him of old Shirley Temple movies. He couldn't describe her as cute—he was too attracted to her for that. Maybe pretty was a better word, but it seemed too soft for Van. Of course, she was quite a bit younger than he. She was thirty-three and he was hitting forty.

He remembered the day Captain Markakis had introduced them. "Take her under your wing, Thornton," the captain had said. "She's a rookie with a lot of potential." The captain didn't know Thornton had been admiring Van for weeks; the opportunity to train her was a stroke of luck.

At the end of their first month together, he'd walked her to her car, and she had suggested they get a bite to eat. Delighted at this sign that she shared his romantic interest, he agreed. She followed him to a nearby diner. They talked about the hard month they'd shared and opened up to each other.

Van told him about her childhood. Raised in Boston, she was one of four children born to affluent parents. Her father was a respected attorney who had expected Van to follow in his footsteps, but she headed west with a friend she had met in college, and when she got here she entered the Utah Police Academy. She worked for years as a patrol officer. Later, she joined the Mormons. Her parents still lived in Boston but had withdrawn from her because they disapproved of her career and conversion to Mormonism.

Van had excelled as a patrol cop and worked up through the ranks, passing all the tests, performing beautifully under courtroom stress, and exhibiting extraordinary observational skills. But the quality that brought her from patrol officer to detective, in Thornton's opinion, was her ability to make strangers trust and talk to her.

She'd worked her magic with him that night. In fact, he'd felt so comfortable with her he told her about his childhood, about the rough Montbello neighborhood where he grew up in northeast Denver. Small and skinny, he was always getting roughed up. To find security, he joined a gang in his early teens—the Crips—and by the time he was a junior in high school found himself in jail for robbing a mansion in southwest Denver. He was sentenced to a reform school where he found a mentor in the officer in charge, Joe Montelli. He learned to box and lifted weights, and by the time he left the program, he was stronger and more confident. He didn't let anyone push him around.

That night, as they had opened up to each other, he had made his move. He covered her hand with his, and said, "Why don't we let things go where they want to go?" She pulled her hand away and stood up. "Try that again," she'd said, "and I'll have you reprimanded." Thornton smiled now as he thought of her spunk.

"Thornton?" Van had opened the glass door and was entering the foyer. He felt his face flush. Had she noticed him staring?

"Yeah, what is it, Van?"

"Brad wants to take a look around to see if anything's missing."

"Okay. I'll have Uluave escort him around the main floor, but the second floor is off-limits right now. There's too much going on up there."

Uluave came up behind Thornton, his huge body towering over the lieutenant. Brad walked past them like a sleepwalker, and Thornton wondered what he would do when he awoke from his delusional nightmare to learn he'd killed his parents. Uluave guided the boy toward the kitchen.

"Thornton," Van said, "Brad says his parents had a remote security key that automatically turned their alarm on and off as they came and went."

"Yeah, he told us that too. We found his parents' keys in their bedroom. The remotes are on their chains."

"Well, we still need to account for Brad's remote."

"Don't tell me you believe the kid's story."

"I'm telling you I believe his story."

"He must be a real smooth talker."

"You're the one who told me I have good instincts."

"You do, but maybe your instincts have been influenced by his handsome face."

She rolled her eyes. "Give me a break, Thornton."

"Did he tell you about the one-armed man?"

"What?"

"Didn't you ever see *The Fugitive*, Van?"

"What are you saying, Thornton? You don't believe the kid's story about the man who made threats against his family?"

"A guy in a sweat suit that's too small for him. What's that? It's crazy."

"That's the kind of detail that makes me believe him. Why would he make up something like that?"

"Van, it might as well be a one-armed man."

"There's something you're forgetting about that movie, Thornton."

"What's that?"

"There really was a one-armed man."

CHAPTER 3

After leaving the Armstrong house, Thornton drove downtown to Gold's Gym, gulping his power shake along the way. It was lunchtime, and he needed to work off some of his frustrations. He could never figure out how Van managed to get the better of him before he knew what was happening.

He drove his unmarked Lumina around the crowded parking lot twice before he found an empty spot. While the Salt Lake City Police Department had its own gym, Thornton had found that Gold's was a good place to meet women. He parked, gulped down the last swig of shake, crushed the can and threw it in a trash bag on the passenger side, then grabbed his gym bag and got out. Cold air blew snowflakes in his eyes, making him blink as he pulled up the collar of his overcoat and headed quickly to the entrance.

The locker room was a hot, steamy contrast to the cold, dry air outside. He put on his gym shorts and T-shirt emblazoned with "SLCPD"—Salt Lake City Police Department. A lot of the girls in the gym were impressed by his detective status.

He walked through the maze of shiny steel machines, barbells, sit-up tables, and squat racks that were being sweated over by grunting men and women and greeted everyone with a big smile.

"Hello, sweetheart. You're looking good," he crooned to Alice Ann, one of several petite blond trainers in the gym.

"So are you," she gushed back.

He threw his towel by an empty weight bench, and Joel, one of the trainers, came up to him. "Want me to spot you?" he asked.

"Yeah, thanks, Joel."

"What're you going for today?" Joel asked.

"Four hundred."

"You sure?"

"Do I sound unsure?"

"Okay," Joel said and shrugged. He began to stack the weights onto the bar as Thornton watched.

Whenever he was feeling down, pumping iron put him right back on top. It was a mood elevator. The weights represented life's struggles. Thornton pushed against them and tried to be victorious over them; it was a spiritual thing. Van had her religion; he had his.

He loved the rush of exhilaration as he lifted the massive barbell over his head. He loved the power he felt. He loved the looks of admiration from the women and, even more, the looks of envy from the men.

He knew that feeling of envy. He'd felt it in the weight room back in Montbello Middle School. He was skinny and weak back then. He'd tried to fit in; he read about sports and even tried out for the basketball team once. After seeing muscleman Charles Atlas beckoning to him from an ad in a comic book, he ordered the muscle manual. "Don't let bullies kick sand in your face, weakling." It was like Atlas was talking to him personally; Atlas understood him, knew what he was going through, and appreciated the pain.

But the manual did him no good. He couldn't seem to make it work. He tried doing push-ups and even tried doing chin-ups on the iron crossbar of his mother's clothesline in back of their house. The muscles didn't come.

Of course, deep inside, he knew he hadn't tried hard enough. It was not just his body that wasn't cooperating; it was his heart. He didn't have the confidence to make it work. If he'd had a father who was really there for him, to show him how it was done, maybe he could have succeeded. But all he'd had was Dotty, his mother, who worked all day and came home and drank all night. She would scream at him to wash the dishes and clean the house. She would tell him how lazy he was and how useless he was, what a burden he was. No one would marry her with a deadweight kid to support, she'd said.

He often thought he didn't blame Ralph, his father, for running off with the waitress from the bar down the street. That's where he'd spent most of his time anyway, getting drunk at Al's Bar in northeast Denver. Ralph hated to come home. When he did, he would get into violent drunken brawls with Dotty, the neighbors would call the police, and either Dotty or Ralph would end up in detox for the night.

The welfare services people had once threatened to put Thornton in a foster home. "Go ahead," Ralph had said. "I pay my taxes and should get something back for it." The pain he'd felt when Ralph said that was still acute today.

Back when Dotty and Ralph first moved into the little house in the new Montbello development, they had dreams for a bright future, or so Dotty idealized it. Dotty and Ralph had moved in with three young children, Thornton's brother, Bobby, and sister, Ruth. Montbello was only a year old at the time, and Thornton was only four. He and the neighborhood grew up together. Back then everyone had high hopes for the community. Who could have foreseen the area's gang-plagued future? By the mid-1970s, Dotty and Ralph's dreams had faded into a dreary reality. Both Thornton and the neighborhood were on their way down. Thornton, however, wasn't going to let his past get in his way. He was stronger than his past, and today, as he'd done on other days, he'd prove it.

"Your lift's ready," Joel said.

He looked at the barbells with plates as big as manhole covers, and he felt a little knot forming in his throat. The pulse in his jaw began to throb, and he pressed his finger on it. The memories. He had to shake the memories. They were no good for him. They always brought on anxiety. Why was he feeling this way?

He knew. It was that rich kid and Van's sympathy for him. She found Brad interesting because he was rich and educated. The kid had been polished and pruned in an upscale environment like Van with advantages Thornton never had. No matter how hard he tried, his Montbello upbringing showed through.

Thornton lay on his back, took a deep breath, and focused on the 400-pound bar resting on the rack above him. He was counting on adrenaline to carry him through the lift. There was something primeval about pumping iron, man against the forces of nature. Wide-eyed spectators who knew what he was attempting became a blur in the distance.

With clinched fists wrapped around the bar and a rush of adrenaline flowing through his body, he extended every ounce of energy into the bar. Pushing the bar halfway off his chest, his giant biceps began to shake.

He saw images flashing in his mind—Van, Brad Armstrong, and the house in Denver, that middle-school weight room. His focus was broken. Joel grabbed the bar and helped Thornton guide it back on the rack.

Thornton sat up and looked around. The viewers turned away.

"Let's try it again in a minute," Joel said.

"Yeah, okay," Thornton said.

His T-shirt was soaked with sweat. As he looked across the room at the mirror he saw his face mottled with exertion and embarrassment. He glanced over at Alice Ann, who was looking at him admiringly.

Now that was a girl who didn't put on airs. When she saw something she liked, she let everyone know. There was no holding back with her. She was down-to-earth and fun. He would have to ask her out. They had been subtly flirting with each other for months.

"Let's take a few off," Joel said.

"No," Thornton muttered. "I'm going to work on the leg press over here a while."

He could hear his old mentor, Joe Mantelli, back in the correctional facility, chiding him. "You can't let your ego get in the way of your bench pressing. The important thing is consistency. You don't have to lift the world on your shoulders. The important thing is not to overdo it, not to rush it. Stop trying to show off."

Thornton held his head down as he walked to the leg press and sat down, grasping the handles on both sides of the seat with his feet on the pedals. He pushed forward until his legs were fully extended. After pressing a few times, he managed to look up and scan the room. No one was looking at him now, except Alice Ann. She winked as their eyes locked. He smiled. Yes, he would ask her out.

She looked a little like Monica Parker, the first girl he'd asked out in high school. He'd joined the Crips by then in the Montbello turf war against the Bloods. He was wearing blue and thought he was tough. He'd already helped knock off a couple of big houses in southwest Denver and had even been involved in a drive-by shooting. The Bloods had shot at him and he'd survived.

He shuddered even now as he recalled the disgusted look on Monica's face after he asked her out. "Montbello trash," she'd said.

Of all the names he'd been called, that was the most vicious. Cruel, arrogant, rich kids had no feelings. They had surrounded him. As part of Denver's busing program, he'd been bused to southeast Denver, far from his familiar neighborhood of boarded-up houses defaced with graffiti.

He'd seen hints of what he now called "the Monica look" in the expressions of Vanessa Chandler. She tried to act down-to-earth— *tried* being the operative word. She couldn't quite pull it off. She always carried an air of aloofness. Something she was born with. She had spunk though, he had to give her that.

He once tried to help Van open a warehouse door that was hung. They were at the site of a west-side gang slaying. "Here," he'd said. "Let someone with muscles help you with that."

She'd glared at him and said, "You do have muscles everywhere, Thornton, including between your ears."

After his workout, Thornton sauntered over to Alice Ann. "Want to make a lonely detective happy?" he asked.

She smiled. "What do you mean?" she asked.

"How about dinner Monday night at that Greek restaurant over on Fourth South?"

"I thought you'd never ask," she said.

"I'll pick you up at seven if you'd be kind enough to give me your address."

* * *

Van maneuvered her car through the Wendy's take-out window on her way to the mall. She didn't have time to stop, so she'd have to eat as she drove. She had to buy Mom a gift for Christmas, and it was always a long, drawn-out ordeal. She always wanted to choose just the right gift. Last year she'd bought Mom expensive perfume. The year before that she'd bought her an attractive blouse, and the year before that a gold necklace.

As she bit into her cheeseburger, she tried to think of something new and unusual to buy for Mom. Whatever she decided on, she would take the elegantly wrapped package back to her apartment and store it in the hall closet with all of Mom's other presents. Some were wrapped in Christmas prints, others in bright birthday colors, and still others in floral wraps for Mother's Day.

Someday she would give them all to her. That would be a wonderful day—the day Mom would forgive her for rebelling. It had started in high school. She had outgrown Mom's obsessive control by the time she was sixteen. She knew Mom only wanted what was best for her, but she hated the constant orchestrating of her life. She'd chosen all of Van's clothes, supervised Van's hairdresser, and selected her makeup.

Van winced as she thought of that big fight. "Mom," Van had said, "I'm not your doll to be all made up. You can't make me walk and talk and act just like you. I have my own mind."

Van tried to push the memory from her head as she turned into the ZCMI Center parking terrace. She stopped and pulled a ticket from the machine before continuing through the winding, dark recesses of the garage. She found an empty spot and pulled into it. She sat in the warm Taurus, reluctant to face the cold air. Her mind went back to Federal Heights. It reminded her so much of Louisburg Square on the slopes of Beacon Hill.

Her old Boston neighborhood looked much as it did in the early nineteenth century. The Chandlers were Yankee descendants of Puritan founders. She thought of the rows of stately Georgian brick houses with white doorways and lacy wrought-iron balconies lining the brick sidewalks and cobblestone streets.

Wellesley. That's where her mom had wanted her to go. Mom went there as did Van's grandma. That's where Van's older sister, Sharon, had gone to school and where her younger sister, Emma, was attending now. It was a tradition for the women in her family to attend Wellesley. Her younger brother, Peter, had gone to Harvard. That was the male tradition.

Van had wanted a coed experience and insisted on Boston University. Her mother fought her on the plan, but she had made a deal with her dad. He would let her go to Boston University and she would plan on law school.

She finally stepped out of the Taurus, and the cold air stung her cheeks. She shivered, pulled her collar up around her neck, and headed for the mall entrance. The warmth of the Meier & Frank was a welcome change.

It was the weekend, Christmas was getting closer, and the store was packed. She stood for a moment in the doorway leading from the parking terrace into the store's second floor, attempting to get her bearings, not certain where to start. A group of rowdy teenage girls emerged from the dark parking terrace and pushed past her.

Teenagers seemed so rude these days. Was she ever that rude? She remembered it hadn't been all that long ago that she was a teenager; she was only thirty-three. Then again, maybe it had been that long. She'd seen so much since going into law enforcement that her teenage years seemed a lifetime ago. She had to remind herself she had her whole life ahead of her.

As she watched the teenage girls with their designer jeans and expensive leather bags, she realized she didn't feel this way about all teenagers—just the rich, snotty ones. They'd been handed everything their whole lives and didn't appreciate any of it.

She knew she was being hypocritical. She admitted to herself that she had been a rich, snotty teenager. Scenes of giggling, silly, loud, attention-starved girls raced through her mind. That act had played out a lifetime ago, or so it seemed.

How had it all changed so quickly? It started at Boston University. She met so many interesting kids from so many fascinating backgrounds, people from all over the world who had lived lives that made Beacon Hill seem like a provincial village of closed-minded aristocrats who cared only for themselves.

For the first time, she'd realized how self-absorbed and egotistical she was. It had frightened her. How could she waste her life keeping up with the most fashionable clothes when starving children had no clothes at all?

After changing her major repeatedly, she'd settled on social work. During the summer months she had worked at internships in various social agencies that took her into worlds she never knew existed. She was profoundly moved by what she saw, even transformed by the people she helped.

Van became interested in police work one summer when she worked with a female officer on an abuse case. Van realized that there was an important place for women in the police force and that, in many ways, the police were on the front lines of social work. They helped in a direct way, and Van wanted to be a part of that.

She had promised her father she would try law school, and she did for half of a semester. She hated it and hated the arrogance and self-centeredness of the students. They were the best and the brightest, and they never let anyone forget it. They saw everyone as competition. She dropped out and headed west.

Her parents had denounced "the mess" she was making of her life. "Why can't you be more like your brothers and sisters?" Dad had asked. "You must take after your mother's side. The Chandlers all had good heads on their shoulders. Your mother's family was flighty."

"I blame your father," Mom had said, "for allowing you to watch too much television. You were always more interested in television than the others. You also read too much. Those awful novels you used to read. They affected you somehow."

She wondered if her mom would approve of the romance novels she now found herself absorbed in, and with that she remembered why she had come to the mall. Why the sudden urge to buy the gift today? She knew the death of Brad Armstrong's parents had shaken her up. What if Mom and Dad died before reconciliation? What then? she thought. Would she live out her life beneath a cloud of guilt? Could she ever forgive herself if such a thing happened?

She forced the thought from her mind. She was standing by a rack of kitchen utensils. She smiled. Perhaps she would buy something practical and down-to-earth this year, something sensible.

* * *

On Friday afternoon, Conrad stopped working on the computer program he was writing and turned to look at Brad who was sleeping in a recliner in the far corner of the study. Brad's right arm was stretched over his head, his left lay across his stomach, his long legs laid the full length of the recliner, and his feet hung over the end of the footrest.

Brad had taken a shower and changed into clean jeans and a fresh T-shirt he'd borrowed from Bishop Henderson. His hair's wetness made it look blacker and shinier than usual. His thick, black eyebrows were furrowed as if he were experiencing an intense dream. There was nothing striking about him. He was a nice guy, and that showed in his face. Even though they were the same age, Conrad had always looked up to him like a big brother. Conrad's own brothers were in junior high when he was born and had moved out by the time Conrad was experiencing problems in grade school.

It was still painful for Conrad to recall that he was bullied throughout grade school and into junior high. David, the neighborhood bully, targeted him beginning in kindergarten. Conrad had been physically overweight and emotionally underweight, and David sensed he could not or would not defend himself. Conrad became David's prey.

For four years he was intermittently chased, punched, and called names. Even as an adult he cringed when he thought about it. He'd tried to time his departures from school to avoid David but lived always with some amount of anxiety. Many nights he fell asleep praying David would die. Once when David was calling him names, Brad had walked up to Conrad. "You don't need to listen to that," Brad said. "You're better than that. Just walk away."

He remembered one day after school when Brad took him down the street past David's house. "I want you to understand something," Brad had said.

They walked past David's house more than once and heard through an open window David's parents screaming at one another and at him. "David," they could hear his father yell, "you stupid little crybaby. Go to your room and don't come out. You don't get dinner, you little idiot. What a loser!"

"His dad's a drunk," Brad had said.

Conrad still remembered the pain he felt standing in front of David's majestic house that fall afternoon. He still remembered the orange and red leaves sweeping across David's lawn as he recalled all the prayers for David's death.

He had a new understanding of David after that. After being called a crybaby by his father, David could feel temporarily relieved when making someone else cry.

It was Brad who explained to Conrad that he was being picked on, not because of his weight or red hair but because of the way he carried himself. Brad taught him how to stand up for himself.

The tormenting reached its climax one afternoon when David tried to block Conrad from going into the school bathroom. Conrad had looked straight into David's eyes and summoned courage from somewhere inside to say, "Leave me alone, David. I didn't do anything to you."

David answered by knocking him to the ground, but Conrad picked himself up and pushed past David into the bathroom. That was all it took. David lost his power. As Conrad looked at Brad, he realized that Brad needed him now like he had needed Brad back in elementary school. Brad needed to know he had a friend and was not alone.

* * *

When Brad woke up, he kept his eyes closed. He knew Conrad would want to talk to him and he wasn't ready for that. He wasn't ready for the questions he knew Conrad had, questions for which he had no answers.

He had walked through the morning in a fog, numbed by pain so that nothing seemed to touch him. Bishop Henderson then gave him a blessing and, to Brad's relief, he felt some leaden darkness breaking up inside him. Bishop Henderson then prayed that he would be able to endure the trials he was going through. As he prayed, a peaceful feeling overcame Brad, but the pain, the intense sorrow, remained.

Brad and Bishop Henderson had talked for a long while about the purpose of life, about the spirit world, and eternal families. Brad thought back on that day when his family had gone to the Salt Lake Temple.

They had only been members of the Church for a year, and Brad had not understood everything, but he could comprehend that they were going to be sealed together forever by God's power. He understood that there were men on earth who had been chosen to hold the power to seal for eternity.

While he had always appreciated the fact that his family was an eternal family, he had never understood its significance as he did today. Never had it meant so much to him. He tried to imagine his parents dressed in white as they had been when they were sealed, and entering the spirit world. He was sure relatives and friends had greeted them.

They were in a better place, he knew, but it was small comfort in the wake of his overwhelming emptiness. As he imagined the future, he saw a large void: no parents attending his graduation; no parents to bid him farewell when he went on a mission or to welcome him home when he returned; no parents to watch his sealing in the temple; no parents to love his children as grandparents. No parents.

He said a silent prayer and, once again, a peaceful feeling overcame him. He knew he would be all right someday, that he would be with his parents again; however, he also knew the pain would take a very long time to go away.

CHAPTER 4

On Friday night Van parked her Taurus in front of the large Victorian-style house on G Street in the Avenues. The snow was falling hard again, and sharp gusts of wind were slapping it against the windshield. Narrowing her eyes, she studied the dimly lit interior of the house. The elaborate Queen Anne with towers, bays, and porches had been divided into three apartments. She dreaded going into her ground-floor apartment's emptiness tonight.

A light glowed from the projecting bay window on the second floor. That was her neighbor, a young artist who sold a few paintings in the galleries downtown but was being supported by his parents back in Seattle. There were no lights coming from the tiny windows of the gabled roof where a young university student lived. She worked nights as a waitress in a downtown pub and usually didn't get in before one or two in the morning.

Of course, Van's roommate was home—Groucho, her grouchy old Siamese cat. Van pushed open the car door, and a gust of wind blew cold and snow into the car. She jumped out and slammed the door, then she raced across the slick walk but slowed herself as she stepped up the porch steps. They could be treacherous when icy.

Warm air embraced her as she stepped inside her apartment, and Groucho meowed and rubbed against her legs as was his custom when she came home.

Blinking to clear her eyes of the snow, she glanced down. "Hungry, old man?"

He meowed.

"Okay, Mama's going to feed you. Give her a minute to get her coat off."

He meowed again.

"You're welcome."

As always her apartment offered restful repose. An old oriental rug that she'd bought at a yard sale covered the living room floor. It had mellowed into soft shades of blue and pink long before she had obtained it. She'd reupholstered the couch and chair she bought at a thrift store in light-blue fabric too elegant for her apartment, but it reminded her of her mother's sitting room couch. She didn't use those pieces much anyway. She spent most of her time in the blue recliner she'd splurged on last Christmas. Her entertainment, a stack of romance novels, a CD boom box, and a stack of pop music CDs, surrounded the recliner.

Anyone who had ever visited her apartment found it odd that a police detective enjoyed romance novels. They expected her to read hard-boiled detective novels or police procedurals. *Give me a break,* she thought. *I deal with that stuff all day. I need something soft in my life.* Sure, many romance novels had silly heroines and improbable plots, but they were relaxing and enjoyable to read. At least someone lived happily ever after.

Against the wall opposite the recliner stood her TV. A hopeless insomniac, especially when she was on a tough case that got under her skin, she would lay in her recliner and watch TV or listen to music until she fell asleep in the early hours of the morning. Of course, she had to fight Groucho for a spot in the chair.

The pictures and prints on the walls and over the fireplace she'd selected one by one in small antique shops. Her favorite was of an eighteenth-century mother and daughter wearing frilly dresses and playing on the lawn of their English estate. Oh, how she missed her mother.

Van hung her coat in the hall closet and went into the kitchen with Groucho underfoot. "Okay, okay, fella. I'm getting it."

There wasn't much she could do with the kitchen. It hadn't been changed since it was decorated in the mid-'70s. Orange-and-green linoleum covered the narrow floor and complemented the olive green stove and refrigerator. When she first moved in, the walls had been covered with orange-and-green wallpaper, but after a year she talked the apartment manager into letting her strip the walls and paint them white.

She grabbed a box of Friskies and poured some into a bowl on the floor by the refrigerator. Groucho began chomping the tiny, star-shaped morsels, and the crunching sound seemed louder than what such small pieces warranted. Van emptied the stale water from his bowl, filled it with fresh water, then placed it next to the Friskies. Groucho immediately jerked his head from the Friskies and lapped up the water with his long, pink tongue.

"Boy, you are hungry, aren't you?"

Van pulled the gift she had bought for her mother from the shopping bag. What need Mom had for a stainless steamer, she didn't know. She carried it into her bedroom and dropped it on the pink and blue wedding-ring quilt her Grandmother, Nana, had given her when she was sixteen. It had been for her hope chest. By the time she was eighteen, her hope chest was so full, Dad had to buy her a second. When she left Boston, she left everything in what she now called her hopeless chests, except for the quilt. She couldn't bear to leave it behind. It was all she had to remind her of Nana.

Her Aunt Georgia had called her a year ago, the day after the funeral, to inform her that Nana had passed away. Mom and Dad had not bothered letting her know. She still felt the pain of that indignity.

Van went through the motions of eating dinner, but her mind was in a tumult over the Armstrong case. Her instincts told her Brad was innocent. She had always had good instincts—even Dad complimented her on her intuition. Why was Thornton being so bull-headed about Brad's sincerity? He usually listened to Van, especially when she had a feeling about a case.

Her mind reviewed the day's events. It had been a long one: the questioning and re-questioning of Brad Armstrong and the Hendersons; the search and re-search of the Armstrongs' beautiful home and the memories it had invoked of Beacon Hill; the walk around Federal Heights, knocking on doors, asking neighbors if they'd seen or heard anything; the dead ends and the final, grueling debriefing sessions headed by Thornton. He insisted on a daily debriefing to compare notes and mull over ideas. Thornton's intensity made these sessions stressful. She pressed her fingertips against the dull thuds in her temples brought on by weariness and too much thinking.

After she washed her dinner dishes, she joined Groucho on the recliner and picked up her scriptures. The scriptures could always soothe her nerves. She opened them to where she had left off the night before: "Now, we will compare the word unto a seed. Now, if ye give place, that a seed may be planted in your heart, behold, if it be a true seed, or a good seed, if ye do not cast it out by your unbelief, that ye will resist the Spirit of the Lord, behold, it will begin to swell within your breasts" (Alma 32:28).

Van lay back in the deep, cushioned chair and closed her eyes to ponder the verse. Groucho situated himself on her lap, and she could hear his purrs of contentment.

Her mind went back to her early years in Salt Lake City. She had just returned from work one evening when the doorbell rang and she found two young men standing on the porch, wide warm grins on their faces, both wearing dark suits, white shirts, and ties.

"Yes, may I help you?"

"We don't mean to disturb you, ma'am, but we would like to share a message with you if you have a moment."

"What kind of message?"

"A message about Jesus Christ."

Van laughed. "Don't tell me you're Mormon missionaries. The people back home warned me about you. The guys at work told me it would only be a matter of time before you found me."

"If you'd rather not talk with us, we understand," one of the missionaries said.

Van felt bad. They were so sincere, and she had laughed at them. "No, I'm sorry. Excuse me. I've been very rude. Please come in."

She held the door open wide and urged them in with a smile. The two young missionaries entered and she motioned them to sit on the couch, and Van sat opposite them in a chair.

"Well gentlemen," Van said, "please give me your message."

The tall missionary with dark hair coughed quietly and then said, "We are missionaries from The Church of Jesus Christ of Latter-day Saints. I'm Elder Thomas, and this is my companion, Elder Anderson."

Elder Anderson was also tall but had blond hair and glasses. Elder Thomas smiled and continued, "We would like to tell you what we believe about Jesus Christ."

Van listened and asked a few questions. The missionaries told her about Joseph Smith, the priesthood, and revelation. Some of the things they told her startled her. Yet there was a fascination as well, something that drew her interest and attention.

Before they rose to leave, Elder Thomas offered a prayer. Van could feel his sincerity, and as he spoke, a warm feeling came over her. She took the pamphlets they offered, and thanked them. When she closed the door on the two smiling faces, she was surprised that she had agreed to another meeting. Yet she knew that she wanted to again feel the warmth they seemed to radiate.

That night in her room Van read the pamphlets, then reread part of the one that told about the plan of salvation. It was late when she went to bed, but she couldn't sleep; too many questions and new ideas churned through her head.

On their next visit, Elders Thomas and Anderson stayed for over an hour while Van asked a whole series of questions about the pamphlets they had given her. They answered her questions using the scriptures. Van was impressed with their knowledge of the Bible.

Before leaving, Elder Anderson handed Van a small, blue book that he had opened to a certain section. "Read this," he said softly.

Van took the book and read, "And when ye shall receive these things, I would exhort you that ye would ask God, the Eternal Father, in the name of Christ, if these things are not true; and if ye shall ask with a sincere heart, with real intent, having faith in Christ, he will manifest the truth of it unto you, by the power of the Holy Ghost" (Moroni 10:4).

"This is the Book of Mormon," Elder Thomas said. "All we ask is that you read it and pray about it."

Van thanked them both and saw them to the door. That night she read the Book of Mormon late into the night, then awkwardly knelt beside her bed and closed her eyes. She was surprised at the warmth and sincerity of her own words. It was as though she were speaking to someone she was familiar with, someone she knew and trusted. As she spoke, a warm feeling came over her; a peace seemed to flow through her entire body. After the prayer was over the feeling lingered.

That next week, Van attended church with the missionaries. Everything in the service was different than any religious services Van had experienced, yet nothing seemed really strange. The service was simple and dignified. She could tell there was a sense of reverence for God present in the meeting. Van felt comfortable throughout the service.

After the service, Van was greeted by many people and thanked for coming. A young couple invited Van to have dinner at their house with the missionaries. The missionaries rode with the couple, and Van followed in her car. The atmosphere at their home was relaxed, and the time passed quickly.

Three weeks later, Van walked down into the water where Elder Thomas was waiting. She was dressed in white. Elder Thomas's hand felt firm and warm. When she rose out of the water, she looked up into the smiling faces of so many people that had become a family for her.

When she had dressed and brushed her hair, she entered the little room where her friends were waiting to congratulate her with hugs and kisses. Elder Anderson confirmed her a member of the Church and gave her the gift of the Holy Ghost. As she felt the hands of the priesthood holders on her head, warmth surged through her, and she knew without doubt that what she was doing was right. In the blessing that followed her confirmation, Elder Anderson told her that Heavenly Father had given her the gift of discernment and that she was to use it in her work to help others. For the first time, her intuition had been identified as a gift from God. She had somehow always thought of it as such, but from that moment, she would always think of her police work as a kind of mission from God to help people.

It was this intuition that was now telling her that Brad Armstrong was innocent. Yet the evidence seemed to be pointing to him. She said a silent prayer that she would be led to the truth in the case. She felt that it was important to have the guidance of the Spirit in her work. The mission of the Holy Ghost was to direct God's children to the truth, and the truth was of vital importance in her work.

Groucho stirred, and Van found herself returning to the present. She continued to read from the Book of Mormon for another thirty minutes and then went to bed.

She was restless as she found herself again rehearsing the events of the day. Her mind conjured up images of Brad's bushy-headed man.

Who could he have been? Why hadn't Brad asked his father questions about the man? What kind of relationship did Brad have with his father?

Her mind continued to race for the next forty-five minutes. Irritated with her constant fidgeting, Groucho jumped out of bed and found himself a spot on the floor.

Van, too, jumped out of bed. "Oh! This is driving me crazy."

Groucho looked annoyed and meowed.

"I'm sorry, old man. I should have been a cat so I could sleep all day and prowl all night. I'm going to get dressed and drive by the crime scene again."

Groucho meowed with a questioning lilt.

"I don't know why. I'm just doing it."

* * *

On Friday night, Brad was lying on his side on the bed in the Hendersons' guest room, his face toward the far corner where Conrad sat in a chair.

"I can't believe this has happened," Conrad said. "I mean, it's like something out of a movie. It's not something that happens next door to your best friend's parents. How're you handling it?"

"I'm not sure I am."

"You're probably in shock. How do you feel?"

"Alone."

"I'll bet so."

"When I was little—maybe four or five—I rode my bicycle down the sidewalk and around the corner," Brad said. "I went farther than I ever had before and got lost. When I realized I was lost, I felt alone. It was like I was the only person in the world. There was no one around to help me find my way back."

"What happened?" Conrad asked.

"I started crying. I mean I was screaming at the top of my lungs. Dad showed up and took me home. Except now, he's not around. He'll never be around again. I don't have anyone to take me home. I don't even have a home now." Brad felt hot tears streaming down his cheeks and dashed them away with the back of his hand.

"It's okay to cry. I mean I would if I were in your shoes. Don't forget to pray. You still have Heavenly Father. I really believe He listens. I wish there was something I could do. I'm not any good at this."

"Who is?" Brad said. "Thanks for letting me stay here. I don't think I could have stayed in our house tonight."

"Mom wants you to stay with us through the Christmas holidays. When school starts again, you can go back to the dorms with Jess."

"I wish I could talk to Jess."

"Did you try to call him again?"

"Yeah. I called Uncle Gordon's office too. His secretary said that on his way out the door to the airport, he mentioned something about staying in the city so he and Jess could go Christmas shopping early tomorrow morning. She didn't know where they would stay— probably a hotel. I hate to ruin your family's Christmas, Conrad."

"What're you talking about? You're part of the family. We've known each other our whole lives. Mom thinks of you as a second son."

Brad leaned up on his elbow and studied Conrad—short, stocky, a full head of bright red hair. They couldn't have been more different. Conrad had always been fascinated with computers. He learned programming as a child and breezed through a two-year technical training program at night while still in high school. He'd picked the right career track; Salt Lake City was a high-tech powerhouse with more high-tech companies than fast-food restaurants. He now had a job as a programmer and was able to work from home a good deal of the time.

Brad, on the other hand, knew enough about computers to use a word processor. There was no understanding of technicalities in his makeup; he hated math and despised statistics. Even knowing that, his dad wanted him to be a doctor. Well, that was one thing he wouldn't have to worry about anymore. Even as he thought it, guilt stabbed him in the heart. He leaned back, placing his hands behind his head.

"What're you thinking?" Conrad asked.

"Empty thoughts." Brad found it strange that he felt nothing now, nothing except weariness. He must put his parents out of his mind now or he would go crazy.

"Who do you think did it?" Conrad asked.

Brad's body became rigid. His eyebrows furrowed as he looked at his friend. Anticipation showed in Conrad's expression. Did he think Brad knew who killed them? Did he think Brad himself had killed them?

"How would I know?"

"Take it easy. Don't get so defensive. I was wondering if you had any ideas, that's all."

"I'm sorry, Conrad. It's just that the police treated me like a criminal. They think I killed Mom and Dad. They think I'm a murderer."

"It probably just seems that way right now because they have to ask so many questions. I'm sure they're just following some kind of normal procedure. At least your mom and dad's lawyer called you back."

"Yeah, it's just my luck that our attorney would be on vacation in Idaho when I need him."

"What did he say to you?"

"He told me to be cooperative and polite to the police and to wait for his return on Tuesday before I said anything else to the detectives."

"Sounds like what Dad told you today."

"I just want to get this thing over with, Conrad. I'm not lying about anything. Everything I told them was the truth. I don't even know my parents' attorney. What's he going to do, tell me what to say? It'll just make me look guilty if I have a lawyer."

"You know, Brad, innocent people need legal advice too. A lawyer can take care of a lot of things with the police so you won't have to deal with it. My advice is to wait until Tuesday when you can talk with your lawyer. Your head will be a little clearer by then."

"You don't know what it feels like, Conrad, to lose the two people you love the most in the world and to be suspected of murdering them. It's torture." Tears welled into his eyes again, and he brushed them away as fast as they appeared.

"I'm sorry, man. I really, really am sorry. I know you must be in pain. That's why I think you should let my family and your attorney take care of things for you right now. You need time to clear your head."

"You're right about that. My head is so full of details that seemed so unimportant before all of this happened—the time I woke up, the time it took me to drive to the airport, that man who was angry with Dad last week. Things I hadn't given much thought have become vital."

"What did the lady detective say about the man who threatened your father?"

"She didn't say much, but she seemed more interested than that other detective. I think she believed me. At least she pretended to believe me."

"Did you see anything unusual when you looked around the house?"

"No, but it's hard to concentrate when you're being escorted around your house like a dog on a leash. I wish I could have looked upstairs. No one can walk into a house with an alarm, kill the occupants, and walk away without a trace. There must be something there."

"Brad, the police went over every inch of that place. They took photographs, fingerprints, and drew sketches of just about everything. They said they were finished there. I don't think they would have left the place unsecured if they thought there was anything else that would help them. When did you all of a sudden become a forensic expert who can outsmart the police?"

"They said a patrol would drive up the street every half hour or so."

"Yes," Conrad said, "only because the neighbors are paranoid that a killer might be roaming the neighborhood at night, which is a very good possibility."

"With the police patrolling all over the neighborhood tonight, I doubt that any prowlers will be out and about, at least any intelligent prowlers."

"I don't like where this conversation is leading, Brad."

"Conrad, I won't sleep at all tonight unless I satisfy my curiosity to see upstairs in my house."

"I think that's a bad idea. You're tired. It's been a long day and it's dark out there, really dark. There's not even a moon. You'll have to turn on lights. You told the police that you were going to stay at our house tonight. The patrol will stop by and start asking questions. I'm sure there are neighbors on all sides looking out their windows tonight. It'll cause a ruckus."

"Don't you have a flashlight somewhere around here?"

"Why?"

"It won't cause a ruckus if no one knows I'm there."

Brad stood and walked to the window. Moving the curtain aside, he looked out at the black silhouette of his own house across the snowy lawn. "I'll sneak out this window so your mom and dad won't get all hyper about it. I'll hide behind that spruce tree. I'll make sure the patrol is not in sight, and then, I'll run to the back door and go in. I'll quickly check the upstairs out, and be back here without anyone even knowing I was there."

"Are you sure about this?"

"Positive."

CHAPTER 5

Shivering, Brad huddled behind the spruce and watched the two patrol cars that were stopped in opposite directions on the dark road in front of his house. The officers' muffled voices were lost in the gentle rumble of their engines. He heard a muted laugh, a cough, and then cars disappeared into the darkness like ghosts. He stood up, and the cold of his pants stabbed his legs and sent a tingle through his whole body. He felt numb and wondered if his blood had frozen in his veins.

He trudged toward the house accompanied by the muffled tramping of his feet in crisp snow, the faint clicking of his loose boot buckle, and the straining creak of his leather gloves.

He fumbled with the key and the back door came open. Ironically, the alarm had been left off. He supposed it was his responsibility to turn it on. He was a little paranoid about that considering the trouble the alarm had caused him that morning, and it seemed to him that the worst damage possible had already been done. The house was full of things, but they meant nothing to him now.

He left the door ajar. That gave him the security of a quick exit, although why he would need such an exit was not entirely formulated in his mind. The house was colder than he ever remembered it. It was like walking into a freezer or, more grimly, a morgue. An image flashed in his mind of his parents lying on their backs in bed, their eyes staring vacantly at the ceiling. Brad closed his eyes, trying to erase the image from his brain. Yet, in the back of his mind, he knew they were in a morgue, closed away in a drawer, their eyes still staring idly up.

He drew a deep shuddering breath. He couldn't let himself think about it. He'd get scared and run. He wanted to retreat to the warm comfort of the Henderson home, but he must look around first, find something to help determine what had happened. He forced his mind to imagine his parents in the spirit world. He imagined their joy and could almost see them smiling. Selfishness made him long to have them back in this world with him.

He stepped through the back hall and to the front foyer, holding his hand over the head of the flashlight to soften the glow. With a deep breath, he started up the stairs. The floors creaked beneath his weight, and every sound the house made sent his heart pounding. He forced his legs up the stairs. He had to be brave; he had to focus on his task despite the dead silence of the house.

He moved down the hall to the open door of his bedroom. Flashing the light in the room, he saw his duffel bag was gone. The police had, no doubt, taken it. They were interested in the gun, but that was to be expected, he guessed, considering that someone had used a gun to shoot his parents.

About two months before, his dad had approached him about buying a gun. It was such a strange thing for his peace-loving father to suggest; he had never shown an interest in guns before, but suddenly he was concerned for his personal safety. Sure there had been a few break-ins in the neighborhood last year, but wasn't Dad overreacting? As Brad thought again of his murdered father, cold reality settled on his mind. Had he known he was in danger?

Shaking the memories from his mind, Brad went on into his bedroom and scanned the bed. He reminded himself he had broken no laws by owning the gun.

Brad heard something—a muted fumbling. Was someone in the house? Was it his imagination? He walked to his closet, opened the door, and reached into the darkness. Brad felt around until he found his baseball bat. He clutched it in his right hand, the flashlight in his left.

Brad stepped back into the hall. It was probably just the sounds of an empty house, but moving down the hall to his parents' door required all the strength he could muster. At last it was done and he turned the knob. The door squeaked as he pushed it open. He started in, the floorboards creaking mournfully at every step.

Brad's eyes grew misty when he shined the light on the blood-stained mattress. The police had taken the bedding as evidence. Wearily he walked to the bed.

His taut nerves almost cracked at a sudden noise behind him. He turned and flashed the light toward the door. Hinges squealed and light illuminated a tall form standing behind the door dressed in black and wearing a ski mask.

As the man lunged at him, Brad dropped the flashlight and swung the bat fiercely. The bat hit the man but with no apparent effect. The man returned the favor by throwing Brad onto the floor. Brad started yelling, but his voice was quickly obstructed by the grip of large hands around his throat. He gagged and struggled for breath and soon felt himself slipping into unconsciousness.

He heard a crash. "Hold it! Police!"

The heavy body lifted itself up and dashed toward the window. Brad heard the breaking of glass, the cracking of wood, and a gunshot. The lights came on, and Detective Chandler raced to the window, her gun raised for action. A uniformed policeman stood in the doorway, his gun also poised for action. Detective Chandler grabbed a radio from her side. "Dispatch—Delta 512. Suspect is on foot headed southeast toward the university wearing black pants, black shirt, and a black ski mask."

Into Brad's swaying, darkened mind, cold sanity came back with a rush and he remembered what he'd forgotten for the moment—that he was frightened, scared nearly to death.

Detective Chandler turned toward Brad. "What're you doing here?"

Rage flowed into Brad and stiffened his spine. "This is my house."

"Then why are you wandering around in the dark? A neighbor called this in as a burglary. The back door was left open."

Brad glanced at the uniformed officer in the doorway, and then at the detective. "Why are you wasting your breath on me?" he shouted. "Why aren't you out catching the man who broke into my house? He's probably the man who murdered my parents. You haven't forgotten that, have you? Two people died in this room."

Brad fell into silence, and then began to cry.

More uniformed police officers appeared in the doorway. One of them stuck his head into the room. "Detective, they lost the guy."

Detective Chandler sighed and looked at Brad. "Look, I'm sorry I barked at you. It's been a long day. I know you loved your parents. I know it must be hard."

"What are you doing here?" Brad asked.

She sighed. "That's a good question. The truth is I'm a hopeless insomniac. When a case gets under my skin, I lie awake at night thinking of all the possibilities. Tonight, I found my mind racing over it. Questions started whirling around in my head. The racing and the whirling made me nauseous, so I decided to make use of my nervous energy by driving by the crime scene. It's not something I usually do at night, but since I live down in the Avenues, I found the urge hard to resist."

Detective Thornton walked into the room. "Chandler, what are you doing here?"

Looking up into the jeering humor of his blue eyes, Van felt swift anger stir, but she subdued it. "I couldn't sleep so I came to get another look at the crime scene location. Just as I was driving into the area, a call went out that a burglary was in progress here."

"Are you striking out on your own now? You know a few months of training doesn't mean you know it all."

The now familiar irritation and antagonism Thornton roused in her made her yearn to speak her mind, but she didn't dare. "What are you doing here, Thornton?"

"I was just leaving the office when a thought struck me. I couldn't remember the exact layout of the street so I decided to drive by on my way home."

"Sounds familiar," Van said.

"Detective Chandler saved my life tonight," Brad said.

"Look kid—"

"My name is Brad."

"Well, Bradley, I hope you don't mind my pointing out that Detective Chandler here wouldn't have had to save your life tonight if you hadn't put yourself in danger by coming back in here. I thought you said you were going to stay away for a while."

"It's my house. I have a right to be here. Besides, your patrolmen let an intruder inside my house. Who knows what damage he would have done if I hadn't caught him."

"What were you doing here, Bradley?" Thornton asked.

Brad looked at Van uncertainly. "It's like she said. I couldn't sleep so I decided to check out the house again. I thought maybe I would see something I missed earlier. I was disoriented then."

"Well," Thornton said. "We have a bunch of insomniacs here tonight. You did seem bewildered this morning, Bradley. It seems you've regained your composure. What did you expect to find here tonight?"

"Well, not my parents' murderer, but that seems to be who I came across."

Thornton smirked. "We don't know that the intruder was the person who killed your parents. He could be a looter or a curious sicko. It happens. A deranged person reads about a murder in the newspaper and then goes to check the place out. Maybe he figured there would be no one home after a murder. What I want to know is why you are sneaking around your house at night. It looks suspicious."

"You keep treating me like a suspect. I told you I don't know anything about what happened to my parents. You wouldn't even let me come upstairs today. I came here tonight to see if I could find anything that might help you find out who did this."

Van walked in front of Brad and took Thornton's arm. "Can I talk with you a minute alone?"

"Sure," Thornton said.

Thornton and Van walked out in the hall. "Why don't you take it easy on the kid? He's just lost his parents. Why don't we walk him through the upstairs? Maybe he'll find something."

Thornton's arm tingled beneath her firm grip. There was a tension, electricity, between them. "Van, we gave him a chance to look around today, and he didn't come up with anything."

"Yes, but that was downstairs. Maybe he'll find something upstairs."

"The kid's bluffing. I know it's a natural instinct to protect your own, but this is going too far."

"What're you talking about? What do you mean 'my own'?"

"You know what I mean. The upper class always sticks together through thick or thin. It's only natural you want to protect the kid. He probably reminds you of your little brother or something, but you're walking on thin ice."

She let go of his arm and her gaze bore through him like a diamond bit. She started to walk away. "Okay," he said. "Let's walk the kid through, show a little interest in helping him. I suppose it can't hurt."

"Officer," Thornton said, "could we put some plastic or something over that window in there?"

* * *

Brad walked through every room of the second floor, but could find nothing of any significance. The detectives would ask questions from time to time, but for the most part, they followed quietly behind him. He could feel their eyes boring through his back. He had a creeping realization that he was becoming the prime suspect in this murder investigation.

"I would like to look downstairs again," Brad said.

"Like you said, it is your house," Thornton responded.

As they walked down the stairs, Brad saw the Hendersons talking with a uniformed policeman. Darlene was in her bathrobe with a panicked look on her face. "Bradley Armstrong," she said in her southern drawl, "what on earth were you thinking? You've got my heart pounding. I won't sleep a wink tonight."

Bishop Henderson gave Brad a weak smile of reassurance, but it was weighted down with worry.

Brad stopped in the foyer and looked into Conrad's face. "Sorry, Conrad."

"Sorry!" Darlene shouted. "Why, he should have stopped you from coming over here."

"Are you okay?" Conrad asked.

"You could have been killed," Darlene said. "It chills my blood thinking that murderer came back here. He probably came back to get you, Brad."

A chill tingled through Brad's body, and the hair on the back of his neck stood up.

"That may not be the case, Mrs. Henderson," Thornton said. "It's not likely the murderer would break in here again."

"I heard murderers often return to the scene of the crime," Brad said.

Thornton sneered at Brad. "Where did you hear that, Bradley? On TV?"

Brad had met few people as chronically irritating as Thornton.

"Escort these people home, Officer," Thornton said.

"Come on, Brad," Darlene said. "Let's get you in a warm bed."

"Bradley stays," Thornton said sternly.

She marched to Thornton's side. "What do you mean? Brad has been through a traumatic experience today. He needs rest."

"Mrs. Henderson, Brad wants to take another look around, and Detective Chandler and I have agreed to help him."

The police officer guided the Hendersons toward the door. "I won't sleep a wink until Brad is safely in my home. Do you hear me, Detective?" Darlene threw over her shoulder as she left.

"I hear you, Mrs. Henderson. Welcome to the insomnia club," Thornton said as soon as Darlene was out of earshot.

Brad continued to hear Darlene's garbled protests as the policeman guided them down the front walk.

"We might as well start in the living room and work our way back." Detective Chandler said.

By the time they made their way to the study, Brad was exhausted. As he entered, he saw his father's sweater still hanging on the back of his desk chair, and picked it up. He held it to his nose. It smelled like Dad. Tears again welled in his eyes, and he quickly put the sweater down. Scanning the room, he saw his dad's papers were scattered on his desk with masses of disks—just as they always were.

"Didn't you say you were writing a paper last Friday when that man showed up?" Thornton asked.

"Yeah."

"Did you save your paper on that computer?"

"Yeah. Why?"

"Bradley, if you keep being defensive over everything I say, we're not going to get far. If you want our help, you need to work with us."

"I'm not being defensive. I just don't see what difference it makes if my paper is in the computer or not."

"That paper will help verify your story. I'm trying to help you here. You say you were working on a paper, and somewhere down the line someone is going to look in our report to see if we checked your story out. It's just a simple loose end we can tie up and go on to something else."

"He's right," Detective Chandler said.

Brad sat in front of the computer and turned it on. After it loaded, he opened WordPerfect and, after a brief search and several clicks, opened his paper. "It's there," he said. "I don't see how it really proves anything though."

"I'll show you," Thornton said. He closed the document and then navigated to the file's location on the desktop. When he found it, he right-clicked the icon and accessed the document's properties.

"There," Thornton said. "It shows that this document was last modified last Friday, which fits with your story, but still doesn't prove that a man threatened your father."

"You'll just have to take my word for it," Brad said.

"We only deal with hard evidence," Thornton said.

"You know, there's something wrong here," Brad said as he studied the computer screen.

"What do you mean?" Detective Chandler asked.

"I use this computer all the time. There used to be a lot more folders than this. There used to be a 'Biotech' folder just above mine. It looks like all of Dad's work-related folders are gone."

"Maybe your dad did some housecleaning this week," Thornton suggested.

"Why would he do that?" Brad asked.

"You tell me," Thornton said.

"He wouldn't," Brad said. "He worked at home a lot. He transferred documents from home to work all the time. He wouldn't suddenly change work habits for no reason."

"So let me see if I understand you, Bradley," Thornton said. "You're saying that someone broke into your house this morning, someone who somehow bypassed your security system. This same person killed your parents and then came down here and deleted work files from your dad's computer."

"Not just any files," Brad said. "Only Dad's work-related files. I know you think I did it," Brad said. "What can I do to convince you I didn't kill my parents?"

Thornton cleared his throat. "Would you be willing to come down to the station on Monday morning where we can ask you a few questions using a tape recorder?"

"Of course. Like I said, I don't have anything to hide."

"Would you also be willing to take a polygraph test?"

"A lie detector?"

"You said you would like to try to prove your innocence."

"My lawyer told me to wait until he gets back in town on Tuesday before I talk with the police."

"That's up to you," Thornton said. "I'm just trying to give you an opportunity to help us get this case moving."

"What time do you want me to be there?"

"Nine o'clock. I'll have Sam Potter, our polygraph examiner, administer the test. Then we'll have Bart Hogan take some fingerprint samples from you."

"Why? Are you arresting me?"

"No. Your prints are all over this house. We need to be able to distinguish your prints from the other prints in order to identify alien prints."

"Oh."

"And while you're down at the station," Detective Chandler said, "I'll have our sketch artist work with you on a composite of the man you saw here on Friday night. I'll also have our forensics examiners check this computer out. It's possible to retrieve deleted files."

Thornton frowned at Detective Chandler. "Let's finish going over the house so we can all get out of here."

CHAPTER 6

Saturday, December 13

Van was eating breakfast at her apartment when she got the call from Thornton. A body had been found down by the tracks on Rio Grande Street. The Rio Grande neighborhood surrounding the old depot was Salt Lake's version of skid row, a vast network of religious and social agencies established to help the vagrants who often came in on the rails. They begged in the streets during the day and slept in them at night. *When it rains, it pours,* she thought.

She parked near the scene beside Thornton's Lumina, and he approached her Taurus as she stepped out into the cold air. Snowflakes carried by a light but frigid breeze brushed across her face.

"What now, Thornton?" she asked.

"Uniform division gets this call from the shelter saying one of their regulars has spotted a pair of lifeless legs sticking out from under a sheet of damaged drywall in this vacant lot. They thought some wino had probably climbed up under the drywall to keep warm and was sleeping."

"But that wasn't the case?"

"He was sleeping all right—sleeping forever."

"Has the body been identified?"

"No."

They walked to where a group of uniformed officers and medical technicians were gathered around a weed patch against a backdrop of decaying brick buildings with broken and boarded-up windows and graffiti-covered walls.

"Is somebody getting a search warrant for these surrounding buildings?" Van asked.

"Scarface should be here with it soon," Thornton answered.

"Looks like he climbed up under the drywall to keep warm," Van said. "Probably froze to death. I don't know why they don't go to the shelters on cold nights."

"Well, I don't think that's how it happened," Thornton said.

Van looked at him curiously. Thornton always had a theory. He was usually good at sizing up the situation at a glance, but he'd been wrong enough times for her to know that his talent still needed developing.

"The disposition of the body," Thornton said, "tells me the body was moved here and covered with the drywall by someone other than the victim. Someone tried to cover their tracks here."

Two men wearing dark suits were walking toward them.

"Feds," Thornton muttered with disdain.

"What do they want?" Van asked.

"Your guess is as good as mine," Thornton answered.

One of them, a tall black man with a big smile, stepped forward and extended his hand to Thornton. "Detective Thornton?"

"Yes," Thornton said, shaking hands.

"I'm Agent Karl Morrison, FBI. This is my partner, Agent Roger Wingate."

Wingate, a young blond who looked like a California surfer, greeted Thornton.

Thornton nodded. "This is my partner, Detective Vanessa Chandler. How can we help you gentlemen?"

"We'd like to be involved in the investigation," Morrison responded.

Thornton chuckled, the fake, sarcastic laugh that Van had learned to hate. "Why would the FBI be interested in the death of a local wino?"

"So you have identified the body as that of a local vagrant?" Wingate asked.

Thornton eyed him. "No, not yet. Why don't you take a look? Maybe you'll recognize him."

Thornton was on the defensive. He was growling like a mutt whose territory was being invaded by two larger mongrels. Everything was a power play for him. He had to jump to conclusions and assume the worst, the worst always being the undermining of his authority.

The men walked over to the victim and looked down for a moment. Morrison looked back at Thornton, his white teeth shining from his dark face. "Yeah, I know a guy on the Salt Lake Police force who looks like this," he said.

Thornton smiled stiffly back. Van could sense the tension building. She decided to break the ice. "I'm interested to know how this case relates to the FBI," she said. "If you guys know something that can help us solve this thing, we'll be happy to take whatever we can get."

Thornton glowered at her. Morrison smiled and stepped away from the body toward Van, extending his hand. "Thank you, Detective Chandler."

She grasped his hand, which was warm in hers.

"We're special agents assigned to investigate the FTRA," Morrison said. "We were just recently transferred from the Denver office. Are you familiar with the FTRA, Detective Chandler?"

"Uh, no," Van said, glancing at Thornton.

Thornton smiled. "My rookie here is learning the ropes, gentleman. She hasn't worked the rail yards enough to know about the FTRA."

"But you have?" Wingate asked.

"I know the legend," Thornton said. "I know a lot of rail legends. I can tell you about Casey Jones if you're interested."

Morrison smiled. "I've heard that one. Detective Thornton, the FTRA is more than an urban legend. It's real. As many as 300 rail killings have been traced to this group, as well as many assaults and thefts."

"You mean it's a gang, a railroad-related gang?" Van asked.

"That's exactly what it is," Wingate said. "FTRA stands for Freight Train Riders of America. A Vietnam veteran formed it in the '80s. The gang has at least two thousand identifiable members."

"What's their purpose?" Van asked.

"Well," Morrison said, "some say it's a network to help vets read-just to mainstream life. Maybe it started out that way, I can't say, but it turned into something dark and violent."

"It's a male-dominated gang," Wingate said, "with violent initiation rites involving mob beatings."

"They also have discipline squads," Morrison added. "One takes care of internal discipline, and the other takes revenge on outsiders."

"What kind of internal discipline are you talking about?" Thornton asked. "I mean there aren't a lot of rules on the rails."

"That's where you're wrong," Morrison said. "The FTRA has blood oaths and internal secrets, especially about how the organization functions and its involvement in crime. Any member who slips with a secret or tries to leave the organization is killed, sometimes brutally."

"How many FTRA members have been prosecuted for these crimes?" Van asked.

"One that I know of," Wingate answered. "By the time the bodies are found, the suspects and witnesses could be twenty states away. Investigations usually turn up nothing, and the victims are typically homeless transients."

"So you think our victim here was killed by the FTRA?" Thornton asked.

"We don't know," Morrison answered. "We have to chase every lead. We can't be sure this isn't a local murder. That's why we have to work with local law enforcement agencies to try to get what little information we can. If it's a local matter, we don't want to interfere, but we're grasping at straws here. We just need information, and this is the only way we can get it."

Van saw that Thornton had lowered his tail. He was feeling more secure. The FBI was asking him for help, and Thornton clearly felt a sense of importance.

"Well," Thornton said, "we'll be glad to help you in any way we can. We're still searching the crime scene."

"We'd like to look around," Wingate said.

"Be our guest. Just don't touch anything," Thornton said.

They stepped back to the body where Uluave was standing with something in a plastic evidence bag. Again, self-satisfaction radiated from his dark face.

"What've you got, Tau?" Thornton asked.

"The body had no identification, but we found this paper in the pants pocket. Looks like it has a phone number on it."

"Let me see that," Thornton said, taking the bag. Peering through the plastic at the number, Thornton pulled his cell phone from his pocket and dialed. Everyone watched in anticipation as Thornton listened. A minute later his eyebrows rose.

"What is it?" Van asked.

"An answering machine," Thornton said.

"Whose?" Uluave asked.

"The office of Allen Armstrong at the University of Utah," Thornton said.

CHAPTER 7

Monday, December 15

A cold wind was blowing, and the scudding clouds overhead were the deep gray of slate when Brad parked in front of the Salt Lake City Police Department at 8:55 A.M The dim setting matched his mood: he felt like a condemned man going to his doom.

He had considered backing out more than once, but he knew that would make it look like he had something to hide. Thornton had questioned him so vigorously, and the others—Detectives Chandler, Jensen, Jones, and Carmichael, and even Conrad—had accused him with their eyes. He knew that look—the same look his father had given him when he had once lied about his grades. He knew the look, except this time he didn't deserve it.

Before he left that morning, Bishop Henderson had tried to convince him to cancel the appointment and wait until his lawyer could be with him. But the thought occurred to Brad that Bishop Henderson would not be so anxious about it if he didn't think Brad had something to hide. What did they all think he was hiding? Even after talking with his parents' attorney, he felt guilty, like he really was a criminal.

"Wait until Tuesday when you can tell me everything," the lawyer had said. But Brad could have told him everything he knew in a few minutes over the phone. What big story did he think Brad had to tell? He felt guilty because everyone around him was making him feel guilty for something he didn't do and had nothing to do with. Would this guilt show up on the lie detector? Maybe. That's another reason he didn't want the lawyer there. He would just create that sense of guilt that Brad had felt when he had talked with him on the phone.

A policeman was sitting at the front desk. Brad asked for Detective Chandler. The officer called her and told her that Brad was there. He stood and waited.

Detective Chandler greeted him with a smile. "Good morning, Brad."

"Good morning, Detective."

She escorted him into a dim, gray room with bare walls and a row of chairs lining one wall. One chair stood beside a table covered with inkpads and cards. He knew Thornton wanted to somehow use the fingerprints against him, but how? His prints must be all over the house—but they should be. His prints were on his gun, but again, they should be, and Thornton already knew they would be. How could the prints possibly help Thornton's cause? He felt the detective was out to get him and wouldn't stop until Brad was behind bars.

"Brad," Detective Chandler said, "this is Bart Hogan, our finger-print technician."

The short, stocky man reached out and grasped Brad's hand. "Hello, Brad, we met on Friday at your house. Why don't you sit in that chair?" Brad felt the cold limpness of his own hand as Hogan let go.

Brad sat, his knees shaking as the detective pushed the small table closer. He handed Brad a white card. "This is a ten-print card."

"Now," Hogan said, "I'm going to press each finger onto this ink pad, and then I'm going to direct your finger to the appropriate box on the card and press your finger from one side to another to get a clean print. Okay?"

"I thought you guys used computers to fingerprint these days."

Hogan smiled. "Computers can't do everything. Most police agencies still fingerprint the old-fashioned way. Computers help iden-tify and compare prints."

"How does it work?"

Hogan took the card from Brad. "Looks like you've already provided us with some prints." Brad felt his face blush as he looked at the marks from his sweaty fingers on the card. "I'll get a new one," the detective said.

He took Brad's right hand and took prints as he talked. "The system's called AFIS—Automated Fingerprint Identification System.

We take your right index fingerprint from this card and submit its numerically designated fingerprint sequence to the system. The computer tries to match it with prints already in the system."

"Why only the right index finger?" Brad asked.

"The right index finger pool is the largest. Let's say you were arrested under the name John Smith two years ago. Now you tell me your name is Brad Armstrong. The computer can send your numeric sequence right now through its network of computers, checking it against millions of prints, and within an hour the computer will spit out about ten possibilities based on some of the numbers in the fingerprint matching a known print sequence. I'll compare them and decide if there is a match. We'll know you're John Smith with a criminal record in no time."

"So the computer doesn't even make the final match?"

"No, but it does more than enough."

"But how do you get the prints you found in my house into your computer?"

Hogan started on Brad's left fingers. "Well, when we go to the scene of a crime, we are working with latent prints, which come from perspiration. There is a thin film of perspiration on the fingers, palms, and feet. Powder, alternate light sources, chemicals, and photographic techniques bring out a latent print. The print is usually lifted with tape. The computer will analyze the print and assign appropriate numbers to the ridges."

"So you'll scan these prints to match with the ones you found in the house?"

"Actually, I'll compare them visually and only scan the prints we can't identify," Hogan answered. "You've got an interest in police work, don't you? Maybe you should go into the field."

"When I was a kid, I wanted to be a policeman," Brad said.

"It doesn't pay much," Thornton said as he walked into the room—the overpowering smell of his cologne wasn't far behind. "If you want to make a decent living, don't do it."

"So why did you go into police work?" Brad asked Thornton in an effort to be friendly.

"I like the adventure," Thornton said and smirked.

More like you like the power, Brad thought.

"Well," Hogan said, "if you decide to go into police work, give me a call. Good fingerprint technicians are hard to find."

"I might do that," Brad said.

"Okay," Hogan said. "We're all done here. Here, take these Wet Wipes and clean your fingers."

Brad absently wiped his hands as he stood and turned to follow Detectives Chandler and Thornton to another room just like the one he'd left. Again, a chair stood in the middle of the room, this time beside a table that held a machine with wires.

Brad gulped once and found his voice. "Is the electric chair for me?"

Thornton laughed. "Yes, Bradley, we have it all ready for you."

Detective Chandler frowned at Thornton's heartless response. "Brad," Detective Chandler said, "this is Sam Potter, our polygraph examiner."

"Hello, Brad." Potter smiled and shook his hand. "Sit right here. Don't worry, it's not set up to hurt you."

"You're in the hot seat now, Bradley," Thornton said with jeering humor.

Brad's heart was pounding as he sat. His palms were sweating.

"Brad," Detective Chandler said, "you understand that we use the polygraph as an investigative tool, since the test usually isn't admissible in court?"

Thornton scowled at Detective Chandler.

"Why should I bother with this if the test doesn't count for anything?" Brad asked.

"On the contrary," Potter said, "it counts. It's hard to beat the machine. It measures stress—the greater the lie, the greater the stress, and the higher the reading."

"But what if you're nervous anyway?" Brad asked.

"The machine takes that into consideration," Potter replied. "Everyone is nervous when they take a polygraph."

"Let's get on with this, Potter," Thornton said.

"Okay," Potter said. "First I'll ask the good detectives here to leave the room and close the door behind them."

"We'll be waiting outside," Detective Chandler said as she followed Thornton out the door.

Potter turned on a tape recorder. "Okay, Brad. You have the right to remain silent and refuse to answer questions. Do you understand?"

"Yeah, but are you arresting me or something?"

"Anytime we ask potentially incriminating questions, we have to advise you of your rights."

"Oh."

"Anything you do say may be used against you in a court of law. Do you understand?"

"Yes."

"You have the right to consult an attorney before speaking to the police and to have an attorney present during questioning now or in the future. Do you understand?"

"Yes, but he won't be back in town until tomorrow."

"If you cannot afford an attorney, one will be appointed for you before any questioning if you wish. Do you understand?"

"Yes, I can afford one."

"If you decide to answer questions now without an attorney present you will still have the right to stop answering at any time until you talk to an attorney. Do you understand?"

"Yes."

"Knowing and understanding your rights as I have explained them to you, are you willing to answer my questions without an attorney present?"

"Yes."

Potter proceeded by interviewing Brad extensively, asking open-ended questions. He then said, "I need you to unbutton your top button and pull your shirt out for me."

Brad did as he was told. Potter placed sensors from a machine on Brad's chest, stomach, and the fingers of his right hand. He placed a blood-pressure cuff on Brad's left arm. "How do you feel, Brad?"

"Nervous."

"Now, Brad, are you eighteen?"

"Yes."

"Are your parents Allen and Peggy Armstrong?"

"Yes."

"You live in the dorms at the University of Utah with your cousin, Jess Armstrong?"

"Yes."

"Were you in the house when your parents were shot?"

"No."

"Do you use guns?"

"No."

"You've never used a gun?"

"No. I mean yes."

"You shoot guns at the gun club?"

"Yes."

"Do you own a gun?"

"Yes."

"Have you ever shot anything?"

"No."

"Have you ever shot an animal?"

Brad knew he'd just said he'd never shot anything, and now he felt trapped. He could hear his heart now, pounding like an African drum in his ears, temples, and head. "Yes. I went hunting once years ago with Jess and my Uncle Gordon."

"Yes or no only please. Do you shoot at targets at the range?"

"Yes."

"Do you shoot targets that are in human form?"

Brad felt the blood throbbing in his ears. "Yes."

"Have you ever shot a human being?"

"No."

"Did you love your parents?"

"Yes, of course."

"Did you ever argue with your parents?"

"Yes."

"Did you ever get angry with your parents?"

"Yes, sometimes."

"Yes or no only please. Did you ever argue with your parents about money?"

"No, that was never really an issue with us."

"They gave you whatever you wanted?"

"They gave me what I needed, and I was satisfied with that."

"Yes or no, please."

"Yes."

"Did you kill your parents?"

"No!"

"Did you pay someone to kill your parents?"

"No!"

"Do you know who shot your parents?"

"No!"

"Okay, Brad, we're going to start over and go through this a couple of more times."

After being given essentially the same interview two more times, Potter said, "Thank you for your time, Brad."

"That's it?"

"That's it."

"How did I do?"

"Our test shows that you told the truth during the test."

Potter helped Brad remove the wires. Brad walked out into the hall and smiled at Thornton. "I passed. Satisfied?"

Thornton smiled. "The polygraph is an excellent tool for getting at the truth, but it's not the only tool. Solid forensic evidence is what we depend on in court."

The euphoria that had overcome Brad like a great wave now washed back out, leaving him empty and depressed. He tried to think of something to prove his innocence, anything.

"What about Jess?" he asked. "Have you talked to him yet? He knows I was at the airport with him yesterday morning."

Thornton grunted. "We're still trying to get in touch with your uncle and cousin. Even so, there's about an hour where you don't have an alibi, Bradley. You were alone. You claim it took you almost an hour to drive from the airport to your parents' home."

"Yeah."

"Well, I drove it in less than thirty minutes yesterday in heavy traffic."

"I told you. It was snowing and the roads hadn't been plowed. There were accidents, I was driving slowly, and I stopped to help get that Bug unstuck."

"But all we have is your word for that, Bradley," Thornton said and walked away.

"Come on, Brad," Detective Chandler said quietly. "Amy Saunders is waiting to do a composite for us."

Detective Chandler led Brad down to Saunders' office, which was bright and cheerful with flowers in a vase and colorful paintings on the walls. Saunders was so absorbed in a sketch, she didn't notice Detective Chandler and Brad until Brad spoke.

"Nice paintings," he said.

"Thanks," Saunders returned, looking up with a smile.

"Wow. You're really talented," Brad said with obvious admiration.

"Thanks again."

"Brad," Detective Chandler said, "Amy Saunders is our official sketch artist, but she's also a respected artist outside the precinct."

Saunders was tall and thin with long, blond hair. "Why don't you sit, Brad?" she invited. He sat on a comfortable couch near Saunders' desk and only then noticed Thornton had not followed them. "Detective Thornton's not coming?" Brad asked.

"No," Detective Chandler said. "He's following leads and investigating other aspects of the case."

"You mean the aspects that implicate me in the crime?"

"Not at all, Brad. He's getting ready for his interview with you."

"I think it's funny he stood by while I was fingerprinted and polygraphed but disappeared when it came to identifying a suspect other than me."

"Let's get started," Saunders interrupted and sat behind her desk with a sketch pad, pencil, and eraser. "First and foremost I want you to understand that this is your drawing, okay? The only thing that I'm going to be is your hands for it."

"Okay."

"So Detective Chandler tells me you were sitting in your dad's study last Friday night working on a school paper."

"That's right."

"What happened next?"

"The doorbell rang. Dad was in the study with me working from his laptop."

"Your dad has a laptop?" Detective Chandler asked.

"Yeah, didn't I tell you that?"

Detective Chandler pulled out her notepad. "No. Where does your dad keep his laptop?"

"He keeps it in the study on a recharging tray on the desk."

"I didn't see it there, did you?"

"No," Brad said. "I don't think it was there. Maybe it was stolen."

"Would it be somewhere on campus?" Detective Chandler asked.

"I don't think so. He brought it home every night. He used it for the consulting he did on the side," Brad said after some thought.

"What kind of consulting?"

"I don't know. Pharmaceutical research with different companies. That's what he was, a pharmacologist at the U's med school. I think he's even done consulting for the Salt Lake Police Department."

"Really? So he was a medical consultant for the police department?" Detective Chandler was furiously taking notes as Saunders waited patiently.

"Yeah, I think."

"Brad," Detective Chandler said, "we could be on to something here. I'll try to find any cases your dad worked on. Will you be okay here with Amy?"

"Sure," Brad smiled.

Saunders laughed. "I don't bite, Van."

"I'm sure Brad's safe with you, Amy."

Detective Chandler left the room.

"Okay, Brad," Saunders said, "let's get back to it. Now, your father left the study to get the door."

"Yeah, and he started arguing with a man at the door. He came back into the study and got something out of his briefcase. When he went back into the foyer, I went to the study door and looked out to see who it was, but I didn't recognize him."

"Okay, I want you to describe in your own words the overall shape of the man's face and whether you thought it was more of a circle, more of a square, or more of a triangle."

"A circle, definitely a circle. He was round and pudgy."

"What do you mean 'pudgy'?"

"Kind of bloated."

"You mean his features looked swollen?"

"Yeah."

"Like he was retaining water or something?"

"I don't know. I guess."

"Was the man fat or overweight?"

"Yes and no."

"What do you mean?"

"Well, he was muscular like a weight lifter, but a weight lifter who was getting flabby and soft. You know what I mean?"

"Yeah, I think so," Saunders said as she began to sketch. "So he was a little heavy?"

"Yeah," Brad nodded.

"Where's Van?" Thornton asked, sticking his head inside the open door to Saunders' office.

"She went to check on something," Saunders said as she continued drawing. "She'll be back in a few minutes."

"Great." Thornton disappeared into the hall, but he didn't go far; Brad could hear him talking to another man in the hall.

"We got the warrant to search the dorm room and Armstrong's campus office this morning," Thornton murmured.

"Who did the search?" the other man asked.

"Van, Uluave, and me."

Brad felt his heart jump. They had searched his dorm room early that morning. Why did they get a search warrant? Why didn't they ask? And Detective Chandler had been involved in the search and hadn't told him. Could he trust her? Even as he thought the question, he knew the answer. Yes, he could trust her. First of all, Bishop Henderson told him she was a member of the Church. Even if he hadn't been told, he could tell she was a member. She radiated something that made him sense that she was a member. Second of all, he felt inside that he could trust her. He could sense that she wanted to find the truth and was not likely to jump to careless conclusions.

"Find anything?" the unidentified man asked Thornton.

Why were they talking in the hall where he could hear them? Was this another one of Thornton's tricks? Maybe Thornton was trying to make him nervous. Maybe he wanted to force him to make a move. Maybe they thought he'd lead them to the murder weapon or something. Brad smiled to himself. Thornton must think I'm an imbecile.

"Not really," Thornton said, "but you should have seen Chandler. Uluave and me, we tore the dorm apart. Chandler was running around like a mother hen, putting things back in place. I mean she put all the clothes back in the closets, remade the beds, picked up the trash we had dumped on the floor. She wanted to leave the place neat like we found it."

The unidentified man chuckled in the hall. "Why did she do that?"

"She likes the kid, thinks he's telling the truth," Thornton responded with a snort.

"Huh."

"Yeah, I'm telling you she's gotten emotionally involved in this case."

Saunders cleared her throat to regain Brad's attention. "I want you to describe in your own words, Brad, the overall shape of his eyes."

"What?" Brad could feel that blood had rushed to his face, burning his ears and neck.

"The man. What was the shape of his eyes?"

He had a hard time pulling himself back on task. "Round like his face and dark. He had big bushy eyebrows that grew together. His hair was dark and bushy. He had a mustache."

"How old would you say he was?"

"Probably about Dad's age."

"Which is?"

"Dad's forty-three."

"What kind of chin did he have?"

"Round and short."

The questions continued for thirty minutes. Saunders drew, erased, and drew again. "That's him," Brad finally said. "We've got to find him."

"Well, the problem with sketches," Saunders said, "is they sometimes look to a police officer like everybody."

Brad felt his heart drop. Even the sketch offered him little hope. "Yeah, I remember reading about a guy once who was shot by police in New York because he looked like a police artist sketch. The guy was innocent," he glumly recalled.

"It happens," Saunders said.

Detective Chandler walked into the office. "Well, we're gathering information on your father's police cases. How did the sketch go?"

Saunders held it up.

"Great," Detective Chandler said. "I'll start with the homeless shelters and food kitchens as soon as I get a chance."

"Why?" Brad asked.

"Because I have an idea that this person was homeless."

Detective Chandler and Brad walked out into the hall. Brad turned to her. "Why didn't you tell me you searched my dorm room?"

"We didn't need your permission, Brad. Is there a reason you wouldn't want us to search your dorm room?"

He frowned. "No, but it looks like I've gone from being a source of general information to being the prime suspect."

Thornton approached them. "Bradley, I've got one of our interview rooms ready. We would like to tape your statement for the record."

Brad frowned. Thornton was playing games with him; he could feel it. He was going to try to find discrepancies between the statements Brad made yesterday and the statements he would make today. What a fool he had been to play Thornton's game this far; what a fool he'd been to come without a lawyer; what a fool he'd been to think he could convince everyone of his innocence by himself.

"No, Detective Thornton," Brad said. "I have said all I have to say to you. If you need anything further, you can talk with my lawyer tomorrow."

Thornton frowned as Brad turned to walk away.

* * *

Brad was emotionally drained when he returned from the police station. As politely as possible, he made his way past Conrad's frantic questions to the guest room where he collapsed on the bed and fell into a deep but restless sleep. He dreamed he was staring into the cold eyes of a man holding a syringe with a large needle. The look of indifference on the man's face chilled him to the marrow.

"Ready?" the man asked.

"No, wait!" Brad screamed.

The man jabbed the needle into his arm.

"I didn't do it! You have the wrong man!"

"Too late," the man said.

Brad saw death coming and fell.

"Are you okay?"

Brad started awake and looked up into Conrad's concerned face.

"Yeah, I'm okay," he said after a moment. He lifted himself up and realized his shirt was soaked with sweat. He collapsed back on the bed, his long frame stretching the bed's length, his feet hanging over the end. "I'm a coward, Conrad."

"What? Are you kidding? You've always stood up to everyone and everything since I've known you."

"I don't want to die, Conrad."

Conrad stood beside the bed. "No one wants to die. That's natural. I'd be worried if you did want to die. But you don't need to worry. What happened to your parents was terrible, but that doesn't mean it's going to happen to you."

"I guess it's not the dying part that bothers me. It's the way I die. It's the pain and the horror of it. Do you think lethal injection is less painful?"

Conrad leaned back, revulsion showing in his face. "What?"

"I wonder whether it is painful, but it's not like you can ask someone who's been there."

Conrad grasped Brad's arm tightly. "Brad, what happened down at the police station today? What did they say to you?"

"They gave me a lie detector test."

"And?"

"I passed."

A wide smile formed on Conrad's face. "That's great. You're home free. That proves your innocence."

"I wish it were that easy, Conrad."

Conrad's smile dulled. "What do you mean?"

"Thornton still thinks I did it. He said the polygraph didn't mean anything. It's not even admissible in court. He hinted that he had some kind of forensic evidence on me."

"Like what?"

"I don't know. I'm scared, Conrad."

"Come on. You didn't kill your parents. You have nothing to be scared of. You don't have anything to hide, do you?"

Brad felt hot tears sliding down his face and tried to brush them away and regain his composure, but it was no use this time. He had lost control and began to sob uncontrollably.

Conrad placed his hand firmly on Brad's shoulder. "Don't worry. Everything's going to be okay. No one's going to hurt you. Mom, Dad, and I will make sure of that."

Brad marveled at the sudden reversal of roles. Now Conrad was his protector. He was being beat up by bullies, and now Conrad was there for him. He felt a sudden warmth, a sense of safety. He wanted to keep it forever, but it was elusive, fading in a moment. It was going to take more than Conrad's reassurance to get him through this; it was going to take real faith.

He realized that to this moment he had been relying on his parents' faith. He believed because they believed. If he was going to get through this, he was going to have to rely totally on Heavenly Father. He was going to have to do a great deal of soul-searching and praying to develop the kind of faith he needed. He said a silent prayer as he wiped away the tears that were still running down his cheeks.

"It's going to work out, Brad," Conrad said. "I just know it."

CHAPTER 8

Around noon, Thornton quietly approached Van's office. Her door was open, and he gazed in on her as she worked at her computer. That's the way she worked when she thought she had the tiger by the tail. She didn't let go until she was satisfied it couldn't get loose.

Too bad she's expending so much energy on a hopeless cause, Thornton thought. Bradley Armstrong was guilty. It was almost a textbook case. A good detective always starts with the family. Bradley was the only close family the Armstrongs had, and he had enough of a motive for Thornton. If a jury wouldn't buy the freedom motive, they would surely go for the money motive; everyone understands greed.

And there was the opportunity issue. Brad had access to the house around the time of the killings, and he had no solid alibi. It was so simple. Why couldn't Van see that? Didn't she know enough about human psychology to know that the killer instinct can come out in anyone who fails to suppress and control their natural desire?

He scrutinized her expression. Her beautiful face was marred by worry. He could see it wasn't adding up for her. She was fighting with herself on this one, with deep-seated biases, an upper-class indoctrination she wasn't even aware existed. This was the type of case every rookie had to face, a case where they had to fight with their own values and prejudices. The good detectives survived and were strengthened by the experience; the bad detectives dropped out and somehow had to learn to live with their weaknesses.

He had a partner who dropped out a few years ago because he couldn't handle it. Police work wasn't for the squeamish. You had to be tough. Often you had to be willing to accept the lesser of two evils.

That's where Van was going to run into trouble. Her values were so clear to her. Life was so black and white. She didn't see that gray no-man's-land between good and evil. Thornton hadn't always seen it either. Years of experience had brought it into focus for him. Maybe he was underestimating her, maybe she would survive. He wasn't yet sure.

She stopped typing and looked up to see him staring at her. "Can I help you, Detective Thornton?" she asked.

He smiled. "Just seeing your beautiful face among all these ugly mugs around the station helps me."

She frowned. "You should read the sexual harassment guidelines on the bulletin board, Detective."

He threw his hands up. "Since when is it sexual harassment to compliment a woman on her looks?"

"Since people started suing over it," she said.

He stepped into her office. It was always neat and orderly. Even the papers on her desk were sorted and stacked. "How do you work in here?" he asked.

She looked around defensively. "What do you mean?"

"It's so neat."

"I can't think in a pigsty," she said. "That's why I never go into your office."

He tried to look hurt by her comments but found himself chuckling.

"What are you working on so intensely?" he asked.

"I've been on the Internet looking for information about the FTRA."

"What're you doing that for? Let the FBI worry about it. We need to solve a local homicide. I don't think the FTRA had anything to do with it."

"What if they did? What if they killed the man down at the tracks as well as the Armstrongs?"

Thornton found himself staring at Van with an open mouth. "Where do you get these ideas, Van? That transient's death most likely has nothing to do with the Armstrongs."

She looked at him with wide eyes. "Of course it's connected to the Armstrongs. That man had Allen Armstrong's phone number in his pocket. Come on, Thornton. Don't tell me you think it was a coincidence."

He walked up to her desk and leaned over it, supporting himself on it with the palms of his hands. "No, Van, I don't think it was a coincidence. Our friend Bradley told you that his father often hired transients to do his drug testing up at the U. I talked to some people in the shelter and at several of the soup kitchens. They all confirmed that Allen Armstrong often gave out his card to transients in need of money. He even talked to the director of the shelter about recommending vagrants who would be around for several months or years. Sometimes, when he ran out of cards, he left his phone number with transients. There's nothing strange about finding his phone number in that man's pocket. It only proves that the man was a vagrant. We may never find his real identity."

"Well, I still think the FTRA is worth looking into. These people are dangerous. I think there must be a connection between Armstrong's work with transients and his death. Obviously some of the transients knew where Armstrong lived."

"What makes you say that?" he asked and lifted himself from her desk.

"Bradley told us a transient came to their house a week ago Friday."

"And you believe that story?"

"Yes."

"Well, even if it was a transient who came to the house, he probably has nothing to do with the killing of the Armstrongs. One of this guy's guinea pigs was trying to get some more money, that's all."

Van turned toward her computer monitor. "Did you know, Thornton, that there were over five hundred deaths along rail tracks last year?"

"No, Van, I can't say that I did know that. I guess I need to brush up on my rail trivia."

"I found an article about Agent Morrison."

"Really." Thornton found his interest aroused despite his efforts to assign Morrison to the nobody files of his mind. "What did it say?"

"Morrison went undercover as a hobo to try to infiltrate the FTRA. Do you know where the term *hobo* comes from?"

Thornton found his lips curling into a smile. She was so darn cute when she was in her knowledge-dispensing mode. "No, I don't."

"Well, after the Civil War, many Confederate soldiers returned to find their farms destroyed. One of their only options was to go to work building railroad tracks. Since they were farmers, they were dubbed 'hoe boys' and later 'hobos.'"

"That's all very interesting, Van, but I'm not sure it's going to help us with our cases."

"I am. I think that Allen Armstrong mingled with an underworld he knew nothing about. He either found something out he wasn't supposed to or irritated one of the gang leaders. Did you know Allen Armstrong consulted with the Salt Lake City Police Department on several drug-related cases?"

"No."

"I don't think it's a coincidence that Brad said a homeless man came to his house and threatened his father and then another homeless man shows up dead by the tracks with Allen Armstrong's phone number in his pocket. There's some connection here."

"Well, the man down by the tracks doesn't have the physical dimensions described by Brad so he can't be the man who threatened Allen Armstrong."

"No," Van said, "but maybe the man who killed the Armstrongs also killed this man by the tracks. Maybe this vagrant was a member of the FTRA, and he wanted out. Maybe Allen Armstrong told him he would help him get out. Maybe the gang sent someone to kill Allen Armstrong."

"You have a lot of maybes there," Thornton observed.

"That's how a good detective works, right?" she replied.

"Right. But a good detective also relies on hard forensic evidence. I'm going to reserve judgment until I get the coroner's reports and the ballistics reports. I'm not much for conspiracy theories. Usually, the most simple solution is the right one."

She looked up at him in a thoughtful pose. "Maybe. We'll see."

"Yeah, we'll see."

* * *

Van arrived at Thornton's office later that afternoon to discuss developments in the Armstrong murder case. Thornton sat behind his desk in a navy jacket, pleated trousers, blue-and-tan-striped shirt, and navy designer tie.

"Got a date tonight, Thornton?"

"As a matter of fact, Van, I do."

"Good for you. Anyone I know?"

"Why?"

"Just curious, that's all."

"Don't worry, Van. She's of the same social standing as me. We're two peas in a pod."

Van ignored his preoccupation with status and pulled out her notepad. "Okay, Thornton, let's get to this so you're not late for that hot date."

"Maybe you're in a hurry because you have a date tonight, Van."

"Not that it's any of your business, Thornton, but I do have a date tonight."

"Anyone I know?"

"As a matter of fact, you do."

"Who?"

"None of your business."

Thornton cleared his throat. "I just talked to the D.A. and he'll probably go for the death penalty on this one."

Van could feel the blood draining from her face. She'd received a stunning blow without warning and, in the first moments of shock, did not realize what had happened. Through it all, she felt Thornton's gaze on her, pitying, annoyed at her obvious concern. He'd been right. She knew that. Somehow, she'd become emotionally involved in the case. Maybe Brad was like her little brother. Maybe she did want to protect him. She swallowed hard and found her voice.

"What about the polygraph?"

"What about it?"

"You know Brad couldn't have beaten the test. He's telling the truth. Why can't you accept that? I hope your objectivity hasn't been compromised in this case."

"Van, it's not my objectivity that we need to be concerned with. You know we can't just plug a person into a machine and determine whether or not he's lying."

"You wouldn't be saying that if it had shown he was lying. You'd be praising the accuracy of the test."

"It doesn't matter what I'd be doing. The Utah Supreme Court has rejected the polygraph because it's unreliable. Besides, we have hard forensic evidence pointing to Brad."

"What kind of hard evidence?"

"The ballistics report says the kid's .22 was used to kill both parents. Also, the kid's prints were all over the gun, the two empty casings, and the four remaining rounds."

"His father was with him when he bought that gun. He bought it to go shooting with his father, not to shoot his father."

"So where's his dad's gun? We found no other gun in the house."

Van cleared her throat. "I don't know about the other gun, but anyone could have broken into that house, taken the gun from the duffel bag, shot his parents, and returned the gun to the bag."

"Not just anyone, Van. It had to be someone with the security code who had a motive to kill Allen and Peggy Armstrong and who knew where the gun was. The kid had means and opportunity. There were no signs of a break-in, remember? And we questioned all the neighbors. No one saw anything that morning except Bradley Armstrong in his fancy BMW."

"No one heard shots either," Van retorted. "It's not like these people were aware of what was going on around them. And what about the person who broke in last night? There was no sign of a break-in there either. And I called the security company. Unfortunately the Armstrongs had an older system. The company only monitors alarm activity. No log of activation or deactivation is maintained. If an alarm situation occurs, the system is designed to communicate a signal to the monitoring system, and a security representative calls the local police with the address. The representative said that someone could arm the system without the security code by pressing the ARM key. They have sixty seconds to leave the house."

"So?"

"So maybe the system was off when the intruder entered the house, and the intruder turned it on when leaving by pressing the ARM key."

"Why would they do that?"

"I don't have all the answers, but I have a lot of questions. Something's not right here. What happened with that intruder last night? How did he get away?"

"He disappeared into the university somewhere. There was no way we could find him. Think like a detective, Van. Why would someone break in the house, kill the Armstrongs, and put the gun back in the kid's duffel bag? My bet is the kid went to the house that morning while his parents were still sleeping, shot them, and set the alarm off to make it look like he had just gotten there to find his parents dead. He knew the security company would call the police, and he would pretend he had just stumbled onto his parents. The kid's smart. I'll hand him that."

"If he was going to do that, why wouldn't he play it up right? Why didn't he break a window or jimmy a door? Why set up a ridiculous situation where someone broke in without setting the alarm off?"

"Breaking a window or a door would have set the alarm off. The police would have come right away and caught the perpetrator before he killed the Armstrongs. The kid had to set up a situation where the intruder slips in without setting off the alarm. That way the intruder has plenty of time to go upstairs, find the Armstrongs in bed, and kill them. When I was questioning him, he kept reminding me that burglars with knowledge of electronics could get past security systems."

"So you think he worked this whole bizarre situation out?"

"Yeah, the only problem was getting rid of the gun. Maybe he didn't anticipate a search of the whole house. He doesn't know how it works. Maybe he thought we would only search his parents' bedroom."

"But we didn't find gun powder residue on his hands or any of his clothes—even those in the duffel bag," Van pointed out.

"He wore gloves and then tossed them and the clothes he was wearing," Thornton guessed.

"Thornton, your scenario is more fantastic than his."

"Truth is stranger than fiction, Van."

"Except my instincts are telling me that his story is true."

"Van, you're grasping at straws. I know this is hard, but you're going to have to face facts. The kid either paid someone to murder his parents or he pulled the trigger himself. The only footprints in the snow going to the house belonged to Brad, the paperboy, and the milkman. The only tire tracks in the driveway matched the kid's BMW."

"The weather reports from that morning say it didn't start snowing until 5:20 A.M," Van pointed out.

"Look Van, the kid hated premed, he hated the direction his father wanted him to go. We found half a dozen diaries in his dorm room. The kid wrote down everything. He wanted to be a journalist, not a doctor. He was apparently frustrated and angry. Van, you're not the first person to be taken in by boyish charm."

"When are you making the arrest?"

"As soon as we screen the case with the district attorney. Hopefully he will sign off on the charges and issue the arrest warrant this afternoon."

Van looked into Thornton's blue eyes. "You're jealous of him, aren't you? You resent him. Please, Thornton, don't let your feelings get in the way of doing what's right in this case."

"I don't know what you're talking about, Van."

"I want to be there when you make the arrest."

"Don't worry. You'll be there. You're my rookie, and I want you to learn all you can. Watch, listen, and learn."

CHAPTER 9

Brad had just sat down for dinner with the Hendersons late Monday afternoon when the doorbell rang. Bishop Henderson went to answer the door. Brad could hear Thornton's voice.

"Mr. Henderson, is Bradley Armstrong here?"

Brad walked to the foyer. Thornton, Detective Chandler, and a couple of uniformed officers were standing on the porch. "What do you want?" Brad asked as he approached the door.

"Bradley Armstrong, I have a warrant for your arrest for the murder of Allen and Peggy Armstrong."

Brad stood stunned. Bishop Henderson put his hand on Brad's shoulder. Thornton motioned for him to come outside, and Brad obeyed like a zombie. The bright sunlight in the front yard clouded, and the bare trees blurred through tears. Brad dropped his head and struggled not to cry. Crying was so useless now. Squeezing his eyes shut to keep back the tears, he was startled by a hand on his arm. It was Thornton.

Darlene and Conrad had made their way to the foyer. "No!" Darlene gasped.

"I can't believe this," Conrad said. "Brad didn't kill his parents. He couldn't have."

Brad looked up. Conrad looked confused, and doubt showed in his eyes. He was probably wondering if a murderer had stayed in his house last night. Everything Brad had said or done the previous night was probably going through his mind.

"Put your hands against the wall, Bradley," Thornton said.

Brad placed his hands against the brick wall. Thornton frisked him and jerked Brad's hands behind his back. His head hit the hard wall, and he felt the tight grip and cold steel of the handcuffs. Thornton pulled Brad up from the wall. Brad could only glance into the horror-struck eyes of the Henderson family before he bowed his head in shame as Thornton read him his rights and pushed him to the patrol car.

As the police cruiser drove away, Brad looked back at the shocked family standing on the porch. Somehow he had to prove his innocence. If it was the last thing he did, he wanted to see the look on Thornton's face when the real killer was caught. He wanted to hear an apology from Thornton's arrogant mouth.

But he didn't have time to think about all that now. He had to somehow get himself out of jail.

At Salt Lake City's Adult Detention Center, Brad was greeted by a group of reporters. The snapping of the cameras and hollering from the press corps faded in the background as the car drove around a wall onto the jail grounds.

Brad was pushed into an indoor waiting area. "Not nearly the number of reporters who were waiting for that killer they brought in here last month," the officer standing at the main desk said and checked the arrest warrant. "Proceed."

Brad was placed in a holding area to wait his turn for booking. There were phones, and he called Bishop Henderson. They only talked for a few minutes. The bishop assured Brad he would get in touch with his lawyer and apprise him of the situation.

After waiting for what seemed like forever, Brad was turned over to two guards, a short stocky one and a tall thin one, who searched him again.

The tall officer took everything from Brad's pockets, catalogued the items, and placed them in a brown envelope.

"Sit!" the short officer growled.

Brad sat in front of a steel desk. The short officer conducted a brief, preliminary interview, then the tall officer hustled Brad into another room where he was placed in front of a gray screen. A Hispanic woman behind a digital camera took the photograph without any warning. "Turn to your right," she said with a heavy accent. Brad turned. Another photograph without warning.

Next the tall officer jostled him into a room where they pressed his fingers in gooey ink and turned them on a card. "I was finger-printed yesterday."

"Doesn't matter. Now just keep your mouth shut."

The officer shoved him into a small office for more information before moving him on to a gray shower room where an officer removed his handcuffs.

"You'll take a shower here."

Brad enjoyed the icy shower as much as the orange jumpsuit and matching flip-flops they issued him.

A tall, bald officer escorted Brad down a long hallway lined with steel barred doors as the cellblock occupants called out.

"Hey, kid, what did you do, skip school?"

"Watch your back!"

One occupant howled like a wounded canine, another sang a tuneless melody with the words "rottin' in the jail block." Many simply pounded on their doors.

The officer unlocked the next-to-last cell and pushed Brad in. "Is it always this noisy?" Brad asked.

The officer chuckled. "Yeah. Most of these people are insane, you know."

"When can I leave?"

He chuckled again. "Maybe tomorrow, maybe never. You'll have to talk to the judge about that."

The officer closed the solid-steel door which had a small horizontal slot apparently used for food trays. The twelve-by-twelve-foot cinder-block cell was painted institutional gray. "Big Jake," "Hard Head," "Bad Roy," and other nicknames were scratched into the paint. Brad found this impressive when he considered that sharp objects were among the possessions taken from those arrested.

Above the stainless steel urinal in the corner of the cell, "TTB," "Mohawk," and "Black Beard" were smeared on the ceiling in what appeared to be the fingerprint ink used in booking. Against one wall a three-inch cloth-covered pad topped a metal rack. This was the bed. Another like it was on the opposite wall with someone on it, apparently sleeping. Brad stepped over, sat on his bunk, and thought of his dorm room. He'd been whining to Jess all semester about how bad it was. Compared to this, his dorm room was a luxury suite.

"You snore?" a rough voice asked from the opposite bunk.

"I—don't think—yes—sometimes."

The face of his jail mate was turned toward the wall. He imagined someone with a hideously distorted face. "You snore tonight, and I'll kill you. You understand me? I'll kill you. It's easy, you know. I'll put your pillow over your face and smother you. You'll never know what hit you."

"I'll try not to bother you."

Brad stretched out on the hard bed. Staring up at the gray ceiling, unable to sleep due to the constant clanging of hard steel doors, he reflected on what had gotten him into this. His parents had been killed, and the police were blaming him. This was the sort of thing that only happened in the movies. People didn't really get wrongly accused of murder, did they? He couldn't imagine spending the rest of his life behind ugly steel bars. He would rather die.

Even as he thought it, a cold fear rose in his chest. Maybe he would die. Maybe he would be executed for the murder of his parents. No one would care; everyone he loved most in the world was now dead. His remaining friends and family would believe the police and turn against him.

The image of the doubt in Conrad's face surfaced in his mind, and for a moment he doubted too. Perhaps he'd killed his parents in some psychotic rage. Perhaps he'd gone temporarily insane. It happened. He saw it all the time on television. Maybe that would be his only defense—temporary insanity. He pushed the wild thoughts from his mind. He couldn't give in to such craziness. He didn't kill his parents and he knew it. He had to figure a way out. He longed for some paper and a pen. He needed to write his thoughts. Writing was practically an addiction with him, and he was suffering from withdrawal. He pacified himself by imagining what he would write if he could.

How did Bradley Armstrong, who had been raised in an affluent neighborhood and had never really had a serious crisis in his life, get into this situation? His parents had always taken care of his minor headaches and problems. They coddled and catered to him. He had lived his life in a sort of wonderland: life was great, school was great; everyone loved him, he loved everyone. He had existed in a comfort zone of the highest order. Now he was alone and didn't know what to do. He realized he didn't know how to take care of himself.

He had planned to start serving a mission in the summer after he finished spring term at the university. How could someone who didn't know how to take care of himself go on a mission? Of course he didn't have to worry about that now. He would probably never go on a mission now. He knew his parents would be terribly disappointed if he didn't go on a mission—but, of course, he didn't have to worry about that anymore either.

As he lay, his worries circled and swooped above him like buzzards, diving down to tear claws and sharp beaks into his tired mind. For a long time he was still, remembering people who were dead, remembering a way of life that was gone, and looking upon the harsh reality of a dark future behind bars. Youth and innocence had gone out of him forever. He could never regain it.

He said a silent prayer, and in his heart he told himself he would live through this. He closed his eyes and tried to concentrate on a happy thought—something positive and bright. He thought of his parents sitting with friends and family in the spirit world. They were smiling, happy. He drifted to sleep with that happy thought playing in his mind.

* * *

Van was walking toward her Taurus in the parking lot of the police station when Thornton approached her.

"You've been quieter than usual today."

"I've been wondering how Brad's going to survive the detention center."

"He'll be brought down a notch or two in there."

"That gloating air is so unbecoming on you, Thornton."

"Your emotions are showing through that thin skin of yours, Van."

The familiar anger that Thornton roused in her came to the surface. "I think you're wrong on this one, Thornton. I think you just arrested an innocent man. I think deep inside you know that."

"Don't start with me, okay? You're a lousy detective who's gotten emotionally involved in a case. You'll never amount to a hill of beans in this business, Chandler. Your skin's too soft, and you bleed too easily."

"Let's put my feelings for this case aside a minute—"

"Oh, so you admit you're emotionally involved?"

"It's called compassion, Thornton. Something you wouldn't understand."

"You know, Chandler, you've got claws like a tiger."

"And if you could put your feelings toward Brad aside a minute too—"

"Feelings? I don't have feelings for that punk. He's a name on an arrest warrant to me. Just another criminal statistic."

"Don't kid yourself, Thornton. You're jealous—not only of Brad but of 'his kind' as you put it. You're not punishing Brad; you're punishing all the rich kids in the world. Are you so insecure with yourself—"

"Shut up, Van! You don't know what you're talking about. You're a rookie. I had nothing to do with what happened. I'm an investigator. I gather the evidence, and the evidence speaks for itself. If the evidence says the kid murdered his parents, I can't change that. The D.A. takes what evidence I gather and makes a case. If the D.A. can prove the kid killed his parents, he deserves to be punished."

"I don't care what the D.A. thinks he can prove. The kid's innocent, Thornton. You know it. I know you know it. If you let Brad take the rap for this, it'll be on your conscience."

"I'll see you tomorrow, Chandler. I've got a date I'm going to be late for, and I thought you said you had one too."

"I'm not going to let you get away with this, Thornton. I'm going to prove you were wrong on this one, and that should scare you because you know you're wrong. And you know my investigative instincts can match yours any day."

* * *

Van reluctantly stepped out of the warmth of the Taurus. It was cold and a lousy night to be alone. Of course, her date was waiting on her in the apartment—Groucho. She pushed open the door and stepped into the warmth of her apartment and Groucho meowed and rubbed against her legs. *Who needs a husband when I have Groucho?* she mused

Blinking to clear her eyes of the snow, she glanced down. "Hungry, old man?"

He meowed. It was the same routine every night.

"Okay, Mama's going to give you something special tonight."

He meowed.

"You want to know what? Why, a nice juicy can of Fancy Feast."

Groucho meowed again.

"Why? Because we're on a date tonight. Didn't I tell you?"

She went through the motions of eating dinner, but her mind was in ferment over the dreadful outcome of the case. She dropped some chicken on the floor for Groucho who had polished off his Fancy Feast. "Thornton would have a good laugh if he could see my date tonight, wouldn't he Groucho?"

She looked over at her worn recliner, which held her nightly relaxers—a comforter, a bag of potato chips, and a romance novel. She would sometimes go on blind dates to make her friends happy, but most of them turned out to be disasters. Either the guys didn't feel comfortable dating a homicide detective or she didn't feel comfortable with their interest in bodies and death and gore over dinner. This evening she didn't have to fight Groucho for a spot. He had moved for her and then found himself a spot on her lap. He seemed to sense that something was wrong.

Van watched the news. There was a report about Brad's arrest. Van could only pray that Brad would have his day in court. He would have a chance to prove his innocence. Hopefully a fair and impartial jury would arrive at a truthful verdict. Each side would be given the opportunity to present evidence and to cross-examine the evidence submitted by the opposing party. The jury would not only be able to hear both sides of the story, but would be able to judge the merit of each side upon cross-examination.

Of course, she realized it wasn't as simple as that. The outcome of a trial depended on the evaluation of many intangibles, most of them subtle and subject to difference of opinion. Only the jury could decide if the prosecutor had proven his case beyond a reasonable doubt. And while she could think of a lot of doubts the defense could throw at the jury, the prosecutor had a solid case with the motive, means, and opportunity. A gut feeling that he was innocent had no place in the courtroom.

The prosecutor would be persuasive. Even Van had been astonished at the amount of evidence Thornton had compiled against Brad. She had momentarily gone into her logical mode of police procedure. If she relied on it alone, she might be on Thornton's side—Brad could be guilty.

But she had never been one to rely on reason alone. She always went with those instincts she was born with. Her confirmation blessing said it was a gift, and she had since accepted it as such. There was no way she could communicate her feelings about the case to Thornton. He was a hard-nosed cop who relied on reason and hard forensic evidence. It had served him well all these years. He was good, and Van knew it. But there was always that case, that one case where reason didn't apply. That's where she came in. That's why she was in the position she was in. Her gift of intuition had helped her in many cases. She couldn't deny that gift now, no matter how persuasive the evidence to the contrary was.

The phone rang, and she picked up the receiver. "Hello."

"Hi, Van. This is Tau Uluave."

"What's up, Tau?"

"I wanted to let you know that I searched the Armstrong house again this afternoon. The laptop isn't there. I also checked out his university office again. The laptop's not there either."

"Thanks, Tau."

"Sure, Van."

"Good-bye."

She decided to get a good night's sleep. She had a lot of work to do tomorrow. She would map out the whole case on the old corkboard in her office. It always helped her organize her mind to have the case visually before her. Maybe her reason and intuition could work together to help solve this case. She also had to take Amy's sketch down to the homeless shelter.

Van felt a heavy burden weighing on her. Somehow she felt like it was her responsibility to help Brad get out of this mess. She knew Brad was innocent, and she felt a moral obligation to find the truth. She had often felt that the Spirit was directing her in her work and that Heavenly Father increased her intellect and physical strength. Yet, somehow, she found the burden of this case too heavy to bear.

She went into her bedroom with Groucho running ahead of her and knelt beside her bed to pray. She explained to Heavenly Father her concerns and asked that He comfort her in this time of distress.

CHAPTER 10

Tuesday, December 16

For a moment, stiffened by the cramped position in which he had slept, Brad could not remember where he was. The steel bunk under him was harsh against his body. Then he remembered. He popped up to a sitting position and looked around. Thank goodness, he hadn't been smothered in his sleep.

It all came back to him now: his parents' vacant eyes, the house swarming with police, the intruder, his humiliating arrest, his ominous cell mate. The man was sleeping but had turned toward him now. He was a young man who looked old. Dark circles surrounded his eyes, and his face was marked with the deep lines of hard living.

A few years in prison and Brad would look like that—old, tired, and broken. He had to get out. He had to figure something out.

A door clanged, and his cell mate snorted, opening his eyes. "What're you looking at?" he asked.

Brad turned his head away, avoiding the question.

"Look at me when I talk to you!"

Brad looked into steely eyes.

"Now answer me!"

"What was the question?" Brad asked nervously.

"I asked you what you were looking at."

"I—I wasn't really looking. I was thinking."

The man smiled, showing crooked, yellow teeth. "Yeah, I know how that is. The worst part of the day is the wake-up moment. The dreams stop, and everything comes rushing back. Sometimes I wish I could go on sleeping without ever waking up."

"Me too," Brad said softly.

A man wearing heavy rubber gloves slipped two trays through the door. His cell mate jumped up and grabbed the tray, then returned to his bunk where he sat cross-legged, eating wildly. "Better eat. They take it away real fast," he said between mouthfuls.

Brad went over and got his tray and sat on his bed, staring for a moment at the biscuits covered by dark gravy sauce with specks of meat. He couldn't stomach it. He put the tray aside.

The cell was darkened by the shadow of a massive guard. "Armstrong!"

"Yes?"

"Your lawyer's here."

* * *

His flip-flops slapped against the cement floor as he walked in the room toward the slim, white-haired man sitting at a table. The fixed stools were no doubt a safety feature. The guard left them alone in the room.

Brad looked into the lawyer's glassy blue eyes.

"I'm Foster Kline, your attorney."

"Boy, am I glad you finally showed up."

"I'm sorry it wasn't sooner. Truly I am. I was so sorry to hear the news about your parents, and you have my deepest sympathy."

Brad looked down. "Thanks."

"Your neighbor, Mr. Henderson, has filled me in on almost everything. I talked with your Uncle Gordon today and briefed him on the situation."

"Situation? Is that what this is?"

He ignored Brad's remark. "Your uncle wants you to know that he is concerned about you. He's sorry it took so long to reach him. He met his son at the airport on Friday, and the two of them stayed in a hotel in the city to get caught up and to do some Christmas shopping."

Brad imagined Jess and Gordon's father-son outing. Tears came to his eyes as he realized he could never again have an outing like that with his dad.

Jess had lost his mother, but at least he had Uncle Gordon. Of course Brad wouldn't have to live with the guilt like Jess had. It had been a tragic accident. Jess was only sixteen at the time. He had just gotten his license that year. He and his mom had been visiting relatives in Oregon. Jess was driving too fast on the winding mountainous roads, and the car went over an embankment and plunged into a river. Jess somehow freed himself, but the car sank fast. He had kept diving in an effort to free his mom, but he couldn't save her. Brad remembered talking to Jess at his mom's funeral. Jess was crying. He said he could never forgive himself and would never get over it. He said the hurt would last forever. Jess was in a deep depression for months, but time had apparently healed some of the wounds. No doubt, though, Jess would carry scars for the rest of his life.

"Your Uncle Gordon," Mr. Kline continued, "wanted you to know that he will get to Salt Lake as soon as possible. He is making the funeral arrangements with Mr. Henderson."

"Will I get to go to the funeral?" Brad asked.

"I believe so. We hope to get this whole misunderstanding cleared up as soon as possible."

Mr. Kline's voice was kind, firm, and reassuring. He made it sound so simple. It had all been a terrible mistake. It was like fifth grade when he had been sent to the principal's office when Joel Clark tried to beat him up. "We'll get this whole matter cleared up," Mom had said, and within minutes, everything was forgotten. Could it be that simple this time? Was the nightmare almost over?

"How are you going to clear it up?" Brad asked.

"Well, first we're going to get you out of here. There's a bail hearing set for later this morning."

"What's that?"

"That's where you go before a judge. In this case, it's before Judge Mark Higgins of Salt Lake Third District Court. The judge's job is to make sure everything is in order concerning the arrest. The warrant set the bail at $300,000. We'll try to get a reduction."

"That's a lot of money!"

"Brad, you've been charged with first-degree murder. There's substantial evidence to support the charges."

"But they don't have any evidence."

"Oh, my boy, I'm afraid they do. You bought and registered a .22 caliber revolver two months ago. The gun was found in your duffel bag with your fingerprints on it."

"So what? Lots of people own guns, and of course my fingerprints were on the gun. It's my gun. But owning a gun doesn't make me a murderer."

Mr. Kline frowned. "But your gun was used to kill your parents, which makes it appear that you could be a murderer."

Brad felt his head spinning as he again pictured his parents' vacant eyes. "What?" he asked softly. "My gun was used to kill Mom and Dad?"

"That's right. The prosecution is going to make a big case of this. They'll say you planned to kill your parents—planned it for at least two months."

"But I didn't. I didn't buy that gun to kill Mom and Dad. Dad was with me when I bought it. He bought a gun too. He bought a Colt .45 automatic."

"Well, we'll have to convince a jury that you wouldn't have gone gun shopping with your father to find a gun to kill him. Apparently your father's gun is missing. You don't know where it's at, do you?"

"No, I don't," Brad said. His head was spinning faster now. Maybe he was psychotic. Maybe he killed his parents without realizing it. He tried to force the thought away, but it tortured his mind.

"Are you any good?"

Mr. Kline smiled faintly. "The best. Your father only accepted the best."

"Where do we go from here?"

Mr. Kline cleared his throat. "I have a little time now to review your case. I want you to start at the beginning and tell me everything. I don't care how insignificant the details may seem. You understand, Brad?"

"Yes, sir."

"Then let's get started."

"Well, it might have started last Friday night with a man in a sweat suit that was too small . . ."

* * *

An hour later Mr. Kline left and Bishop Henderson arrived with his first counselor, George Sanders. They prayed with Brad and then gave him another blessing. Brad could feel the strength of the priesthood that radiated from Bishop Henderson. The bishop blessed him with strength to endure the trials of life. Brad reflected that it was funny how he had always thought of major trials as something that happened to other people.

Brad remembered when a young couple in his ward had lost their five-year-old daughter in a car accident. Brad had prayed for them, but couldn't have possibly understood then how they felt. That had all changed.

Bishop Henderson gave Brad a triple combination and said his good-byes. Brad returned to his cell where he stretched out on his bed and opened the book. Bishop Henderson had placed a small card in the front with a list of scriptures. Brad turned to the first verse on the list: "Whosoever shall put their trust in God shall be supported in their trials, and their troubles, and their afflictions" (Alma 36:3). It was Alma speaking to his son Helaman. "God has delivered me from prison, and from bonds, and from death; yea, and I do put my trust in him, and he will still deliver me" (Alma 36:27).

Brad thought of his testimony. He had one. He had read the Book of Mormon and prayed about it. He had received a confirmation by the Spirit. Yet he realized that he had only planted the seed. He had not really worked at nourishing the seed. He wasn't consistent in reading his scriptures. He hadn't registered for an institute class even though his mother had encouraged him to do so. His morning prayers were often quick and incomplete as he rushed off to class.

He continued reading Alma: "I cried within my heart: O Jesus, thou Son of God, have mercy on me, who am in the gall of bitterness, and am encircled about by the everlasting chains of death" (Alma 36:18).

For the first time, Brad could totally relate to Alma. He could understand what he meant. Brad continued reading the scriptures that Bishop Henderson had listed. The next verse was a revelation received by Joseph Smith while he was falsely imprisoned in Liberty Jail in 1839: "O Lord, how long shall they suffer these wrongs and unlawful oppressions, before thine heart shall be softened toward them, and thy bowels be moved with compassion toward them?"

(D&C 121:3). And then came the Lord's reply: "My son, peace be unto thy soul; thine adversity and thine afflictions shall be but a small moment; And then, if thou endure it well, God shall exalt thee on high; thou shalt triumph over all thy foes" (D&C 121:7–8).

Brad felt an inner peace and warmth. It was as if the scriptures were speaking to him directly. He was like Alma who could remember his pains no more. "And oh, what joy, and what marvelous light I did behold; yea, my soul was filled with joy as exceeding as was my pain!" (Alma 36:20).

It was like Mom always said: bad luck can turn into good luck. Brad realized that the Spirit was witnessing unto him, providing him with comfort. His testimony was growing. He remembered hearing a quote by one of the General Authorities that said that a prison could be like a palace to a person who was filled with the Holy Ghost.

Brad was still reading the scriptures when a guard came to get him for his bail hearing. They passed the steel bars and rude voices of inmates. Mr. Kline was waiting for him in the room where they would talk to the judge through closed-circuit TV. Brad wasn't sure how long it took, but Kline managed to get bail reduced. Brad changed back into his clothes, and Kline escorted him through the jail release door. They were greeted by a swarm of reporters. The sidewalk felt slick underfoot, and Brad tried hard not to slip. The situation was humiliating enough without slipping. The hum of the reporters began.

"Why did you purchase the gun, Brad?"

"Were you planning to kill your parents?"

"How long had you been planning to kill your parents?"

"What did they do to you to set you off, Brad?"

"Will you use the insanity defense?"

Kline had pulled his silver sedan around, and, before getting in, Brad looked over the tall buildings of Salt Lake's skyline toward the snow-capped mountains of the Wasatch Front. He took in a deep breath. He had never appreciated freedom so much. He thought of the stale air in the dim jail and shuddered. He never wanted to go back there again. He would do whatever it took to make sure that didn't happen.

The voices faded into the snowy background as he got in the sedan and looked over at Kline, who smiled briefly. The nagging worry on Kline's face sent alarm signals through Brad, dissolving the euphoric sense of freedom he'd been enjoying. He could tell from the look on Kline's face that he was as good as dead. He felt trapped again. Kline might be a good lawyer, but even good lawyers didn't win every case.

As Kline drove through the slush-filled streets of downtown Salt Lake toward the east bench, Brad tried to devise a plan to save his life. The harder he thought, the more muddled his mind became. It was an overwhelming task.

As they drove past his house, he noticed the house looked empty and lonely. Funny how you could tell a house was not lived in. It was like the whole facade was lifeless and still. There was a sadness about an empty house.

Kline pulled through the semicircular driveway of the Henderson home, and Darlene and Conrad hurried out to greet them as Brad jumped out. Darlene immediately engulfed him in her arms and kissed him on the cheek.

"Oh, Brad, I'm so glad you're home. I haven't slept a wink since you were arrested. Now don't you worry about a thing. I want you to come right in and get warm. Lunch is on the table and ready to serve. I know the food at those jails must be dreadful."

Conrad slapped Brad on the back. "Brad, it will all work out. I know it will."

"I know, Conrad. I just don't know how."

"Brad."

Brad turned toward Kline. "Yes?"

"I'll be in touch."

"Yeah. Sure."

Kline got back in the car and drove away.

"Is he any good?" Conrad asked as they walked in the house.

"I hope so."

Bishop Henderson stepped into the entryway, holding a cordless phone. "Brad, it's your cousin, Jess, from California."

Jess! The thought of family sent a momentary thrill through Brad. Someone was calling for him, checking on him, caring about him.

The bishop handed him the phone. "Go into my study, Brad, where you can talk in private."

Brad took the phone and rushed into the study. "Hello, Jess."

"Are you okay, Brad?"

"I'm hanging in there, Jess. It's good to hear your voice."

"It seems like forever since I last saw you, Brad, and it was only Friday morning."

"Is that all? Just four days ago?"

"Yeah, I guess a lot has happened since then. When your lawyer called yesterday and told us what'd happened, it was like we were both in shock. We sat there looking at each other for the longest time, and Dad started to cry. I didn't know what to do. It was like—" Jess's voice broke. "Well, you know, like when Mom died."

"I know, Jess." A hard lump formed in Brad's throat. He tried to swallow, but it only caused a sharp pain in his chest. "At least you have your dad, Jess."

"I know, I know. If I could do anything to bring Uncle Allen and Aunt Peggy and Mom back, you know I'd do it. Anything."

Jess's sobs broke through the receiver, and Brad swiped the tears from his face. "Jess, you know they think I did it."

"That's insane!" The anguish in his voice had turned to quick anger. "Anyone who knows you, knows that's crazy. Everyone knows how close you were to your parents. Everyone knows how much you loved them. You would do anything to make them happy."

Brad's sense of futility and misery deepened as he heard the panic in Jess's voice. Jess, who always faced life with a determined effort to cut to the chase, get the job done, check off the list. "Except for the pre-med thing. You know Dad and I didn't agree. I don't know what to do, Jess."

"Brad, don't think about that now, and don't worry. Dad will take care of everything."

Brad cleared his throat. "Jess, someone used my gun to kill them. It's got my fingerprints on it."

"I know, Brad. Dad and your lawyer are working on it. They're trying to figure out what happened. Do you have any ideas, Brad? Is there anything you saw or heard that might help them?"

The thoughts raced through Brad's head, spinning like a top and disturbing the contents of his stomach. "I've gone over this, Jess, with the police and with Conrad and with the lawyer. I've gone over it again and again in my mind. I don't know what happened. There was a man who came to the house a week ago last Friday night when I was working on my paper. He threatened Dad. He might be connected."

"Brad, don't think about it now. You need to get some rest. Dad and I will come in on Thursday for the funeral. Let's talk about it then."

"Okay, Jess. I'll see you Thursday. I can't wait to see you."

"Me too, Brad. You hang in there."

He hung up. Jess and Uncle Gordon were as shaken and dumbfounded as he was. Somehow he had hoped they could step in and provide the same comfort and security Mom and Dad had always provided. He bowed his head and said a silent prayer. Prayer was all he had left.

CHAPTER 11

Captain Emmanuel Markakis, chief of detectives, was a big, broad-shouldered man in his late fifties who displayed no emotion of any kind. He was all business as he sat behind his cluttered desk.

"I'm disappointed with your conduct, Chandler. I had high hopes for you."

"Captain," Van said, "let's be specific. What conduct are we talking about here?"

"Okay, Chandler. According to Detective Thornton, you've gotten emotionally involved in the case. He feels that your ability to remain objective in this case is in question. Do you deny this?"

Perhaps she had become emotionally involved in the case, but Thornton wasn't being objective either. Somehow in his mind, he had convinced himself that Brad was guilty. He couldn't see the forest for the trees. The evidence was compelling, but sometimes a good detective had to take a step back and look at the whole picture. Brad Armstrong didn't kill his parents. The evidence was too compelling, too neat. He was being framed. Why couldn't Thornton see that? How could she make Thornton see the truth?

"Captain," she said, "I cannot deny that I have gotten emotionally involved in this case. My only defense in the matter is that I see an innocent kid being accused of a crime I know he didn't commit. As a human being, I can't sit back and let an injustice like this happen."

"What makes you think the kid's innocent, Chandler?"

"Well, though the evidence is compelling, there are a lot of holes in it, and some of the evidence is contradictory. Something just isn't right."

Something like a smile, grim and humorless, tugged at the corners of his mouth.

"Instinct," he said, "is much like a polygraph. It's a tool. It can be used to direct us in the right direction so we don't run around wasting time on dead ends. But instinct, like the polygraph, is not admissible in court. The only thing that the courts want to see and hear is hard evidence."

"How can I follow my instincts to hard evidence when I have Thornton thwarting my every move?"

"You know, Chandler, I called you in here today to tell you I was taking you off the Armstrong case."

"I know."

"Thornton wants you off the case."

"I know."

"But after talking with you, I think I'm going to leave you on the case. The D.A. thinks he has a solid case and Thornton's come up with some good forensic evidence, but I'm going to let you run with your instincts. Why not? Tie up any loose ends. Answer those questions that are gnawing at you. Besides, if there are any holes in our case, you can bet Foster Kline will find them. It won't hurt to have one of our own looking at the questionable pieces."

"Thank you, Captain."

"Okay, get out of here."

Van hesitated.

"You're excused, Chandler."

She started to get up but still hesitated.

"Something else on your mind, Chandler?"

She wanted to rag on Thornton, to tell the captain how totally vindictive he was. She glanced into the captain's waiting eyes. Anticipation was there, and she sensed he knew she wanted to complain about Thornton. It would look like sour grapes at this point.

Van stood up. "No. I appreciate this opportunity, Captain."

"Sure, Chandler."

* * *

Tuesday afternoon, Van's usually immaculate office was now a mess. She had tacked notes and pictures of the crime scene all over her bulletin board. She had taped police reports and printouts about the FTRA on her walls. She had even checked out a library book about the pharmaceutical industry. Reference books about homicide and family killings also littered her floor. Her wastepaper basket was overflowing with balled-up pieces of paper. Someone whistled from her doorway. She looked up. Thornton stood there, a smirk covering his face.

"What are you doing?"

"I'm thinking," Van said.

"Well, I hope your mind is more organized than this office."

"You're a good one to talk about messy offices, Thornton."

"I guess you heard the wino was identified."

"Yes. I guess you heard I'm still on the case."

"Yeah, the captain's a softy, can't resist a pretty face. What, did you cry or something?"

Blood rushed to her face. She clenched her fist. "The captain is a reasonable and fair man. He believes everyone should have a fair shot, that good detectives shouldn't rush to conclusions."

"Well, can we move on to our new case, our railroad wino?"

"You could use his name, you know. Mark Wilson. Everyone down at Rio Grande called him the Clown because he was always joking."

"Well, someone got the last laugh on him. He was killed by a blunt blow to the head. I watched the autopsy."

"I talked with Gordon and Jess Armstrong today, Thornton."

"The skull was cracked at least eight inches. I talked with the Armstrongs today too. So what?"

"So Jess Armstrong confirmed Brad's story. He was with his cousin at the airport when his parents died. Did the medical examiner have any idea what type of weapon was used on Wilson?"

"Jess Armstrong confirmed that Bradley was with him until around 7:20 A.M So what? He had plenty of time to get to his parents' house and kill them. The medical examiner says it was some kind of club like a baseball bat or something that killed Wilson. He probably would have died soon anyway. He had a malignant tumor."

"Thornton, you're not taking into consideration the condition of the roads on Friday morning. They were pretty bad. I checked with the highway patrol. They had three accidents just on the stretch of highway Brad traveled. Do you think Wilson was moved to the lot after being killed?"

"It takes about twenty or twenty-five minutes to get from Brad's house to the airport on a fair day. A little snow would not add forty minutes to that. The time factor is exaggerated, which seems to implicate Brad even more. I mean, why lie about it if you found your parents dead? The crime-scene boys say that Wilson died at the scene. It's dark at night. Few streetlights. Someone probably hid in the shadows of one of those warehouses and sprang on Wilson. They covered his body with an old piece of drywall that had been thrown in with the rest of the junk in that lot."

"Did you know that another vagrant was found in the Jordan River yesterday?"

Thornton moved some books from a chair by the door and sat down. "I heard something about that."

"His name was Albert Richards. He frequented the shelters and soup kitchens around Rio Grande. He was also killed by a blunt blow to the head."

"There could be a connection. Maybe someone's sick of being nickled and dimed."

"I think there must be a connection."

"I have some friends on the force over in West Valley City. I'll give them a call and find out what they have. I'm glad to see you're going forward with this new case. The Armstrong case is coming to an end, just a few more loose ends to clear up. The district attorney is happy with what we have. I'll let you know what I find out. We could have a serial killer on our hands, someone who hates the homeless."

Van watched Thornton walk down the station hall and disappear into his office. She had decided to keep her mouth shut for now. She couldn't think with Thornton breathing down her neck. He didn't need to know that she was sure there was some connection between the Armstrong murder and the deaths of these two homeless men. She didn't need to tell him. She could pursue her leads and make connections without giving Thornton any reason to hassle her. And then she needed to start looking into the pharmaceutical angle. Armstrong did testing for pharmaceuticals. There was a lot of money there.

* * *

Later Tuesday afternoon, dressed in jeans and wearing a heavy ski jacket, Van drove from the station with Detective Carmichael. It was time to show Amy's drawing around. The snowfall had let up momentarily, and the sun had decided to come out and melt the snow enough for an evening freeze that would leave the streets slick. Van looked out the window at the bustling sidewalk full of Christmas shoppers. Salvation Army workers rang shiny brass bells on each street corner.

As Van pulled onto Rio Grande, she caught sight of the old depot. She continued down Rio Grande, a scabby street and a dumping ground for diesel smoke and coal dust. The street housed a smorgasbord of homeless shelters and social services offices.

"What makes you think you're going to find this guy down here?" Carmichael asked.

"Instinct."

"Oh."

Van parked on the street by the homeless shelter. She jumped out into the cold, and as they made their way down the street, a transient rode by on a bicycle. He had attached a shopping cart to the back of his bike and crammed it with clothes, blankets, and a sleeping bag.

"Got any change?" asked a young hobo leaning against the wood siding of one of the many rescue missions in the neighborhood.

"Sorry," Van said.

Van recognized two transients sitting on a bench just ahead. The man called Davy Crockett wore a skunk-skin hat, and Lucky Charms had a full head of tangled red hair. Both men were in their late forties.

"I'll talk to these guys, Carmichael. Why don't you get the guy standing by the wall there?"

"Sure thing," Carmichael said as he sauntered toward the other transient.

"It's supposed to dip below zero tonight," Van said, handing each man a bright pink flier from a stack she had picked up at the station.

The fliers contained a warning for those transients who could read: "Traveler's Aid Society Warning: temperatures to drop below zero in the early morning hours of Wednesday, December 17. For shelter information, please come by the Salt Lake Community Shelter and Resource Center, 200 South and Rio Grande. For a hot meal, stop by St. Vincent de Paul Center at 400 West and 200 South or the Salvation Army soup kitchen."

"My sleeping bag and the fresh air suit me just fine," Davy Crockett said. "I don't like all those rules in the shelter."

"I'll sleep under a bridge somewhere. I got my friend to keep me company," Lucky Charms said and pulled a liquor bottle from the breast pocket of his coat.

"Well, if you men change your mind, you know where to go. By the way, have you seen this guy around?" Van pulled a copy of Amy's drawing of the bushy-headed stranger from under her fliers.

"No, ma'am, never seen anyone like that," Davy Crockett said.

"I know all the faces down in this neighborhood," Lucky Charms said, "and I ain't never seen that face."

"Okay, thanks."

Van and Carmichael continued down the street and stopped on a muddy corner of Rio Grande where melting snow had leached into a parking strip. A teenage boy with long, greasy hair and acne stood in the water, leaning against a light post. Van handed him a flier.

"I prefer the streets," he said, glancing up from the paper and focusing briefly on them, before turning away.

"It's going to get cold," Van said and walked away. She hated to see kids on the streets. She knew that many of the homeless kids were runaways from abusive homes. They pretty much lived their whole life from a backpack. It was them against the world, and they were losing. Drug use was the number one means these kids used to deal with fear and loneliness and cold. When they couldn't find a place to sleep during the winter nights, they kept warm by walking around the city.

Van and Carmichael showed Amy's sketch to at least a dozen transients without any luck. They crossed the street into Pioneer Park. The ten-acre square was where the Mormon pioneers of 1847 built the first fort to protect them against hostile Indians. Now it had become a daytime squatters' camp for Salt Lake's homeless and a den for drug dealers and users. Van hadn't missed the irony of the pioneers' safest haven becoming the most dangerous spot in the city.

They approached two old men sitting on a park bench. One had a Rip Van Winkle beard and wore a stocking cap with a large red ball of yarn on top. The other man appeared frail and had a hunched back. Van passed fliers to them.

"It's going to get cold tonight," she said to the bearded man.

"Yeah, I know."

"You hear about the big raid down here?" the frail man asked Van.

"Yeah, we heard," Carmichael said.

"They cleared us all out of here. Told us to go someplace else."

"So are you two coming to the shelter tonight?" Van asked.

"No," the bearded man said. "I'll find a bridge to sleep under."

"They treat us all like trash up at the shelter," the frail man said, "but these people need to wake up and realize that if it wasn't for us, they wouldn't have a job."

"You're right," Van said. "Would you do me a favor?"

"Anything," the bearded man said.

"Name it," the frail man added.

Van pulled out the sketch of the bushy-headed man. "Have you ever seen this man?"

They stared at the picture. "Looks like Samson," the bearded man said.

"I was thinking the same thing," the frail man added with a nod.

"Who's Samson?" Van asked.

"Big man who shows up around here at night," the bearded man said. "He sells drugs and makes money to get high. He's hooked on coke. He injects. He sells needles for two dollars."

"Will he be around here tonight?" Carmichael asked.

"Usually is," the frail man said.

"Will you be around tonight?" Van asked.

"We might. Depends," the bearded man said.

Van pulled some money from her pocket and handed it to the men. "You be here tonight to point Samson out to me, and I'll have more for you."

* * *

On Tuesday evening, Van sat in her messy office. It was at times like these that she realized that she really needed to get a life, a real life. To Van, a real life would include a family, but the opportunity had not yet presented itself. Of course, she hadn't done a lot to make it happen either.

She wanted to someday get married in the temple. Going to the temple and being sealed for eternity was important to Van. Bishop Henderson told her that Brad's family had been sealed in the temple. She remembered feeling relieved when he told her that. She thought of how blessed Brad was to have been sealed to his family. What a comfort that must be to him now that his parents were dead.

She thought of her own parents. In spite of their differences, she loved them. After all, they were the only parents she had. She sometimes fantasized about her entire family joining the Church. She could imagine them all dressed in white, kneeling at the altar, being sealed for eternity.

If she couldn't have that with her parents, she wanted to at least make sure she had it with her husband and children. She was very careful about whom she dated, but perhaps she had not tried hard enough to meet people. Perhaps marriage had taken second place to her career. She felt that her career was important, but her patriarchal blessing told her she would someday get married in the temple and have children if she lived worthy of it.

Her friend Amanda attended the same ward as Van and had been trying to set her up with her brother, Matthew, but Van had resisted because he was a lawyer. Perhaps she had been narrowed-minded about lawyers. She had judged the man by his profession without giving him a chance as a person. Here she thought she was so openminded. She got angry when people tried to judge her by her profession, and yet she was doing the same thing to Amanda's brother, Matthew. She made a mental note to ask Amanda about Matthew at church on Sunday.

The ringing of her phone brought Van back to the present.

"Hello?"

"Detective Chandler, there's a Brad Armstrong here to see you."

"I'll be right there.

She went to the station lobby and saw Brad. He was well groomed and dressed in an oxford shirt and tan trousers, but the worried look on his face aged him.

"Brad. Is anything wrong?"

He stepped in the door. "I'm going crazy just waiting around. I have to know if you've come up with any new leads."

She smiled grimly. "Well, I have a few ideas, but I can't talk with you about them. I will tell you that I have a lead on the guy in Amy's sketch. I'm going to follow it up tonight."

"What kind of lead?"

Van hesitated, but the glimmer of hope in his eyes made her give in. "It could be a drug pusher down on Rio Grande. I won't know until I check it out tonight."

"I want to go with you."

"No, Brad. That's impossible. I've already told you more than I should have."

"But I'm the only one who can positively identify the man. She said her sketch could look like anybody. How will you know if you've got the right man?"

"You're just going to have to trust me, Brad."

* * *

It was around eight o'clock in the evening when Detective Chandler walked out of the police station with another detective. Brad watched them as they crossed the street and got in an unmarked vehicle, then waited for them to pull out before he put his car in drive and followed.

He kept a safe distance and allowed a few cars to get in front of him. Knowing that they were headed for Rio Grande made his job a little easier. They carefully wound their way through downtown traffic and took the route Brad had expected.

They turned onto Rio Grande and found a parking spot in front of the homeless shelter. Brad stopped where he was and parked in front of a dark warehouse. He watched as they got out of the car and went into the homeless shelter, then jumped out into the cold night air to follow them.

"Got any change, man?" a transient leaning against the warehouse asked. Irritated, Brad ignored him and passed by as quickly as possible. He knew he was in a dangerous part of town; he heard the stories on the news about Rio Grande, the rail yards, and Pioneer Park. The area was an oasis to transients from all parts of the country. The extensive rail yards divided Salt Lake City into east and west, the haves and the have-nots. Just across those tracks was the west side, which meant nothing more to Brad than a news report of a gang shooting or a meth bust. Rio Grande was the gateway to a sordid world Brad knew little or nothing about.

As Brad made his way up the street, a man stood out in the middle of the sidewalk as if to stop him. Brad kept walking toward him, hoping he would move when he got close enough.

"Do you have any change?" he asked.

Brad looked up into his sad countenance. Silver hoops sparkled in his ears and nose. Two silver necklaces—a cross and a peace sign—clanked together on his chest, which was exposed to the cold by his open jacket and unbuttoned shirt. Brad dug into his pocket, pulled out some loose change, and handed it to the man. "Thanks, man," Brad heard as he walked past.

He couldn't believe he had done that. There were better ways of helping the poor. Why had he done it? It was something about those eyes. He made his way against the sharp wind to the homeless shelter. The lobby was crowded, and he couldn't see the detectives in there. He opened the glass door and pushed himself into the crowd. The air in the shelter was stale and stuffy.

Brad walked up to a harried-looking woman at the front desk. "I'm looking for Detective Vanessa Chandler," he said.

"She went down to the offices," the woman said, pointing to a long, dimly lit hall. "She'll be back this way in a minute."

Brad's clothes felt wet and sticky on his skin. He wanted fresh air more than anything. A myriad of voices reached his ears:

"I'm in therapy, see? Getting better, see? My family don't know where I am, see? I'm running and I landed here. I eat, sleep, move on."

"I believe in God. My mom's religious. She prays for me. Out here I don't have a lot of time to think about God or praying."

"My main philosophy is don't freeze to death."

Brad put his hands in his coat pockets and made his way back through the crowd to the front doors. By the door, a tired-looking man sat in a worn, plastic chair with two small children who sat at his feet with their faces dirty and their eyes anxious. Brad stopped and looked at them.

"They've reached capacity," the man said as if Brad had asked for an explanation. "They're trying to find an overflow shelter for us. It's hard to know where to look for a place to live if you're not from here."

Brad looked at the two small girls. They looked tired. One had obviously been crying. "Where're you from?" Brad asked.

"Phoenix. We camped at Phoenix Air Park and then checked out the street life in Southern California. Someone told us it was better for families in Salt Lake City. Someone said they had programs to get us back on our feet. They say there's work here, too."

"What kind of work are you looking for?" Brad asked.

"Janitorial. That's all I've ever done. The place I worked for closed down. My wife died of pneumonia right after we lost our camper. I took the station wagon and headed for California with the girls. And of course there's Christmas to worry about. I have some things I've put up for them and I've said we'll try to get them some new shoes, but I don't know."

Brad only then noticed their shoes. One girl was wearing plastic sandals; the other was wearing tennis shoes with holes in them. A knot formed in Brad's throat, and he gulped hard.

Brad pushed past several people, making his way out into the cold, fresh air. He waited down the street a ways until he saw the detectives leave the shelter. They headed south. He followed at a safe distance.

"Got any change?" a deep voice asked from the recess of a warehouse door front. Brad just rushed past.

The detectives made their way into Pioneer Park, where the streetlights threw a smoky glow on an old woman digging through a garbage can and some teenagers huddled in a circle smoking cigarettes.

Brad stopped beside a light pole. He could see the detectives talking with two old men. Detective Chandler handed them something and continued south.

Brad followed them toward a complex of viaducts and bridges south of Pioneer Park. Brad had heard about the notorious vagabond campsites under the viaducts.

As Brad walked across the tracks and rounded the corner of a great cement pillar, he came into full view of the camp and halted. A few hobo camps were scattered throughout the area under the viaducts, along the railroad tracks, and on haggard patches of dead weeds between sheds and chain-link fences. Lying on blankets in the snow were small groups of tramps huddled around campfires.

The detectives stopped and were talking to a haggard old woman huddled beneath the bridge who pointed to a group of men hunched around a campfire. Brad looked up to see homeless people hiding in the nooks and crannies of the viaduct.

As the detectives approached the men, Brad stood shivering and watching. The glow of the fire cast an eerie glow on their faces, and their shadows stretched across the tracks. He tried to see the face of the big man but couldn't discern it. He wanted to get closer. He stepped up to a scraggly tree.

Brad was beginning to move closer when he felt two strong punches in the right side of his back. It happened so quickly he barely felt the blinding pain. He felt his undershirt sticking to his back and gasped. He clumsily sank to his knees and slumped forward, his forehead taking the impact of the fall. As he slipped into unconsciousness, he tried to call for Detective Chandler.

CHAPTER 12

Wednesday, December 17

The pain. It was so hard to think with the pain shooting up through his body. If he could only get up, but his back was a mass of burning flesh. His head was pounding. What time was it? Tuesday night. Was it still Tuesday? Was it Wednesday yet? Who were those people who kept looking at him? How could he get out of here? He could hear the moans coming from his own lips and tried to stop them. He tried to think.

"Brad?"

He opened his eyes and looked up into Detective Chandler's face. "Where am I?"

"A hospital room at University Medical Center."

"What happened?"

"You were stabbed."

"Stabbed? By who?"

"I don't know. I found you slumped over and bleeding. Your wallet was beside you. There was no money in it. Someone obviously wanted quick cash for drugs or alcohol and didn't want to bother with credit cards."

"That wasn't him. I saw his face. It wasn't him."

"I know. I figured that out after talking with him."

He could feel that he had a large bandage on his forehead where he had fallen forward. His eyes were cloudy. How foolish he had been to follow them to the park.

"What day is it?" he asked.

"Wednesday morning."

"You're kidding."

"No. You've been on painkillers. They knocked you out. You have a good doctor, a friend of your father's, Peter Cummings."

"Oh, yeah. That's good."

"Mrs. Henderson and Conrad came to see you. They waited for nearly three hours, but when we realized you were going to sleep longer, I sent them home."

"Good. I don't think my head could handle Sister Henderson."

Detective Chandler smiled. "At least you still have a sense of humor."

"That's good. You'll need it." It was Thornton's voice.

Detective Chandler turned. "What do you want, Thornton?"

"I came to pay a visit to poor Bradley here. Word down at the station is he was mugged last night while searching for a bushy-headed man down by the viaducts. Did the bushy-headed stranger stab you, Bradley?"

Brad looked at him in silence.

"I talked to the doctor. He told me your wounds were superficial, that they didn't penetrate the chest cavity, and that it didn't appear that any internal organs had been damaged. All they did was sew a few stitches in the wounds."

"Thanks for the report," Brad said and glowered at Thornton.

Dr. Cummings walked in. "I hope we're not upsetting our patient here."

"No, Doctor," Thornton said and smiled smugly at Brad.

Dr. Cummings scowled at Thornton. "Well, Brad needs to get his rest. He has a funeral to attend tomorrow."

"It's good to see you again, Dr. Cummings," Brad said.

"It's been too long, Brad."

"You two know each other?" Thornton asked.

"Dr. Cummings is an old friend of Brad's father," Detective Chandler answered.

"Really?" Thornton said. "How long have you known the Armstrongs, Dr. Cummings?"

"I've known Allen since high school. We graduated in the same class."

Thornton took out his pad and pencil. "That was here in Salt Lake City?"

"Yes."

"East High?"

"No, Allen and I went to West High."

"Really?"

"Yes."

Thornton scribbled some notes. "And you both became doctors? That's impressive."

"Not everyone's born to privilege, Thornton," Detective Chandler said. "Some people work their way up."

Thornton glared at Detective Chandler.

"Allen, Gordon, and I worked hard to get through medical school," Dr. Cummings said. "It was not always easy."

Thornton stopped writing. "Gordon?"

"Allen's younger brother," Dr. Cummings explained. "He and Allen were always interested in pharmacology. Drugs didn't interest me. I liked the people aspect of medicine. Allen liked the research, and Gordon liked the money."

"So your Uncle Gordon's a doctor too," Thornton said, looking at Brad.

"Yes," Dr. Cummings said. "Gordon is one of those rare scientists who has good commercial sense. He started Armstrong Pharmaceuticals in the University of Utah Research Park, and then went public with it when he moved it to San Francisco. He's a successful businessman now."

"So the younger brother outdid his older brother?" Thornton asked.

Dr. Cummings glanced at Brad. "I wouldn't say that. In my opinion Allen was the bigger success. He was a well-known professor of pharmacology and toxicology at the university's medical school. He's internationally known for developing a strong painkiller that produces little, if any, addiction. He was a respected consultant to major pharmaceutical companies and even your police department. And he was a financial success, especially with Armstrong Pharmaceuticals. Gordon paid his consulting fees with stock options, and the company has done quite well. Of course, Gordon has paid a price for his success. He had a heart attack last year. I believe he almost died."

"Really?" Thornton looked interested.

"I think Brad needs to rest now," Dr. Cummings said. "I'll show you two out, and Brad, I'll come in later to check on you."

"I'll call you, Brad. Your days of detective work are over," Detective Chandler said as she walked out.

In the hall, Dr. Cummings frowned at Van and Thornton. "I will not have you upsetting my patient. Do you understand?"

"Oh, come on, Doc," Thornton said, "we weren't upsetting the kid. It's not like he's dying. The wounds were superficial."

Dr. Cummings grabbed Thornton's arm. "From my standpoint, no wounds are superficial. Brad could have died out there last night. Hasn't he been through enough without you harassing him?"

Thornton jerked his arm away and straightened his jacket collar. "The only harassing I see going on around here, Doc, is by you. I suggest you stay out of the way or I'll charge you with assault."

Van laughed. "Oh, come on, Thornton, stop trying to throw your weight around. Let's go."

Thornton stepped close to Van and put his finger in her face. "Don't push me, Van. Your charm may work with the captain, but I see right through you for the lousy detective you are."

He walked away, the clicking of his shiny black wing tips echoing in the hall.

* * *

Van spent the latter part of Wednesday morning going over the files for the cases Allen Armstrong had consulted on for the Salt Lake City Police Department. Her instincts were telling her they could have something to do with his death. While one interesting case dealt with illegal pharmaceuticals, the others were narcotics related. A strange thought occurred to her. What if Allen Armstrong was dealing drugs? He had a lot of money. Maybe he decided he needed more. That would explain the bushy-headed man's demands.

She set up the scenario in her mind. While gathering vagrants for his studies, Armstrong came across a lot of heavy narcotics users living on the streets or in a shelter. These people were vulnerable. They not only had the daily necessities but also the never-ending craving for drugs to contend with. She had seen people with 500-dollar-a-day habits.

Armstrong was perhaps in a position to get drugs for users. He may have had a large clientele. Suppose Armstrong decided to get out of the business. Junkies had been known to kill when they were denied drugs, when their supply was cut off. There were loose ends to this theory—the alarm being set, the use of Brad's gun. And why would a man worth ten million dollars peddle drugs? Besides, there was nothing to indicate that Armstrong had a dark side and every indication that he was a faithful member of the Church. All the same, there were many possible theories. Thornton had jumped at the most obvious, had taken the lazy detective's way out. Speaking of the devil, he stuck his head in the office.

"Get your coat, Chandler. We've got a body up in the cemetery."

* * *

Van sat on the passenger side of a department SUV as Thornton drove in silence. The heavy clouds had dissipated, and she had to lower the visor to block the afternoon sun. They were headed north of the Avenues to the Salt Lake City Cemetery.

"You ever walk in the cemetery?" Van asked, trying to break the silence and tension.

"Not the type of place I usually hang out."

Van responded with silence, staring out the window. Thornton drove off the plowed road onto a snow-covered path full of holes. The vehicle's bobbing and swaying made Van feel sick for a moment.

"Take it easy," Van said.

"You want to drive?" Thornton asked.

"Sure, but you never let me," she snapped back.

The vehicle came to rest by three patrol cars. As Van stepped out of the vehicle, a frigid wind hit her full in the face. "It's windy out here."

Van knew the cemetery well. Since it was located in the upper Avenues, she often hiked up to the cemetery to explore the fascinating sites. It was one of those old-fashioned cemeteries with statues and tombs and decorative fences. Van's graveyard explorations usually took place in spring and summer. Now, in the dead of winter, the various monuments and headstones looked like macabre snowmen beneath the snow cover.

A patrolman came rushing up to them. "The body's behind a tombstone over here. It was found about an hour ago by someone walking through."

"They've got good eyes," Thornton said.

"Well, he's wearing a bright yellow rain slicker," the patrolman said. "You couldn't miss him."

The snow crunched under their feet as they made their way to the body. They approached the slicker sticking out of the snow behind the tombstone. The jacket was open, revealing a bloodstained shirt pulled up above a fat belly. Van looked down into the face, his eyes and mouth reflecting a permanent look of terror. He was Polynesian, probably Tongan or Samoan.

Most outsiders were surprised to learn that Salt Lake had one of the largest Polynesian communities in the country, some twenty thousand islanders. Most had come to the valley for religious reasons. Language, improved education, and occupational training made acculturation easier for the more westernized Polynesians. Others had struggled to fit into the strange intermountain society. This alienation had spurred gangs like the Tongan Crips.

Van would have probably prejudged this as another gang-related killing had it not been for the age. The victim was probably in his forties, too old for the typical gang member. He had no identifiable gang clothing or jewelry. Perhaps he had tattoos. The medical examiner would determine that.

"What do you think, Chandler?" Thornton asked.

Van shivered and pulled her collar up around her neck. The strong winds blew snow into her face. "Looks like he was shot in the chest. Maybe a drug deal gone bad or something. They drove out here and dumped the body where no one would see them."

"Let's hurry and search the crime scene so we can get out of this place."

CHAPTER 13

Brad was exhausted. He'd spent the afternoon assuring visitors he was okay. Darlene lingered by his side the entire afternoon, long enough to drive the nurses crazy calling for things with her oversolicitous care of Brad. Conrad endured his mother for about two hours before he made an excuse and took off. Bishop Henderson had come by and assured Brad that prayer would see him through this. He agreed and asked the bishop to pray for him.

Alone now, Brad used the remote to raise his bed. A pain shot through his right side, so he turned until it felt better. He then used another remote and turned on the television. It was time for the six o'clock news.

A commercial was just ending. The familiar face of anchor Rob Baxter filled the screen. Unsmiling, his voice subdued, he spoke: "A string of frigid nights has caused steady overflows at Salt Lake City homeless shelters, even forcing the opening of a rarely used and little-known emergency building in Liberty Park. Homeless services officials on Wednesday were reluctant to openly discuss the small building's existence."

"It's an overflow to the overflow," an official said. "We only open it when everything else is full. It's a contingency shelter for when the weather's too cold and the shelters are too full. We don't want the neighbors to think we're opening another homeless shelter here."

Brad lifted himself up in the bed. "Who cares what the neighbors think? People are cold."

"Temperatures in Salt Lake dipped below zero last night," Rob said. "With a major storm headed our way for Friday, officials want to make sure no one dies on the streets this winter."

A commercial advertising snow shovels came on.

Brad felt a lump in his throat. He thought of the man with the two little girls. He hoped they'd found shelter and safety. It was a world he had known existed, but not really. Sure, he had seen the commercials on TV for the Save the Children Foundation. He had even seen a few PBS specials on starvation in Africa. But it was just television, something distant and unreal. Now he had seen it for himself. People were cold and hungry on the streets of Salt Lake. People were sick and needed care.

Rob's face appeared on the screen again and behind him was a picture of Brad. He grabbed the remote and turned up the volume.

"In other local matters," Rob said, "suspected parent-killer Bradley Armstrong is in the hospital tonight after suffering a knife wound to the back. A transient under the Fourth South viaduct allegedly stabbed Armstrong last night. Police could not confirm why Armstrong was in the area, but an inside source says he was looking for the man he believes killed his parents. This video footage you're seeing here is of Detective Douglas Thornton, who is heading up the case."

Anger flowed through Brad's veins as Thornton's face filled the screen, which was surrounded by microphones.

"Detective Thornton," a reporter asked, "if Bradley Armstrong killed his parents, why would he be risking his life to find their killer?"

"I have no official report that Armstrong was looking for his parents' killer," Thornton said.

"Then why was Armstrong in that area of town on such a cold night?" the reporter asked.

"Your guess is as good as mine," Thornton said. "The area is known for drug deals."

"Are you saying Armstrong is a drug user?" the reporter asked.

"I'm saying we have to look at all possibilities," Thornton answered.

Rage flowed through Brad. He picked up the remote and threw it at the television screen. It fell short and landed on the floor. A sharp, burning pain shot through Brad's back. He stared at the television screen.

Rob was speaking again. "Police this afternoon discovered a body in the Salt Lake City Cemetery. Detective Thornton, also on this case, said the body was spotted by a man walking through the cemetery."

"All I can say is that this is a homicide," Thornton said.

The door opened and Peter Cummings walked in. He picked up the remote from the floor and turned the television off. "You okay, Brad?"

Brad sat in silence. Dr. Cummings walked to his bedside and placed his hand on his arm. "I'm sorry about your parents. I wish there were something I could do. I'll miss playing golf with your old man. He was a good friend. I wish I could have seen him before— well, never mind. I was disappointed he didn't come to the class reunion last Friday night though."

"Reunion?"

"Yeah, it was the West High class reunion. Your dad probably didn't want to come in costume," Dr. Cummings smiled.

"Costume?"

"Yeah, Renée Bridge was in charge of the reunion this year, and she had this 'cute' idea that everyone should come wearing something they wore when they were in high school. I wore my letter jacket. It was embarrassing because it didn't fit. Your dad was smart to stay clear."

"West High School's colors are red and black, aren't they?"

"That's right. Listen, you'd better get some rest and leave the TV off, okay?"

"Okay. Thanks, Dr. Cummings."

As soon as Dr. Cummings left the room, Brad picked up the phone and dialed Conrad's cell phone. "Conrad? This is Brad."

"Brad, how're you doing?"

"Okay. Hey, can I trust you?"

"Of course you can trust me. I've been your best friend since before either of us can remember."

"Do you think I killed Mom and Dad, Conrad?"

There was a pause. "No!" Conrad said. "I was confused when they arrested you, but I know you didn't do it. I just wish there was something more I could do to help you."

"Well, actually Conrad, there is something you can do for me."

"Name it."

"I need you to go in my house tonight."

"What? No way. I'm not going near that place, especially at night. Are you forgetting what happened last time?"

"Please, Conrad. This could be life or death for me. Do you want to live with that on your conscience?"

"Okay, okay, man. Why do you want me to go in your house?"

"I want you to go in the study and find Dad's old yearbooks. They're on the bottom right shelf over his desk. I want you to bring me his senior yearbook. Bring it to me tonight."

"Well, that doesn't sound too hard. Why do you want his yearbook?"

"I think the man that came to our house and argued with Dad might be in there. Just don't tell your mother. You hear me? Don't say a word and don't do anything to make her suspicious."

"Okay, but we're getting ready to eat dinner. You're going to have to wait until after dinner."

"Thanks, Conrad. You're a good friend."

As soon as Brad hung up the phone, it rang. "Hello."

"Hello, Brad? It's Jess."

"Hey, Jess. I guess you've heard the latest?"

"Yeah. What's going on back there? When I left on Friday, Salt Lake was a sleepy little town. Now you're getting stabbed down on Rio Grande. I told you to hang in there until we could come."

"I'm trying. Believe me, I'm trying."

"What were you doing down in that part of town, Brad?"

"I was trying to find the man who killed Mom and Dad."

"And you thought you would find him under some viaduct?"

"Yeah, but I was wrong. Now I know where to look."

"Where?"

"In Dad's old class yearbooks. I know they have the answer."

"What are you talking about?"

"Never mind. I'll explain it to you when you get here."

"Okay, but listen, Dad talked with your doctor this morning. He said you'd be able to attend the funeral tomorrow. I called, but you were still asleep. We want you to know we'll be in tomorrow morning at 8:50."

"I'll ask Bishop Henderson to pick you up."

"Don't bother. We're renting a car. Dad needs to get around town. He has a lot of people he needs to talk to about your case. And he said I could stay in Salt Lake and spend the holidays with you. He has to go back for a business meeting, but I can stay."

"No, Jess!" The sharpness of his response surprised even him. "I mean, it's Christmas. Spend it with your dad. You never know how long you're going to have with him. You never know if this is going to be your last Christmas together."

"But Brad, I want to spend Christmas with you."

"No, really, Jess. It's okay."

"Are you sure?"

"Yeah, I'm sure," Brad said. "I won't be happy until I know you and Uncle Gordon are together for Christmas."

"Okay, Brad, if that's how you want it."

Jess sounded hurt. He was the only family Brad had now, but he couldn't let Jess spend Christmas away from home. He knew how much Jess had been looking forward to spending time with Uncle Gordon over the holidays. Brad didn't want Jess to sacrifice his holiday because of him.

"I'll see you tomorrow, Jess," Brad said.

"Yeah, Brad—tomorrow."

* * *

Conrad could see his breath as he trudged across the snow toward the Armstrong house. The freezing air bit at his face and he huddled into the warm fur hood of his parka. At the back door, he fumbled in his gloved hands trying to fish the key out of his pocket.

A sudden, sharp spitting sound, and a snarling yowl came from a shadowy corner of the lawn. Conrad let out a frightened cry and almost tumbled over backward. Cats. He regained his balance, but dropped the key, which fell with a ping at his feet. He bent down to feel on the ground for the key. When he felt the outline of the key, he sighed with relief.

He unlocked the door and stepped in, fishing in his oversized pocket for his miniflashlight. Finally he took one glove off to get it. He shuffled his way through the kitchen and into the foyer, where the stairs loomed dark and still. He thought of the Armstrongs dead up there but quickly forced the thought from his mind.

He looked at the doorway to the study and sighed. Ten more shuffling steps carried him into the room and he flashed the light on the shelves over the large desk. Four yearbooks lined the right side of the bottom self. He grabbed the last one and stepped back to examine it. At that moment, a squeak sounded from inside the house. A floorboard? A door opening? Was someone in the house?

With a trembling hand he turned off the flashlight and listened but could hear nothing above the pounding of his own heart. He hesitated, shrugged, and walked out into the foyer. A sound from the kitchen sent him into the sitting room where he ducked behind the settee.

He could see the silhouette of a tall man now. The streetlight glowed through a crack in the sitting room curtains and fell on the form now in the foyer. The man was wearing a mask—a ski mask. In his right hand, Conrad could see the glistening of a gun. His heart continued its pounding and he feared it would divulge his hiding place. The form slid past the doorway. Maybe he was going into the study.

Frantically, Conrad looked toward the front door in the foyer. He had to do something. Run. He would have to make a run for it. But what if the intruder was waiting in the foyer for him? Maybe he had seen him and was hiding around the corner of the door to attack.

His pulse was pounding in his head. He had no choice. What else could he do? A reflex in him pushed him up. He bumped the settee, making a loud noise, but still his legs moved beneath him. He grabbed the front doorknob, fumbling with the bolt. Footsteps sounded behind him as something grazed against his back. He gasped and yanked the door open to run into the cold night air, clutching the yearbook to him.

"Hey you! Stop!"

A patrol car had stopped in front of the house, so he turned and ran into some overgrown evergreens. He heard a shot. Was someone shooting at him? He had to keep running. He could hear the crunch of snow beneath his heavy boots as he raced through back lawns and over rock barriers. A fence, tall and dark, loomed before him with a snarling, barking dog on the other side.

"JoJo! Quiet, JoJo!"

He ran to the end of the fence, turned the corner, and opened the side gate.

"Over here! There are footprints over here!"

The police! They were following him. That was better than the masked man, but he would be arrested, he was sure. He scrambled on his hands and knees into JoJo's huge doghouse and retreated to the back corner. As the voices got closer to the fence, JoJo barked wildly, snarling and growling.

Someone jumped up on the fence. "Wow, there's a monster of a dog over there. The guy can't be there. He must have gone into the woods."

The voices trailed off. Conrad was sorry for all the times he complained about taking care of JoJo for Agnes Miller while she was away. He looked out of the doghouse, and JoJo licked him across the face. The house was dark. Agnes always went to visit her daughter in Florida for Christmas.

Cautiously, Conrad made his way across the lawn and onto the back patio. He realized his heart was still beating wildly. He looked down and saw he was still clutching the yearbook. He needed to get back to his car and get the book to Brad.

* * *

Conrad walked into the hospital room, his green parka covered in mud, his hair disheveled, and his face scratched.

"What happened to you?" Brad asked. "You look like you've been through a war."

"I have," he said and flopped down on the chair beside Brad's bed. "Someone tried to kill me."

"What?"

"Someone took a shot at me. I don't know if it was the police or the man with the gun."

Brad sat up in bed. "What are you talking about?"

"A man in a ski mask with a gun. He came into your house while I was there getting the yearbook."

"He came back? What did you do?"

"What do you think I did? I ran."

"And you got away?"

"Well, I'm here, aren't I? What do you think? I'm too fat to get away?"

"I didn't say that, Conrad."

"But you were thinking it."

"Well, it looks like you got the yearbook," Brad said, changing the subject.

Conrad handed it to Brad. "Yeah, and it almost got me killed."

"Sorry about that, Conrad. I didn't think that guy would return to the house after last time. I wonder what he wants. There must be something in the house he's looking for. Something that none of us have thought of yet. I guess we should tell the police about this."

"Are you crazy, Brad? I ran from the police. I could be in big trouble here. Besides, they were there. Maybe they saw him."

"But you said they ran after you. It doesn't sound like they knew he was in the house. At least you got the yearbook."

"Well, the guy that you're looking for in that book can't be the guy who was in the house tonight."

"Why not?"

Because he doesn't fit the build. You described a bodybuilder who carries a lot of weight. This guy was tall and slender. Maybe muscular, but a tall, slender kind of muscular. Not a fat kind of muscular."

"Well, they might be working together."

"Maybe. Look, I've got to get home."

*　*　*

After Conrad left, Brad scanned through the yearbook and tried to concentrate. He had to recognize a face that would have been younger and maybe not as pudgy back then. His head was throbbing. He hoped Dr. Cummings had left for the night. If he came back, he'd be furious that Brad was exhausting himself. Dr. Cummings had wanted to give Brad a stronger painkiller but Brad refused so he would be alert to look at the yearbook. He had to find the bushy-headed man. He said a silent prayer that if anything was there, he'd recognize it. As he turned the pages, one face started to look like another.

The door opened a crack and the nurse looked in at him. "It's all right. I'm getting ready to go to sleep," he whispered.

"Okay, but lights out soon," she whispered back.

"All right. Just a few more minutes."

Thirty minutes had passed, and he'd gone over every individual photograph in the album. Nothing triggered Brad's memory of the man in the sweat suit. He flipped back to the front of the book. Now he would start looking at the group shots. The clubs came first. He was so tired his sight blurred. His head was spinning by the time he looked at every face in every club.

He flipped the page to the team sports. Suddenly, he sat up and brought the book closer to his face. Yes, it could be the same pudgy face, only younger. The body frame was the same, only firmer. He had bushy, dark hair. He stood in the middle of the picture of the West High football team. Brad looked down at the caption: Otto Von Hauser, quarterback. It looked like it could be the same guy, but what were the chances? From quarterback to vagrant? Maybe he was wrong about the sweat suit anyway. Maybe it had nothing to do with the reunion.

Brad leaned over toward the side table. There was a flick of pain, but he kept reaching for the drawer until he opened it and with some effort lifted the phone book inside onto his lap. He flipped through to the Vs: *Vogel; Volt; Vonharten; Von Hauser, Otto.* He lived on Apricot Street in the Marmalade District. It was a residential area on the western slopes of Capitol Hill that had once been dotted with fruit orchards.

He could call Detective Chandler and tell her what he had found, but maybe he was wrong. That photograph was taken more than twenty years ago. Maybe he should get a look first. He would be careful, just park near the house, stay in the car, and watch. If he was right, he would call Detective Chandler immediately. If he was wrong, nothing was lost. Brad was the only person who could identify the man who had come to his house. If Detective Chandler were to question him before Brad could identify him, perhaps he would run.

* * *

On Wednesday night, Van was lying on her stomach on her apartment floor with the Armstrong files strewn in front of her. Groucho was throwing himself amidst the papers in an attempt to get attention. He was getting it, but it was the wrong kind. Van pushed him aside and continued reading.

Her eyes were getting blurry. She was tired. It had been a long, hard, cold day. She and Thornton had walked through the afternoon's crime scene with the gusting winds slapping against their bodies. It was as if the wind had sapped the energy out of her. She and Thornton made sketches and measured the body's distance from the road. Finding evidence was difficult because anything that might have been dropped on the ground was covered with an inch or more of snow.

The crime-scene boys showed up to take the photographs and mark the location of the corpse with a rope so Manwaring could take the body for autopsy. Van was tired and wanted to go home, which was an indication she was getting sick. She was surprised when Manwaring said he was going back to do the autopsy that afternoon because he had some kind of appointment the next day. She wasn't surprised when Thornton ordered her to witness the autopsy so she could take immediate note of any additional information and to take possession of the slug if it was still in the body.

The autopsy was her least favorite part of the job. She almost passed out the first time, not from the sight so much as the smell. She knew the importance of being there; she could receive any evidence directly, which shortened the chain of custody. Perhaps most important to her was the quick access to any new information. Besides, it got her out of Thornton's debriefing session.

The clothes of the victim were checked first. They were clean—no identification, no money, not even any change. Manwaring was good enough to have found a book of matches in the victim's clutched right hand. Manwaring surmised that the victim had gone into an instant cadaveric spasm when he was shot in the heart. His right hand had been in his coat pocket with the matches when he died. The killer had picked the victim clean but probably didn't bother to fight a dead man's spasmed muscles to check his hand.

The matches came from La Casa, a bar near the University of Utah. This clue told them a lot: the victim probably smoked. He probably drank. He probably had some reason to be near the University of Utah at some point.

There was powder tattooing from the muzzle flash on the clothing and burns on the chest. The shooting had been at close range, perhaps by someone he knew. As it turned out, he was shot with a .45 caliber automatic gun like the one Brad said his father owned. She couldn't wait to tell Thornton, to see the look on his face. Of course, he would pretend to be unmoved and would rationalize the coincidence.

They were able to extract fingerprints from the corpse, and Van stayed several hours after the autopsy to run them through AFIS. Lucky for her, the victim had been arrested once before for disorderly conduct. His name was Tongata Uloa, and the autopsy showed that he had cancer, which Van noted in her notebook beside information about Mark Wilson, who also had cancer. It was another one of those facts that seem a little too coincidental. Of course, Thornton would most likely classify this as a drug-related homicide. Uloa wasn't homeless, although he lived alone. He was shot, unlike the homeless victims.

When she got home, Van had taken a twenty-minute shower. She wanted nothing more than to wash the smell of death from her body, especially her hair. The smell tended to linger in the hair follicles. Afterward, Van found herself drifting off as she went through the cases in her mind. Somehow she knew that the answer to the Armstrong murder involved vagrants, drugs, and perhaps cancer. She had to somehow figure out how it all fit together before it was too late for Brad.

The phone interrupted her concentration.

"Hello?"

"Van, Thornton here. The Armstrong house had another break-in."

"What?"

"Patrol just saw a shadowy figure running from the house. They lost him again."

CHAPTER 14

Thursday, December 18

Brad called Conrad early Thursday morning to come pick him up and insisted Conrad drive Brad's BMW. When Conrad arrived at the hospital at 8:00 A.M, Brad insisted on driving, over Conrad's objections.

"Did you find anything in that yearbook, Brad?"

"Yes."

"What?"

"I might have found the man who came by the house last week and argued with Dad. His name is Otto Von Hauser. He was in Dad's graduating class."

"Did you tell the police?"

"No, not yet."

"Why not?"

"I just want to be sure it's him first."

"How are you going to do that?"

"I have a plan." Brad pulled the BMW around the Hendersons' semicircular driveway and stopped in front of the door.

"Okay, Conrad, this is where you get out."

"What?"

"I have an errand to run."

"No way. Mom will kill me if I let you go off alone. She's already going to be furious that you drove home."

"She doesn't have to know."

"She already knows," Conrad said and pointed to the Tudor mansion's front window.

Brad could see Darlene peering out from behind the heavy drapes with a frown on her face. "Looks like we're caught."

Conrad sighed in relief and got out. As soon as he slammed the door shut, Brad drove around and exited onto the street. He looked in his rearview mirror to see Conrad looking up at his mother in the house and shrugging.

Brad drove through the Avenues and turned onto East Capitol Boulevard, which took him into the Marmalade District. Once he was on Apricot Street, he went past several houses until he found the right one and parked across the street. A chill shot up his spine as he realized how close he was to a person who might be able to explain what had happened to his parents.

It didn't look like the house of a killer. Of course, he wasn't sure what a killer's house looked like. He had expected a grungy apartment. It was a handsome old house with a flat roof, molded eaves, segmented window arches, and a prominent bay window. The house had character. Stairs led to the front porch, and another set of stairs led to a basement entrance under the porch. It was probably a duplex. It didn't look like the house of a homeless man either. Perhaps he had been wrong about that. Perhaps this was the wrong man.

An old man, hunched and with a wrinkled face, was shoveling the sidewalk leading to the front steps. Brad decided he would wait for the bushy-headed man to show up. But what if he had already left for the day? The funeral was at 11:00 A.M He didn't have time to wait very long.

The house looked empty except for the old man. Brad glanced around at the other old houses. When he saw that no one was in sight, he took a deep breath, turned off the engine, and jumped out.

He made his way across the icy street to the old man. "Excuse me."

"Whatever it is you're selling, I don't want none. Can't you read?" The old man pointed to a sign on the front door that read, "NO SOLICITORS!!!"

"I'm not selling anything. I'm just looking for someone."

"Who?"

"Otto Von Hauser."

"Well, you've found him. What can he do for you?"

"You're Otto Von Hauser?"

"That's right. What were you expecting, a beauty queen?"

Brad's heart fell. "Uh, no. I was looking for a younger man with bushy, black hair."

"That's my nephew, Otto. I should have known—another bill collector. My curse in life was for my dear brother—may he rest in peace—to name his only son after me. That boy had real potential, but he's been nothing but trouble since he grew up. He's even been in jail. He's disgraced the Von Hauser name." The old man spit on the ground. "Disgraced, I tell you!"

"Can you tell me where to find your nephew?" Brad asked.

"Well, I'll gladly tell you where Otty lives. He lives out on Abby Lane in Rose Park. You can't miss the place. It's an apartment building called Abby Place. It's one of those rundown joints. Do me a favor and have him arrested and throw away the key."

"Thank you."

Brad ran back to his car and jumped in. He glanced at his watch. He didn't have time to go to Rose Park now. He had to go back to the Hendersons, clean up, and get ready for the funeral.

* * *

From a snowy hillside, Van watched the large group of mourners huddled around the caskets with umbrellas to protect them from the heavy snowfall. The wind was blowing hard, making it difficult for people to keep control of their umbrellas.

Van had met Gordon and his son, Jess, before the funeral at the ward meetinghouse. Gordon was a tall, heavyset man with thinning hair. Jess huddled by his father, rubbing his red eyes. Jess was tall and dark like Brad, but not quite as handsome. They both expressed concern about Brad's state of mind. Jess had told her that Brad seemed to be in some kind of shock and wondered if he should see a counselor.

They both wanted to stay with Brad over the holidays, but Gordon had to get back to San Francisco because apparently the new year was a big time for pharmaceuticals due to all those New Year's resolutions people made. Jess had planned on staying with Brad, but Brad insisted he return home with his father. She could tell Jess was hurt by Brad's attitude.

Van looked for anyone who might have bushy hair, but it was too hard to see beneath the umbrellas. Brad was looking around too. He'd probably heard that killers often attend the victims' funerals and was looking for a face in the crowd.

Bishop Henderson completed his short graveside service and then dedicated the graves. Many of the large group in attendance walked up to Brad one by one to hug him and offer condolences. Van headed for the car.

* * *

The graveside service was not as bad as Brad had expected. He didn't hear much of what the bishop said because he was busy scanning the faces of those in attendance to determine which ones thought him guilty and which ones thought him innocent. It was split about fifty-fifty.

He had returned to Darlene's catered luncheon for about an hour, and then he excused himself.

Conrad followed him to the front door. "Where are you going, Brad?"

"Just out driving."

"You went looking for that Von Hauser guy this morning, didn't you?"

"Yes."

"I take it you didn't find him."

"No. But I'm getting closer. I now know he lives in Rose Park."

"You're not going out there are you?"

"We'll talk about this later, Conrad. I really need to go." Brad walked out the door and got into his car. He had his cell phone in his suit pocket. As soon as he was sure he had the right man, he would call Detective Chandler.

* * *

As he sat at his cluttered desk, Thornton felt the pulse in his cheek begin to throb again. He pressed his fingers on it and received momentary relief. He was tired. He hadn't slept well. He shuffled through his papers on the Armstrong murder case, and, in exasperation, pushed them back, knocking the pencil holder from his desk. The phone rang.

"Hello."

"Is this Detective Thornton?"

"Yes. Who's this?"

"Conrad Henderson."

"Yes?"

"I'm worried about Brad. He's going to be mad that I'm calling you, but I don't want him to get hurt again."

"What are you talking about?"

"He thinks he's found the man who came by his house and argued with his dad. It's a man named Otto Von Hauser in Rose Park. I think Brad might have gone out there looking for him."

"What? Is he putting you up to this?"

"No. Go out there and look for yourself. Just don't let Brad get hurt."

"Okay. I'm going to go out there, but if this turns out to be one of Bradley's games, I'm going to have you both arrested for obstruction of justice."

* * *

As Brad drove into Rose Park on Salt Lake's west side, he was overwhelmed. This was Dad's old neighborhood. Dad and Uncle Gordon had grown up here.

Rose Park was Salt Lake City's first mass-produced housing project. Immediately after World War II, the mechanized construction methods used during the conflict were adopted to build quick housing for war production. While critics complained that the city was turning into a community of look-alike houses fated to become slums, Brad's grandfather had seen an opportunity to own his own home. Fresh back from the war and looking forward to a bright future, he had settled down in the so-called cookie-cutter neighborhood to raise his two boys. It was a safe neighborhood back then.

Brad remembered his dad telling him that Uncle Gordon was a natural businessman. He used to buy bubble gum and licorice at the local market for two cents, then sell it for four cents. Dad once caught Uncle Gordon watering down lemonade and selling it on the street corner for two cents too much. He had taken advantage of the chance to give his brother a lecture on business ethics. Dad was always the moralist. He even taught a class in ethics for pharmacists at the U. It was no wonder that Dad ended up joining the Church. Uncle Gordon took the discussions but could never commit himself to baptism. Brad had grown up in the Church; Jess had not. Brad felt a twinge of guilt as he contemplated what kind of example he had been for Jess.

Brad parked his car across the street from the three-story apartment building where a man stood on a ladder to change a lightbulb by the front door. Brad could sit in front of the building until he saw Von Hauser, or he could go ask the man on the ladder. He decided to ask.

He got out and walked across the street. "Excuse me," Brad said.

"Yes."

"Do you work here?"

"I'm the manager."

"Do you know Otto Von Hauser?"

"Who wants to know?"

"His uncle sent me here to find him."

"Well, he's not here. He's had a job for a while now, leaves around six every morning."

"Do you know what time he usually gets home from work?"

"Well, he rides the bus so it depends on which bus he catches. He's usually here by 5:30 or so."

"Thank you."

"No problem."

Brad went back to his car and got in. He could go home and come back, but it would be dark by then. He watched as the man folded up the ladder and went around the side of the building. Brad drove around the corner and down the street. He got out and walked back. It was a simple brick structure with an alleyway down the side and to the back. He walked inside the front door onto a squeaky wood floor. Upon examining the beat-up mailboxes, he saw Von Hauser was in apartment 2D.

He made his way up the rickety stairs to the second floor. He just had to find out if he was right or not. Maybe there would be a picture or something in the apartment. Brad shuffled his way down the hall. No one in the building seemed to be home. They all were probably at work. He stopped in front of the door. His heart was pounding and his forehead perspiring. He listened—silence.

He found himself knocking lightly. No one. He reached to hold on to the knob, and to his surprise it turned. The door was unlocked. He pushed the door open, and the hinges whined. Quickly he stepped in, closed the door behind him, and locked it.

The place smelled bad. He wasn't sure what the stench was. It was a small three-room apartment, including a living room with a small area for a minirefrigerator and hot plate, a bedroom, and a bathroom. The living room had a well-worn couch, a frayed recliner, a TV, and a small kitchen table covered with dirty dishes. Dumbbells cluttered the floor around a large weight bench. Next to the bench was some kind of rowing machine, an exercise cycle, and a treadmill. As Brad walked into the middle of the room, he tripped over some kind of abdominal contraption like the kind advertised on thirty-minute infomercials.

He picked up a framed picture from a small table beside the couch. His heart jumped as he looked at Otto Von Hauser, the man he had been looking for. In the photo, Von Hauser was in some kind of bodybuilding competition, flexing his muscles, reeking arrogance. Brad put down the frame.

He walked over to the kitchenette with its one small cupboard and pulled the cupboard door open. The shelves were full of Slim Fast, hazelnut bars, and fat-free caramel corn.

The bathroom was filthy. The sink counter was littered with fat-burning skin creams, more vitamins, and various herbal medications. He went into the bedroom and froze: There lying on his stomach was Otto Von Hauser. His head had been bashed in. Beside the bed was a metal trophy covered in blood.

Brad bit his lip to avoid screaming. For a timeless moment he froze. Every irrelevant sound and scent seemed magnified: the quick thudding of his heart, like a drumbeat; the slight creaking of the old building; the far-off sound of a car going down a street.

His trance was broken by the sound of feet shuffling their way up the stairs followed by a knock on the door. Brad's first terrified impulse was to hide in the closet, crawl under the bed, jump out the window, anything to escape. Too cold with fear to move, he listened.

"Mr. Von Hauser? Open up so we can talk with you, sir."

"I told you he's not here. He works." It was the manager's voice.

"Detective Thornton wants us to wait here for him. He's coming with a warrant to search the premises," said a voice that apparently belonged to a policeman. "We'll have to ask you to open the door when he gets here. Do you understand?"

"Yes," said the manager.

At the mention of Thornton's name, rage leaped up into Brad so sharply that it jabbed at him like a knife. His fear mingled now with overpowering fury. He couldn't let Thornton catch him here. The window! He had to get out the window.

Brad opened the window soundlessly and cold air rushed into the warm apartment. He crawled out onto the narrow ledge and gazed down into the alley below. His feet fumbled, and he swayed before catching his balance by leaning hard against the window frame. Luckily the ledge was covered by the roofline and was free of snow. He closed the window.

A large dumpster stood below, a lid covering one side. He had no choice. Before he had time to think about what he was doing, he jumped, his body falling straight toward the opening below. He crashed into the dumpster, his arm hitting the closed lid with a firm thud. He heard cracking as he sank into the reeking trash, and smelled the foul, stomach-churning odor of festering garbage.

Ignoring the burning pain in his arm, he pushed himself through trash bags and empty boxes and crawled to the opening in the top of the dumpster to peer out. The alley was empty. He listened. The still-ness seemed sinister and almost unbearable. He glanced up at the window. He couldn't tell if anyone was there, and he didn't care. He had to get out. He climbed over the side of the dumpster and hung from the rim with feet dangling for a moment before he let go, landing firmly. Quickly he made his way to the front of the alley, dashed around the corner, and raced down the street.

"Hey, it's the Armstrong kid!"

Like lightning, Brad ran down the sidewalk and turned the corner. His heart kept pace with the pounding of his shoes on the pavement. He twisted his way through several alleyways and down a small side street. No one seemed to be following him. Of course, they had no reason yet to follow him. They had no reason yet to chase him. They hadn't yet found the body, but they would soon, and they would find his fingerprints all over the apartment.

A bus! He had to get to the bus. He ran faster than he ever remembered running. His heart was in his throat, and his eyes were burning. Pain shot from his side through his whole system. He could feel the stitches on his side bursting. The bus started to pull away from the bus stop. "Hey! Stop!" he yelled.

He reached the side of the bus and pounded it with his open hand. The wheels squeaked as the bus stopped. The door opened and he jumped on, pulling his university bus pass from his wallet and flashing it. The bus started again. He made his way to the back. The passengers cast quick glances as he passed them. Did they recognize him? Maybe they'd seen him on the news. He sat in the back to avoid their stares.

He had to get off as soon as possible and double back to his BMW. But wait! They would be looking for his car. Thornton would be looking for him. He could try to explain the whole situation, but they hadn't believed him the first time. Why would they believe him now? He was in trouble, more trouble than he'd ever been in. He would have to disappear somewhere. He couldn't go back to Conrad's. He had to find a place to stay.

Brad got off the bus on a downtown street and trudged his way through the snow to the ZCMI Center Mall. He stepped in from the cold, found a quiet corner bench, and pulled out his cell phone. He dialed information for the number to the Salt Lake City Police Department. After receiving the number, he dialed.

"Hello."

"May I speak to Detective Chandler?"

"One moment please."

"Hello."

"Detective Chandler?"

"Yes, Brad is that you?"

"Yeah, I need your help. First of all, no matter what they say, I didn't do it."

"Do what?"

"Kill the bushy-headed man."

"What?"

"He's dead, and Detective Thornton may think I did it, but I didn't. I just went to his apartment because I thought he might be the man who argued with Dad. I just wanted to get a look, make sure. Well, now I'm sure, but he's dead."

"Look, Brad, you need to come down to the station so you can explain this whole thing."

"No way. Detective Thornton will just arrest me again."

"You're only making things worse. Running never works."

Brad ended the call. He rushed out of the mall and caught the southbound transit bus. It made its way slowly, stopping at every block. When it stopped to let a man off by a strip of businesses left to die after the interstate viaduct came in, a neon sign flashed in Brad's face: "Desert Inn." It was a seedy motel built to resemble an old, Spanish-style hacienda of stucco and red tile. Brad jumped off the bus.

CHAPTER 15

The tiny office smelled of strong coffee and stale cigarettes. A TV was blaring in the back room, so Brad slammed his hand on the bell until he got someone's attention. The motel clerk peered around the door frame and eyed him suspiciously. Brad was still wearing his funeral suit.

"Yeah?" the man said, stepping up to the desk so Brad could get a good look at his wrinkled face and bald head.

Brad cleared his throat. "I need a room."

The man pulled out a pad from under the desk. "For how long?"

"One night."

"Okay, that'll be thirty dollars plus tax. Fill this out."

Brad took the form and started to write his name, stopped, and started writing again. Along with the pseudonym John Johnson, he made up an Idaho address and phone number. He pulled his wallet from his back pocket. He had sixty dollars Conrad had loaned him. He would have to get some money from an ATM as soon as possible. He handed the man two twenty-dollar bills. The man reached under the desk and returned with a key and the change.

"You're in Suite 18 on the west side."

Brad smiled as he took the key. "Thanks."

He looked over his shoulder once before walking out. The old man was studying him. Did he recognize Brad from the news?

The rooms frowned on a snow-packed courtyard. Brad crossed to the west side where he found a door with peeling red paint and the number 18. He unlocked the door, pushed it open, and entered.

The dim room had green shag carpet, matching curtains and bedspread, scratched-up old furniture, a broken table lamp, an ugly desert landscape print, a television, and a wheezing electric heater under the window. Brad collapsed on the bed and smelled the elusive but distinctive combination of thrift store and disinfectant or maybe air freshener.

He wanted a shower, had wanted one since seeing Von Hauser's body. He pulled off his jacket and placed it to his nose. Did it really smell like a rotting corpse or was he just imagining it? Maybe it was just the garbage he had jumped into. He quickly pulled off the rest of his clothes and went into the bathroom.

The linoleum floor looked filthy. He stepped across it, pulled back the plastic shower curtain stained by years of hard water, and stepped in. A dark orange stain ran from the showerhead down the tiled wall. He turned the water handle, and the showerhead shook and sputtered before reluctantly producing a weak stream of warm water. He put his head under the water and tried to wash away his aches, but the water only seemed to intensify the pain. His arm still ached. The stab wound in his lower back itched and pricked. A hot pain ran from his lower back up his spine to his neck.

Dark images roamed the corridors of his mind. Von Hauser's eyes. Dad's eyes. Mom's eyes. He clutched his head and moaned. "Get out! Get out!" Tears flowed from his eyes, down his cheeks, and into his mouth, adding a salty taste to the hard water.

Thornton thought he did it. Thornton would be looking for him. Maybe Detective Chandler was right. Maybe he should turn himself in and go quietly to his death. Anything had to be better than living in this torture chamber. He'd stepped over the line into a twilight zone he never knew existed, a place of violence and danger.

He turned toward the dirty shower wall and placed his head against it. Loud sobs were now emerging from his mouth. "Why? Why? Why? Why did this have to happen? What have I done to deserve this?" He stood there under the flow of hard water, sobbing until his skin began to wrinkle. When the water turned cold and he ran out of tears, he turned the water off and stepped out onto the bath mat. He dried himself and wrapped a towel around his waist.

He sat down on the side of the bed by the side table. He clicked on the lamp and pulled out the drawer, revealing a Gideon Bible. He took the Bible from the drawer, opened it to Isaiah, and looked down at a verse: "For I the Lord thy God will hold thy right hand, saying unto thee, Fear not; I will help thee" (Isa. 41:13).

Brad stretched out on the bed to read but fell asleep. When he woke up, it was dark outside. The clock on the side table said it was almost 9:00, time for the Fox news. He got up, walked over to the TV, and turned it on. The first story was about a bad accident on I-15 that afternoon. The roads had been slick, and drivers weren't slowing down enough.

A photograph of a body in the Salt Lake City Cemetery appeared behind the anchorman's head. "Authorities have identified the body found in the Salt Lake City Cemetery as that of Tongata Uloa. His death was apparently the result of a gunshot wound to the chest." Brad's picture then flashed behind the anchor's head. Brad turned the volume up.

"The story of Bradley Armstrong, accused of killing his parents in their upscale Federal Heights home, took a new and bizarre twist today. Philip Morris has the story."

A video clip of Von Hauser's apartment played through the static of the screen. "The unusual story of the Armstrong murder found its way here today in the most unlikely of places—Rose Park, a world away from the exclusive Federal Heights home of the Armstrongs. Police detectives found a man bludgeoned to death in this rundown apartment building. The victim has been identified as Otto Von Hauser, a resident of the apartment complex. What makes this story bizarre is that police spotted Bradley Armstrong coming from the alleyway beside the building moments before discovering the body. Armstrong ran and managed to escape."

Thornton's face appeared on the screen. "We want to make it clear that while Bradley Armstrong is a suspect in this case, we're only seeking him for questioning at this time. His relationship to this murder is unclear at the moment."

"Police find Armstrong's presence disturbing," said the reporter, "and say it is odd that he ran from the scene."

"Thank you, Philip," the anchorman said, "for that twist in an already bizarre case. Meanwhile, friends and family gathered today in Salt Lake City Cemetery to pay their last respects to Allen and Peggy

Armstrong. Cynthia Miller caught up with some of the Armstrong family at Salt Lake International tonight as they prepared to leave for California."

"Gordon Armstrong, president of Armstrong Pharmaceuticals, and his son, Jess, left Salt Lake today with heavy hearts."

Gordon appeared on the screen. "We hope Brad will come of his own volition to the police and explain what happened today," he said.

The reporter asked, "What do you think happened today, Mr. Armstrong?"

"I have no idea, but Jess and I both feel in our hearts that Brad had nothing to do with his parents' deaths or this man's over in Rose Park."

"Why was he there, Mr. Armstrong?"

"I wish I could answer that, but I have no idea. All I know is that I love Brad like he was my own son, and I'm concerned for his safety tonight. It's cold outside. The temperatures are dropping. Brad, if you're out there listening, please give me a call tonight. Let me know you're okay. We'll work this all out."

The reporter then turned to Jess and asked, "Do you have anything to say to your cousin, Jess?"

"I just want Brad to know how much I love him and how much I hate going back to California, leaving him alone for Christmas. I'll be waiting for your call, Brad."

The tall, angular Victor Kline then appeared on the screen. "My client is being persecuted by the authorities and the local press. He is being tried unfairly in the public arena. I want to make it clear that this shadowy figure the police claim to have seen running from the Von Hauser murder was not my client. He was some sort of straw man created in the minds of the police involved."

"How do you explain your client's disappearance?" a reporter asked.

"Just because you don't know where he is, doesn't mean he has disappeared. If anything, he is seeking solitude from the persecution you are heaping on him."

Brad switched off the TV and felt hot tears streaming down his face. At least Kline seemed to be holding the wolves at bay.

Time was running out for him. He had to keep going. He had to think. How was Von Hauser involved with this? What was his relationship to Dad? It must have something to do with Dad's work. Maybe the answer was in his father's office. Sure, Thornton had searched it already, but he didn't know what he was looking for. He wasn't looking for Von Hauser then. Why had Thornton been at Von Hauser's apartment? What was he looking for? What was going on?

* * *

It was 9:15 P.M. when Carmichael and Jensen walked into Thornton's office with the pizza.

"Did you get anchovies on it?" Thornton asked.

"Yeah, yeah, just like you like it," Jensen said.

"Where's Uluave?"

"Still checking out hotels with Scarface," Jensen said. "They checked the Marriott, Hilton, Doubletree, and Little America. They're working their way down from there. What makes you think the kid's staying in a fancy hotel? He may have left town by now."

"He doesn't have a car. We've got the bus stations and airports covered. He's tired. One thing I know about spoiled rich kids, they're creatures of habit. He has to have a place to stay tonight, right? Well, he's not going down to some cheap motel. That wouldn't even occur to him. He doesn't know what a cheap motel is. No, this kid will stay in what he's used to. He'll check himself into a nice hotel with a spa and sauna. I tell you I know the type. Besides, we've got to start somewhere. We might as well work our way down."

Thornton's phone rang. He picked it up. "Yeah, Thornton here."

"Detective Thornton, there's a man on the phone who says he knows where Armstrong is. He wants to talk to you."

"Put him on."

"Go ahead."

"This is Detective Thornton."

"Yes, Detective. I just saw you on the news. I'm the manager of the Desert Inn down on Fourth South. Armstrong just checked in this afternoon. I couldn't believe it when I saw his face on TV tonight."

* * *

Van had passed Thornton on his way out of the station, and he told her to come along for the ride. Lately, everyone seemed to be at the station at all hours of the night. All of a sudden they had several unsolved murders on their hands, and none of them dared let the trail run cold. Van sat in the back with Carmichael, Jensen up front, Thornton driving. The temperature was dropping fast, and the Lumina's windows kept fogging up.

"Where are we going, Thornton?"

"You'll see, Van. Be patient."

"You said it had something to do with Brad."

"It does."

She clutched her sweaty hands together, released them, and clutched them again. They pulled up in front of a seedy motel—Desert Inn, a repulsively gaudy mock-Spanish building. Uluave and Jones were there to greet them. Van jumped out of the back.

"We have the key," Jones said. "The manager said the kid left ten minutes ago in a cab."

Thornton took the key. "Call the cab company and find out where they dropped him. The rest of you follow me."

They walked into a tacky courtyard with a snow-covered statue in the middle. They rushed past rooms 15, 16, 17, stopping in front of 18. Thornton knocked, waited a few seconds, and then unlocked the door. They all went into the room. Everything was bad about the room: bad carpet, bad wallpaper, bad furniture, bad bedspread, bad curtains, and bad print. The room was repulsive.

"I thought you said the kid didn't know about places like this," Jensen said and glared at Thornton.

"What can I say? The kid's learning fast."

"What makes you think Brad was here?" Van asked.

"The manager recognized him."

"He had a shower," Uluave said. "And the bed's messed up."

Jensen came into the room. "The cab company said they picked up a passenger here and just dropped him off near the university."

Thornton grinned. "Well, well, I'll bet Bradley decided to stay in his dorm room tonight. Call university security and have them meet us there to open the building."

* * *

Brad moved down the hall to his father's office. His footsteps echoed in the empty hall. The door had a keyless lock installed to make access easier for research assistants. Brad punched the code into the programmable lock, and the door came open. The dark room oozed musty air. Brad stepped in, closed the door, and switched on the light.

He went over to Dad's computer and turned it on. Dad had let him use his office computer several times; he had shown Brad where he kept his password. He pulled the top drawer open, and, on a post-it note, saw it—Peggy3. When he got the computer up, Brad started searching through program after program. He didn't know what he was looking for. Anything. Dad had nearly a hundred documents in his WordPerfect directory. He went into several database programs and typed in the Von Hauser name with no results.

He went into a directory labeled "Consulting." He pulled up another database program and typed in Von Hauser's name. A dialogue box popped up: Record Deleted. When Brad went to check the document's history, he learned it was deleted at 4:55 A.M the same morning he'd found his parents dead.

Brad rummaged through the desk drawers but found nothing that indicated Von Hauser's connection to his father. He turned to the bookshelves and noticed several books lying sideways on the bottom shelf, and he lifted each one to read its title. He wasn't sure what he was looking for, but he felt compelled to keep looking.

* * *

"For a dumb kid, he's sure lucky," Jensen said as he walked out of the empty dorm room.

"I'm beginning to think there's nothing dumb about this kid at all," Thornton said grimly. "Where else could he be? They're sure they dropped him off by the university?"

"The only other place I can think of is maybe his father's office," Jensen said.

"Of course," Thornton said. "Let's get over there."

CHAPTER 16

Brad looked down at the phone. The light beside the voice mail was flashing. His father had messages he would never pick up. Brad felt a now-familiar twinge of emotion as he picked up the phone and pushed the VMX button. "This is the phone mail service for Allen Armstrong. Please enter your identification code now."

Brad glanced at the computer. Peggy3. He translated the letters to numbers and dialed 734493. "Thank you. Messages are being retrieved."

He waited anxiously.

"Professor Armstrong, this is Ginny Adamson. I need to talk with you about my final grade. I don't think it was fair. If we can get together sometime before Christmas that would be great."

Beep.

"Allen, this is Earl Derr. I have the results back from those tests. Give me a call."

Beep.

"Dr. Armstrong, this is Amazing Computers calling about your laptop. We had to order a new hinge from Compaq to replace the broken one on your monitor. Anyway, it's all ready for you. You can pick it up anytime."

"That was your last message. To review messages, press 1. To delete messages press 7. To hear more options, press—"

Brad hung up the phone. Dad's laptop had been in the shop all along. He picked up the phone book and found Amazing Computers. They were on Wasatch Boulevard. He would go first thing in the morning.

He needed to get back to the motel and get some sleep. He took one last look around, shut the light off, and locked the door. As he headed down the hall, he heard a click and felt a breeze through the hall. Someone had entered the building. He looked to his right, a long passageway. He dashed down the hall, trying doorknobs as he went. Finally, a door that was unlocked. He jumped inside. It was a janitor's closet. He stepped back against the wall and his back hit something hard. He turned and felt a ladder. Looking up, he could see small lights in an opening above his head.

He heard footsteps now. "He's not here. Check down that hall."

He heard doorknobs clanking and his heart pounding. He climbed up the ladder into the hole. The doorknob turned, the door flew open, and a light came on. Feet shuffled in the closet beneath him. He could hear feet on the metal ladder. Someone was coming up. He held his breath.

"Come on, Uluave. He's not here. Let's get back to that sleazy motel before the kid returns. We'll get him before he gets in the room."

They knew where he was staying. How did they find out? The motel manager; he must have told them. He was studying Brad too hard. Now he'd have to find another place to stay, and how did they know to look for him at the U? What about Thornton showing up at Von Hauser's? Brad shook his head. He couldn't take time to think about it now.

He waited in the ceiling until he was sure everyone had left, then climbed down and turned on the light. The room was full of janitorial supplies, mops, and brooms. Brad opened a locker in the corner. A pair of overalls, some old jeans, some work boots, and some dirty shirts were hanging in the locker. An idea came to him. He started changing his clothes.

* * *

A late-night bus dropped Brad off on the corner of 200 South and Rio Grande. He was wearing dirty Wranglers that were too big and held up by his belt, and a thin blue jacket covered a dirty work shirt. A blue baseball cap was pulled down over his eyes. He walked down past the dark windows of the social services agencies, past Pioneer Park, and toward the viaducts. Thornton would never look in the hobo camps for him. It was funny how Brad's perspective had changed. Just a couple days ago, he had been terrified of this area of town. Now he was nervous, yes, but looked to the campsites as a refuge, a place to hide out.

He rounded a huge cement boulder that was holding up an overpass and walked into a campsite lit by the mellow glow of campfires. He walked past several groups of hobos, mainly old men with gruff manners and mean looks. He didn't feel welcome. He heard faint, weird music coming from somewhere in the deep recesses of the viaduct. He strolled over to the viaduct and looked into the darkness at three teenage boys standing around a campfire, singing.

"Jingle bells, jingle bells, jingle all the way. Oh what fun it is to ride in a one-horse open sleigh . . ."

Brad stepped nearby and sat on the cold cement that sloped up toward the overpass. One kid was playing a harmonica while another jingled some bells on a string.

"Dashing through the snow in a one-horse open sleigh. O'er the field we go, laughing all the way . . ."

One of the kids looked over at him suspiciously. He left the group and headed in Brad's direction. His face was pasty, his hair matted, and he appeared to be high on something. He was covered in a long green raincoat that was two sizes too big. "Hey, dude, you new around here? Haven't seen you before."

"I just got here."

"You from around here?"

"Yeah."

"Parents toss you out?"

"They died."

"Oh, sorry, dude. Why don't you come on over by the fire?"

"I don't want to bother anybody."

"Then you better come over 'cause it'll bother me if you sit over here alone."

"Okay."

"They call me Bates. You know, like the guy in that movie *Psycho.*"

"Why do they call you that?"

"'Cause I was put in the psycho center six times for depression, chemical dependency, and fits of rage. You name it, I did it. I got sick of taking the medicines and ran away. That was back in L.A. I went to Vegas first. Got into a ring that was paid by owners to steal their cars. Sometimes we could get four or five hundred dollars."

"Why would anyone pay you to steal their car?"

"Insurance, dude. They wanted the insurance."

"Oh."

"I fell in with Frankie over there. He told me spanging was pretty good in Salt Lake so we took a bus. Been here ever since."

"What's spanging?"

"You know, 'Got any change?' 'Can you spare a quarter?' 'Need a dollar to catch the bus.'"

"Oh."

"Dude, you've got a lot to learn if you're going to make it out here."

"I'm not sure I'm going to make it out here."

"Sure you will. I've learned a lot more on the streets than I ever would have learned in school."

They drifted over to the other two boys. The bonfire glowed and crackled, lighting up the faces of the two teenagers.

"Hey, Frankie," Bates said. "Meet my new friend. What's your name again?"

"Brad."

"Brad. He's new on the streets, dude."

Brad studied the tall, gangly Frankie. He had bad acne and was what Brad recognized as a Goth—dyed black hair, black eyeliner, black lipstick, and fingernails painted a gloomy hue. He stared at Brad with glassy eyes. "Welcome, Brad." He lifted a small container of correction fluid in his right hand. "Wanna huff some White Out, Brad?"

Brad backed away. "No thanks."

Bates giggled. "Don't let Frankenstein scare you. He's a recovering Goth. They did a number on him, but he's cool now."

"Yeah, I don't dwell on the dark side anymore."

Bates walked over to the handsome black boy standing by Frankie. "This here is Boozer."

"Hey man," Boozer said. "Got any pot or booze?"

"No," Brad said.

"Brad's parents died," Bates said.

"Man, I wish my parents would die," Frankie said.

Bates giggled. "Frankie's still mad at his old man for roughing him up a little now and then."

"Roughing me up? Man, he beat the life out of me. I had enough of that stuff. I figured I was tough enough to handle life on my own."

Boozer spit near Brad's foot. "Running away's the only safe thing to do sometimes. It's not safe out here, but it's safer than at home."

"Boozer's dad caught him stealing his pot one day," Bates said. "He stabbed him in the ribs. Show him the scar, Boozer."

"No, man. It's freezing out here. I'm not taking off anything tonight."

Boozer crawled into a sleeping bag by the fire on the viaduct cement. Frankie got into his sleeping bag too.

"Hey, dudes," Bates said, "cough up some blankets for Brad here. You gonna let someone freeze to death at Christmastime? What if Santa finds out?"

Frankie pulled a ragged blanket from his sleeping bag. "Here." He threw it at Brad's feet. "Thanks," Brad said.

Boozer pulled a small quilt from his backpack. "Here, man."

"Thanks."

Bates climbed into his sleeping bag, and Brad made a bed beside him, snuggling into the blankets that smelled like body odor and campfire. "Thanks for your help," Brad said.

"It's tough when someone dies," Boozer said. "My sister was killed. They found her around Christmas two years ago."

"Sorry," Brad said.

"I had to get away," Boozer said. "I didn't want to end up like her. I spent the only cash I had on a bus ticket to Salt Lake. It was the farthest I could go from San Francisco with the money I had. When I got here, I tried to get a job, but none of the stores or fast-food places would hire me because I'm black."

"They said that?" Brad asked.

"No man, they didn't have to say nothing. I knew what they were thinking by their eyes. People are scared of young black men. They think we're going to hurt them or rob them or something. They think we're all gang members out to get them. They think we're no-good trash. There ain't nothing worse than being misjudged."

Brad looked into his sad black eyes. How strange the world was. Brad Armstrong from Federal Heights was lying under a viaduct, using borrowed blankets from homeless teenagers, talking to a young black man, and totally connecting to what he was saying. There was nothing worse than being misjudged. It was perhaps the ultimate injustice, the worst punishment the world could inflict on a human soul. For a brief moment, it was like Boozer's soul met Brad's in some freaky cosmic alliance.

Brad's thoughts were interrupted by the jingling of bells. "It's Santa," Bates said.

"It ain't Santa," Frankie said. "It's Smiley."

A short, shaggy-headed boy approached their camp. "Hey, guys. Been to McDonald's lately?"

Bates giggled. "Don't tell me you're still playing that stupid game? Chances of winning a million are one in a million, Smiley."

Smiley looked offended or hurt or both. "If everybody thought that, Bates, nobody would win and everybody would be losers."

Bates laughed.

"You wouldn't know what to do with the money anyway," Frankie said.

Smiley smiled. "I'd buy a big piece of land out in the country for all runaways. We could take our tents out there and live. We could have a nice community."

Bates giggled. "A nice community? Sounds like those social workers have warped your brain, Smiley."

"Laugh all you want. I'll still let you come live on my land when I win."

"That's a real nice idea, Smiley," Boozer said seriously. "Save me a place, will ya?"

"Sure, Boozer."

"Don't encourage his fantasy," Bates said.

"Why not? None of us could live without our fantasies. Only difference is Smiley talks out loud about his."

There was silence.

"Did you hear they found an old man dead in a cemetery?" Smiley asked proudly.

"Smiley, you love spreading bad news more than anyone else I know," Frankie said. "Where do you get all this stuff?"

"I watch the TVs in the malls. They found a body in some river somewhere, too."

"Thanks for the update, Smiley," Bates said. "We're hitting the sack early so we can go down to St. Vincent de Paul's for breakfast. Roll your sack out and shut your mouth."

"No thanks, Bates. I've got some more game pieces to collect. Someone said Badger went to McDonald's today."

Boozer laughed. "Better not stay out too late, Smiley. You don't want Santa to get mad at you."

"Don't worry, Boozer. I'll be in bed before midnight."

CHAPTER 17

Friday, December 19

Brad woke to the sound of tires cutting through slush. The overpasses to downtown were busy. He looked at his watch. 7:15. The two malls downtown were opening early this week for holiday shoppers.

He sat up and his back cracked. His legs were numb, hands blue and gray. He was a human Popsicle. Bates, Frankie, and Boozer were sleeping. They were probably used to the noise. Smiley had joined them sometime in the night and was snuggled between Frankie and Boozer.

Brad stood up. The blankets clung to him, and he pushed them to the ground reluctantly. He felt his back pocket. He still had his wallet. He didn't have much money, but he had a Visa card. He'd catch a bus to the mall.

* * *

Brad stepped off the bus into the crowd of shoppers outside the ZCMI Center. He trudged across the walk into the mall, slipped on the tile floor, caught himself, and headed to the west entrance. He crossed Main Street and entered the Mervyn's door to the Crossroads Mall so he could pick up some pants, a shirt, and a winter coat.

The shoppers standing around him in line kept their distance. The woman behind him backed away. He probably smelled like smoke. The woman at the register looked up, and the smile fell from her face. She gave him a condescending look. "Yes?"

He pushed the clothes toward her and threw his VISA on top of them. She stuck her nose in the air and started scanning the bar codes.

"That's one hundred and seventy dollars and fifty-two cents."

She took the VISA and scanned it. While she waited for approval, she eyed Brad suspiciously. "Christmas gifts?"

He could hear the disdain in her tone. It was like what Boozer had said. Here was a clerk who got pushed around every day, and now she found someone she felt superior to. She couldn't let it pass without boosting her ego. What would she think if she knew he'd purchased all his Christmas gifts at Nordstrom? Funny how easily one slipped in social status.

"No," he answered.

She frowned at him, tore the slip from the register, and said, "Sign on the bottom line."

After concluding the purchase, Brad headed for the bathrooms. There were two men washing their hands. Brad walked by them and went into a stall, locking the door. He changed into his new clothes as quickly as possible. By the time he finished, the bathroom was empty and he threw the old clothes in the trash. He went to the sink and washed his hands and face.

* * *

Thornton slammed the phone receiver down. "Hey Jensen! Get in here. We have a lead on the kid. He just made a purchase at the downtown Mervyn's."

Jensen ran in the room. "What's he doing, his Christmas shopping?"

"Who can figure this kid out? Come on. Let's go give the kid our Christmas present."

Jensen snickered.

* * *

Brad finished his McDonald's breakfast and headed up to the main level of the shopping mall. As he passed a video store, he could hear the familiar dialogue of the movie *A Christmas Carol* playing on the large-screen TV at the entrance. He used to love watching that movie with his parents during the holidays.

He leaned against the wall and watched for a moment. The ghost of Jacob Marley had appeared to Ebenezer Scrooge. Marley was lamenting his wasted life: "Mankind was my business. Not to know that no space of regret can make amends for one life's opportunities misused! Yet such was I! Oh, such was I! Why did I wander through throngs of fellow beings with my eyes cast down and never once lift them to that glorious star that guided wise men to a poor abode? Were there no poor homes toward which its light might have conducted me?"

Guilt struck Brad's conscience. He thought again of the man and his daughters at the homeless shelter. He would never be able to erase that image from his mind. He could still picture those terrible shoes the children were wearing. He glanced down at his new clothes and he thought of Bates, Boozer, and the others. He had never known they existed. What kind of Christmases had they been having while Brad enjoyed an overabundance of gifts up in Federal Heights? Silently Brad said a prayer of gratitude for this moment of realization.

He was being blessed with an awareness of what was really important in life. Like Scrooge, Brad was being given a chance to see the world in a whole different light. It was the same world he had always lived in, but now the illumination was a little brighter, allowing him to see into the dark corners he had missed before. Silently, he promised Heavenly Father he would try to serve others with the gifts he had been given. He would try to think less of himself and more of others. Of course, he was in no position to help anyone now. He would first have to get himself out of this mess. Once again, he was thinking only of himself, but he remembered once hearing that you can't take care of anyone unless you first take care of yourself. He would have to get through this crisis, and then he would take care of others as he had just promised.

Brad started toward the South Temple exit and stopped in his tracks. Thornton! He was coming through the glass doors with Jensen at his side. Brad's heart pounded. He knew credit purchases could be traced but had no idea they could be traced so quickly. What should he do? Should he run? No. They'd catch him for sure.

He moved to a window with his back to the walkway. He could see their reflection in the glass. They passed without looking his way and pushed their way through the crowd and into the Mervyn's main-floor entrance.

He turned and rushed out of the building.

* * *

"Come on, Thornton," Jensen said. "We've searched every inch of this mall. He's not here. We missed him again."

"He's clever," Thornton said. "The clerk said he was dressed like a bum. I'll bet he's hiding out with the street people. I want you to call Uluave and Scarface. I want patrols to search every street in the downtown area for that kid. Let's get down to Rio Grande right now."

Jensen grinned. "Rio Grande's a long way from the Hilton, ain't it, Thornton?"

"Oh, shut up, Jensen."

* * *

Clouds had darkened the day by the time Brad got off the bus on Wasatch Boulevard. He walked a block to Amazing Computers and rushed in the store. "I'm here to pick up my dad's computer."

"Name?"

"Allen Armstrong."

"Oh, yeah. We wondered when you were going to pick it up."

The clerk disappeared into a back room and returned a few moments later with the laptop in its carrying case. "We had to order the hinge from Compaq, but it's fixed. Let's see. That'll be one hundred and forty-two dollars."

"Do you take VISA?"

"Of course."

Perhaps it was stupid to use the VISA again, but he had no choice. He had to get the laptop. He felt his hands trembling as he thought that the answer to all his problems might be held in the microchips of that small computer.

He handed the clerk the VISA and watched the clerk punch the number into a small box and tap his fingers on the counter as he waited for approval. Brad's heart began to hammer. Would they approve it? Maybe they'd canceled his account. Could they do that?

The machine buzzed and a receipt printed. Brad sighed and wiped the sweat from his forehead.

"Sign by the *X*."

He scribbled his signature, grabbed the laptop, and headed for the door.

"Wait!"

He froze and slowly turned. "Yeah?"

"You forgot your receipt."

"Oh." He grabbed the receipt and rushed out into the cold air. His eyes shifted from side to side as he sauntered down the sidewalk, clutching the computer case. He stopped at the crosswalk and studied the two teenagers waiting at the bus stop across the street. They looked harmless enough.

When the light changed, he started across, fumbling in his pockets for his pass to board the next bus. As he pulled his wallet out, it slipped from his hand and tumbled onto the wet pavement. He was stooping to retrieve it when a black Mercedes with slightly tinted windows turned the corner. With tires screeching, headlights glaring, the Mercedes appeared to be running the light.

Brad stood up. The driver bore down on him. He ran. The Mercedes swerved. He jumped to the sidewalk and rolled. The Mercedes smashed into the newspaper boxes on the sidewalk and veered back into traffic. Horns blared.

Brad jumped up, still clutching the computer case and his wallet. His legs raced beneath him as if they were separate from the rest of him. Rhythmically his heart raced with his legs, and his pulse pounded his temple to the point he thought his head would explode. He ran down a narrow sidewalk lined by a tall chain-link fence on one side and a busy street on the other. He heard screeching tires behind him, horns honking, and a roaring engine. It was coming after him again.

He heard metal smashing into metal somewhere behind him. To his right, behind the chain-link fence, was a school playing field covered with snow's white frosting. He looked back. The Mercedes deviated from the street and, with the left wheels on the street and the right wheels on the sidewalk, bore down on him.

He tossed the laptop over the chain-link fence and hurdled after it. The snow-covered field slowed his steps. He heard the car smash through the fence. Looking back, he saw it swerve like a snake in the snow.

Sirens echoed in the distance, and the Mercedes turned abruptly back toward the street, smashed through another part of the fence, and roared away. Brad ran back toward the fence, grabbed his laptop, and headed toward an alley by the school.

* * *

Thornton was furious at himself for letting Brad get away that morning. No punk from the east side was going to make a fool of him. He would get him before Christmas Day. He'd promised himself that.

He looked out his office window across the Salt Lake skyline. Somewhere out there, Bradley was hiding. His train of thought was broken when Detectives Uluave and Jones entered the room.

"Thornton," Uluave said, "the kid was spotted on Wasatch Boulevard. He picked up his old man's laptop using his credit card. The laptop was being repaired."

"So that's where the infamous laptop was," Thornton said. He could feel the adrenaline rushing through his body. His heart pattered. "The kid's up to something big. I can feel it."

Jones laughed. "Why risk going for a laptop? I mean, the kid's acting crazy."

"There must be something on that laptop," Thornton said.

Jones scratched his head. "Yeah, the kid seems to think so. He probably figures there might be something in there that would clear him."

"Yeah," Uluave said, "and get this, a Mercedes tried to run the kid down after he picked up the laptop."

"What?" The pulse in his cheekbone was throbbing again. He pressed his finger on it.

"Yeah," Uluave said. "Someone even wrote down the plates. The car's stolen."

"Sounds like someone's trying to kill your prime suspect," Jones said and grinned at Thornton. "The kid sure doesn't act like a murderer to me."

"Oh, shut up, Scarface," Thornton said. "We don't have enough evidence to know what's going on now. Maybe the kid wasn't in this alone after all. Maybe he was in this with someone else and now the deal's gone bad. Maybe someone's scared that Bradley will start talking."

* * *

Brad had transferred to several local buses before settling down in one headed to the west side of the city. He would just keep riding until he felt safe enough to get off. He placed the computer on his lap and turned it on. He hoped the repair service had recharged the battery. Beep. Beep. The Windows screen came up. His glance immediately caught an icon labeled "Pharmacology Database." He clicked on the icon and a box popped up: "Power Center Security protects this database from unauthorized use. Please type in your password."

Brad typed in the familiar Peggy3. It didn't work. He tried two more passwords before a box popped up: "You have violated Power Center Security's password protection limitations. This database is now locked and can only be opened by the database administrator."

Brad slammed the screen down. He was so close to finding the truth. How could this happen? What password could Dad have used? He was so obvious about these things. Of course, the events of recent days had proven that Dad was not as obvious as he'd thought. For a moment, he felt like giving up in despair, but he didn't have time for that. He prayed for the strength to go on. He didn't have time for any of the familiar reactions. He was in a race for his life. He had to keep going.

He turned off the laptop and placed it in its case, then reached for his cell phone and dialed Conrad's cell. Conrad's cell phone was off. Perhaps he was in a meeting or something. He probably wouldn't get home from work until at least 5:00 anyhow. Brad would have to hang out until then.

CHAPTER 18

Later that afternoon, Van found herself in a self-imposed mess in her office. Her corkboard was covered with photographs and notes, which she sat studying. There was method to her madness. She glanced at the quote she had framed over her desk: "Discovery is looking at what everyone else has seen and thinking what no one else has thought."

She had obtained everything she could find on the six murder victims. She had pulled from police files, homeless shelter files, Traveler's Aid Society files, and DMV files. She arranged the photographs according to the time, or approximate time, of death.

She studied the first photograph: Peggy and Allen Armstrong. They were the odd couple in the group. They were well-to-do, well educated, well known, and dead. The Armstrongs had been killed by their son's .22 caliber revolver on Friday morning. Their connection to the others on the board seemed to be Allen Armstrong's work among the homeless—or perhaps she should say his work on the homeless. He used them for his purposes, but she was in no position to judge his motives. She had placed a pin beside the Armstrong photograph with yellow thread running to the photograph of Von Hauser and Mark Wilson, the only two men to have a definite connection to Armstrong. Next came Mark Wilson, a.k.a. Clown. His round, cheery face looked like a clown. He was killed by blunt force to the head on Friday night. Someone found his body in an empty lot down by the homeless shelter. Allen Armstrong's office phone number was in his pocket.

The next photograph was Albert Richards, a.k.a. Grandpa. He was homeless and hung out at the agencies on Rio Grande. She had obtained his photograph from the free clinic. She couldn't tell what he looked like from the autopsy photos, and the clinic picture wasn't much better. It was taken last summer when he had gotten into a patch of poison oak in an empty field by the viaducts. His face was swollen and red, making his fat face look like Santa Claus. Richards and Wilson had a lot of similarities: A blunt force to the head had killed them both, they had both been homeless, they had both frequented the Rio Grande agencies, and they were both overweight. That fact had not gone unnoticed before, but she was still mulling it over, trying to put the pieces together. The murderer had dumped Richards' body in the Jordan River on Friday night.

On Tuesday night, Tongata Uloa had been killed. The huge Tongan with a record for disorderly conduct was not homeless. He lived in a small apartment on the west side. His neighbors said he was friendly but had a drinking problem and was always hard up for cash. He had divorced many years ago and had no children. His photo had come from the arrest files. He had been killed with a .45 caliber gun like the one Allen Armstrong had owned, but this could be a coincidence. Detective Chandler had a green thread going from Uloa to the Armstrongs since she wasn't quite sure if there was a relationship. An interesting fact was that Wilson and Uloa both had cancer, and again, both were fat. Just like putting together a puzzle, you gather pieces with similar features, and the pieces usually fit.

Next was a photograph of Otto Von Hauser. He had been killed on Wednesday night by one of his own trophies. He wasn't homeless, although he was obviously at the poverty level. His picture stood out from the others. He was in some kind of bodybuilding competition. The picture was old. He, too, was now overweight. Here was the bushy-headed stranger, dead like the others. Had someone hired him to kill Armstrong and then killed him to keep him quiet? A thick red thread went from his photograph to the Armstrong photograph. He had numerous connections to Allen Armstrong. He had been to the Armstrong house a week before Allen Armstrong was murdered. He had raised his voice, even threatened Allen Armstrong. He had gone to high school with Armstrong. What other kind of connection could he have had with Armstrong?

Under the notes and photographs, Van had placed three-by-five cards, the loose ends. There was a man running around in a ski mask who obviously wanted something from the Armstrong house. Was he the killer? Had he failed to get what he wanted from the Armstrong home when he killed the Armstrongs? There was also someone in a Mercedes running around trying to kill Bradley Armstrong. Again, was it the killer? Had he meant to kill Brad with the Armstrongs?

Perhaps the killer went into Brad's bedroom to kill him that morning. He found the duffel bag, looked in it, found the gun, and decided to use it instead of using a blunt instrument. After he killed the Armstrongs with the .22, he found the .45 in the house. With a better weapon, he returned the other gun where he had found it.

And then there was the University of Utah connection. Uloa had a matchbook from a bar near there. Wilson had Armstrong's phone number from there. The masked man had disappeared there. Allen Armstrong worked there.

Detective Chandler stood back and looked at the tangled web she'd woven on the old corkboard. It was nothing more than a somewhat colorful collage. She was sure it all connected somehow; she just needed to find the one thread that connected them all. It wasn't that they were homeless—only two were. The one thread that connected most of them was that they were overweight. Everyone except the Armstrongs was overweight. Armstrong could have been using these men in his experiments because they were overweight, but how could that lead to murder? Who had he been working for just before he died?

* * *

It was 3:00 P.M. when Thornton called one of his debriefing sessions. Van walked into the bureau conference room. It was the nicest room in the station. A huge oblong oak table was surrounded by comfortable hunter-green cushioned chairs with arms. A whiteboard covered the wall at the head of the table.

Thornton was standing in front of the board. Detective Chandler glanced around the table at the regulars: Jones, Uluave, Carmichael, and Jensen. But there were others there too: Perry Hunsaker, Bart Hogan, Sam Potter, and Amy Saunders. She recognized the FBI agents Karl Morrison and Roger Wingate. A man she did not recognize was sitting between the two agents.

"Won't you join us, Detective Chandler?" Thornton said. "I know you work alone these days, but perhaps we can help each other."

Van ignored Thornton and sat in an empty chair beside Amy Saunders who smiled and grasped Van's hand, squeezing it in reassurance.

"Now that everyone's here," Thornton said, "we can get started. Time is running out."

Van's mind kept flying back to the corkboard in her office. She was close to finding an answer; she knew she was. She always had this feeling when an answer was on the top of her head. She just needed something to jog it out. She felt her irritation rising as Thornton lectured in the front of the room. She wanted to get back to her research.

"As you know, we have two unsolved murders on our hands that could be connected."

"Don't you mean six?" Van said.

Everyone turned to look at her. Thornton scowled. "If I meant six, Detective Chandler, I would have said six. Apparently you've missed some of our debriefing sessions. Perhaps this will be a lesson to everyone here. If the rest of you don't want to make a fool of yourselves as you've just witnessed Detective Chandler do, you'll make sure you're always here and on time," he said with a glare at Van.

"I'm sorry," Van said. "I guess I'm a little mixed up." She pulled out her notepad. "Let's see, I have Armstrong, Armstrong, Wilson, Richards, Uloa, and Von Hauser. I count six. Maybe you can tell me what kind of arithmetic you're using, Detective." She stared straight at his eyes. His face turned crimson, and she could see that one hand was closed in a fist. She grinned snidely. His frown became more intense.

He spoke. "I hope the rest of you will excuse me while I catch my rookie up. Don't be embarrassed for her. We were all new and green and ignorant at one time or another."

They all looked from Thornton to Detective Chandler, waiting for a response. She remained silent.

"Okay, Detective Chandler. We have several different cases here. The Armstrong case is solved as far as this department is concerned. Bradley Armstrong killed the two of them. Our only job now is to testify for the prosecution. We don't yet know his connection to the Von Hauser murder, but we know he is in some way connected there. We need to work on motive. We also have a possible drug-related murder of a man named Uloa. However, we are meeting here today to discuss the killings of two men in the Salt Lake City area in less than a week. The FBI here thinks we may have a serial killer on our hands. Agents Morrison and Wingate have come here today to introduce us to Mr. Abrams, a criminologist from the FBI's behavioral science unit. Now if you'd be so kind as to keep your mouths shut, I'll turn the time over to Agent Morrison."

Van felt her face heating up. She clenched her own hand into a fist, her nails cutting into her palm.

Morrison cleared his throat and stood to go to the front of the room as Thornton sat down. "Thank you, Detective. As you know, my work has involved the FTRA, which has several serial killers connected with it. However, Mr. Harold Abrams here is an expert at studying crime scenes and determining the personality and possible lifestyles of killers. We've asked him to come here today to profile the type of killer you may have working among the homeless in Salt Lake City. Mr. Abrams."

Mr. Abrams was tall with a stern face and high forehead. His hair was thinning and his cheeks were scarred with deep wrinkles. His eyes had dark circles under them that Van assumed were permanent features. He attempted a smile, but it did little to soften the rather morose expression he carried. He cleared his throat.

"Thank you, Agent Morrison. I was talking with a few of you before the meeting, and I realized that there is some confusion about the terms I'll be using today. I would like to start by clarifying definitions."

Van sighed, and everyone turned to look at her. She looked down at her notepad and began writing as if fascinated by Mr. Abrams' words thus far.

"Now," he continued, "a mass murderer is generally one person with four or more victims at one time in one location with no cooling-off period. These are the type of murderers that walk into McDonald's or the post office and start killing. The killings at Columbine High in Littleton, Colorado, and the stock exchange in

Georgia were the work of mass murderers. Another term that applies to this type of killer is "spree killer" because he kills in a relatively short span of time, within days, usually a cluster."

"I noticed you said 'he,'" Amy interjected. "Are we to assume that all mass murderers are men?"

"No," Abrams answered, "we are to assume nothing, but most mass murderers do tend to be men."

Carmichael raised his hand. "You say a spree killing can take place over a period of days so there is no cooling-off period during that time? He must sleep."

"Yes, but his emotional state does not change. He is in such a state of emotional unrest that murder appears to be a solution to him."

"A solution to what?" Jensen asked.

"It depends," Abrams said. "There are spree killers who want to eliminate witnesses or perceived witnesses. There are spree killers motivated by revenge for actual or perceived wrongs. There are spree killers motivated primarily by a desire to control. Some spree killers are totally psychotic. Sometimes their first killing was the result of a great emotional upset, which then leads to more killings that make no sense in relation to each other. In other words, the killer is out of control, not rational. The very act of killing leads the killer into a deeper emotional state which he can't seem to control, so he keeps killing in an effort to establish control."

"So you think these homeless men could have been killed by a spree killer?" Uluave asked.

"It's possible because of the closeness in time of their deaths. However, the killer could also be a serial killer. We don't know how many people he has killed before. A serial killer is generally a person with three or more victims and three or more separate events in three or more locations. In the serial killing a cool-off period is evident, as well as premeditation, planning, and fantasy."

"What do you mean by fantasy?" Van asked.

"He enjoys killing, he enjoys the contest with law enforcement, and he enjoys the methods. In other words, he kills for the thrill. There are different types of serial killers, but it is important to recognize here that we have a pattern. This killer has targeted the homeless.

Some killers target prostitutes, some target the rich and famous, some target doctors, some target lawyers. It's my belief that the killer you have on your hands has had a deep-seated desire to kill for many years. He rationalizes in his mind that he is doing society a favor by killing the homeless. They are worthless, useless. They take up tax dollars. They also lack family and friends who care about them. But the bottom line is he kills for the thrill of the kill."

"Going back to spree killers," Van said. "They don't necessarily have a pattern. I mean victims vary, weapons vary."

"That's right," said Mr. Abrams. "They usually are not coolly planning murders because their emotional state is anything but calm. On the surface they may appear calm, but underneath they're simmering."

"So the six murders I mentioned could all be the work of a spree killer?"

Thornton glowered and then pounded his fist on the oak table. "Detective Chandler, if you want to play out your naive theories, do it on your own time. Mr. Abrams' time is very valuable. Most of us here are open-minded enough to listen to his theories. He's one of the leading criminal profilers in the country. Let him do his work."

Abrams cleared his throat. "That is quite all right, Detective. It's a fair question. The answer is yes. It is possible. Just remember, even though the murders are often the result of irrational behavior, the murders still have to have a link between them. For example, the killer shoots the gas station attendant to steal money. He then runs to a car where a man is pumping gas. He shoots the man and takes his car. The man's wife is in the car screaming. This annoys him so he shoots the wife. He runs out of gas just outside of town. He walks to a nearby farmhouse and breaks in. He kills the farmer and takes his keys. Again he is on the road. A policeman pulls him over. He shoots the policeman. These events are linked by the murderer's emotional state, which is most likely irrational. However, all of the events are linked, and the police will have to establish that link to pin these crimes on one individual."

"Mr. Abrams, I apologize for my trainee here," Thornton said. "New detectives are a lot like teenagers. They think they know it all. It takes years before they realize how little they do know."

Van felt her pulse racing. She stood, rigid and tense. Everyone looked at her in astonishment as she walked to the door.

"Where do you think you're going?" Thornton asked.

She turned to look at him. "I'm going to cool off. You wouldn't want another murder on your hands, would you, Thornton?"

There was muffled snickering in the room. Thornton scanned the table, and the snickering came to an abrupt halt. Van turned and walked from the room.

CHAPTER 19

When Conrad got home from work, he went into the family room and stared blankly at the TV. His mind kept making images of all his troubles. It had been a miserable Christmas season so far. Mom was sulking around the house eating chocolates and crying. Dad had closed himself in the study, pretending nothing was wrong. Mom and Dad's best friends had been murdered, and Conrad's best friend was the prime suspect.

His mind replayed his recent conversations with Brad. Why was Brad acting so strange? Could it be a coincidence that he was at the scene of another murder in Rose Park?

What was going on? Maybe Conrad didn't really know the man he'd called his best friend for over fifteen years. Even as he thought it, he knew it wasn't true. He knew Brad. He was like a brother to him. He couldn't kill his parents. There was no way. Brad was innocent. He knew it in his heart even if his head had doubts.

His cell phone rang. He jumped up and grabbed it. "Hello."

"Conrad, it's me."

"Where are you, Brad?"

"I got the laptop."

"What?"

"Dad's laptop. I got it. I know there's something in it to help me clear my name."

"Like what?"

"I don't know, Conrad, but after today I'm sure someone wants it. I think someone tried to kill me for it."

"Brad, I don't like the sound of this. You'd better go to the police. You could get killed."

"If I go to the police before I find out what's going on, Conrad, I will be the next one to die. I'll be executed."

A knot formed in Conrad's throat and a dull throb began in his temples. "What do you need, Brad?"

"There's a database on the laptop called "Pharmacology Database." It's password protected. I locked the thing up by trying too many passwords. I know you can unlock it, Conrad. You can get through anything."

"I don't know, Brad. Some of those protection programs are tough to crack."

"Please try, Conrad."

"Okay, I'll try. That's all I can promise."

"Great, Conrad, here's the plan. Meet me at the dorms in an hour. I'll be by the side entrance waiting for you. Please don't let me down."

* * *

Thornton slammed the phone down. "Scarface! Get in here!"

Detective Jones sauntered in, rolling his eyes. "What is it now? Look, I stayed for your debriefing. It was all so interesting. I'm on my way out."

"Did Uluave check the homeless shelter again?"

"For the third time, yes."

"What about Pioneer Park?"

"Thornton, we have searched the entire Rio Grande area. We have talked with every homeless person we encountered. We have scoured Federal Heights and the university campus at least half a dozen times. Why don't you give it a rest? Go home."

"I can't rest until I find the kid."

Jones rolled his eyes. "You're working too hard, Thornton. You'll think better if you go home and get some shut-eye."

* * *

The snow was falling hard against the windshield, and Van could barely hear the soft instrumental rendition of "Silent Night" on the radio beneath the resonant swishing of her windshield wipers. The old Victorian house's utter darkness stood out among the other houses on G Street draped in festive blinking lights with bright star-topped trees gleaming through bay windows.

She sat in her car a long while. She didn't want to get out. She didn't want to feel the cold or the loneliness. She had spent the whole afternoon tracking information about the six murder victims. Could there be a connection? Her head throbbed under the weight of her thoughts.

She glanced over at the stack of notes she'd grabbed on her way out. She would miss the old corkboard, but she couldn't stand to stay in that tense station house. The music on the radio stopped, and she heard the news. She turned up the volume. "It's going to be some kind of white Christmas, folks. We've got eight to ten additional inches on the way."

Van looked at the large flakes as they pelted the windshield with a sound like tiny fingers tapping, trying to get inside. She shivered.

The news continued. "Police are still searching tonight for suspected parent-killer Bradley Armstrong. He is now a prime suspect in the murder of Rose Park resident Otto Von Hauser. In another story, local police have called on the FBI's criminal profiling experts to help in the investigation of the deaths of some local transients. Police fear a serial killer may be on the loose. More news after this."

A commercial came on.

"Ho! Ho! Oh!"

"Mommy! Mommy! Santa's stuck in the chimney!"

"Don't get stuck in the same old situation this year. Do something about it. Start the new year out right with Slim Down Diet Systems. Our special combination of diet pills, fat-free dinners, and exercise is a sure winner."

Van grabbed a folder from the passenger seat, pulled out the photographs, and scanned through them. The murders all had to do with Allen Armstrong, consulting, and overweight people, she was sure of that. She then shoved the photographs back into the folder and turned the car off.

As she stepped from the warmth of the Taurus, a gust of cold wind blew snow in her face. She stepped across the slick walk to the front steps, which squeaked beneath her weight. Even though the porch boards gave their familiar creak as she made her way across, and the key clinked as usual when she turned the lock to the deadbolt, there was something unfamiliar about it all, something she couldn't put her finger on. She shook her head. She was tired and frustrated. She tried to shake the feeling as she pushed open the door and stepped inside. Groucho was not there to meet her.

"I'm home, old man. Hungry, old man? Groucho?" She flipped on the light, closed the door, and placed her purse on the kitchen counter.

She heard an anxious meow and a thump down the short hall to her bedroom. She stepped down the hall and saw that the door to her bedroom was closed. Another thump resounded from behind the closed door. Silly cat. Must have been playing around and closed himself in the room.

She opened the bedroom door. Groucho paced fitfully, his tail twitching in spasmodic bursts. Van reached down to rub him. He backed away with a cry and jumped onto the bed, ruffling the spread.

"What's up, old man? Are you mad because you've been locked up all day? I'll bet you're hungry."

She walked to the bed and reached for him. He hissed, swiped his claws at her, and scratched her hand. She drew back and brought her bleeding hand to her mouth. "Groucho! What has gotten into you?"

He stood on the bed, his body stiff and ears pointed and alert. His tail bristled. Just as he dashed off the back side of the bed, she heard the squeaky floorboards of her bedroom and turned. A man in a black ski mask was pointing a .45-caliber automatic at her face.

CHAPTER 20

The tall man, dressed in black, held the gun to Van's head. Her heart rose in her throat. She was frightened but not enough to lose her wits.

Van stared at the eyes that slithered from side to side in the tiny holes of the ski mask.

"What do you want?" she asked.

"I want you," he said in an eerie, hoarse whisper. "We're going for a ride, and if you try anything, I'll kill you."

He pulled her into the living room and shoved her onto the couch where she saw a large duffel bag she hadn't noticed. The man pulled the bag to the floor, reached in, and pulled out a ball of thick rope and a roll of wide bandages, all the while keeping his eyes and the gun on Van.

"What do you want with me?" Van asked with all the sternness she could muster.

"Lay down on the couch," he said gruffly.

"No. I won't."

Van stared at his powerful hands that held the gun. "Lay down!" he repeated.

Van lay face down on the couch. The man looked at her and slowly lowered the gun, letting it dangle from his hand. Van saw her chance and leaped from the couch, hitting the intruder in the face and knocking him back. She grabbed his wrist and struggled for the gun, but he grabbed her neck in one hand and forcefully shoved her back. She toppled to the floor.

The man immediately jumped up, leaned over her, grabbed her arm, and flipped her on her stomach. She felt a pain in her side as he dug his knee into her back and pulled her arms behind her. She felt the rope burning her wrists. As she opened her mouth to protest, he stuffed a wad of gauze into it and wrapped a strip of duct tape over her mouth, cheeks, and around the back of her head. She could barely breathe. He then pulled her legs together and tied them with the scratchy rope. When he wrapped a black blindfold over her eyes, the world went dark.

She felt herself being lifted. Where was he taking her? Why was he taking her?

He opened the front door and cold, wet air stung her face. She felt the heavy snow sticking to her hair, and then she felt her body hit something cold. She tried to calm herself by inhaling deeply through her nose. She had to stop the panic before she started hyperventilating.

She heard the rasping of a door being opened and felt herself falling. Her head grazed against rubber. A tire! He was throwing her into the trunk of a car. She tried to protest, but it only caused her to choke.

"Shut up!"

She felt the stiff, cold gun barrel in her side. His sharp order chilled her. He would kill her if he had to, she was sure of that. He closed the lid with a thud. Crunching footsteps hurried around the car and a door opened and shut. She heard the engine start and felt a jolt as the car began to move.

Frantically she tried to wrench her hands free. The rough rope bit into her wrists. Claustrophobia set in. She felt her pulse pounding in her throat, closing it. She tried to swallow. Her nose produced a soft whistle as she breathed over the edge of the tape. *Calm, be calm, Van. Don't panic. Breathe slowly through your nostrils. You'll suffocate if you don't breathe slowly.*

She said a silent prayer, which helped her feel calmer. She thought of her parents back in Boston. How she longed to be there with them. If I get out of here alive, she thought, I'm going to swallow my pride and call Mom and Dad. I'm going to tell them how much I love them and miss them. She realized how childish she had been. Here she was a thirty-three-year-old woman buying gifts that she kept hidden in a closet and never sent.

It was still snowing. She could feel and hear it under the tires as they picked up speed. Where were they going? Eventually, the car came to a stop, and Van heard the engine die. She had no idea where he'd taken her; she'd lost track of turns a long time before. She heard the door close and crunching footsteps coming toward the trunk. The trunk door popped open and fine, powdery snow stung her face. The man grabbed her legs, and with quick strokes of the knife, sliced the cords from her ankles. He pulled her up and stood her on her feet next to the car. The muscles in her legs were cramping. Her arms were still tied securely behind her back.

"Walk forward," he said.

She was dizzy and staggered. He grabbed her and yanked the blindfold from her face. Cold air rushed into her eyes. Everything was blurry. She felt a sharp prodding against her side and looked down. Her eyes were clearing now. The man in the ski mask held the gun in his hand.

"Walk to the door of that building." He pushed her forward. Unsteadily, she stepped across the slippery parking lot. The university. They were at the University of Utah. She recognized the medical school. It was next door to the medical examiner's office. She took a quick look around. The parking lot was dark and empty except for the man's dark car. No one was around. She could try to scream, but no one would hear her, and he would likely shoot her. Besides, the stuffing in her mouth would muffle any real effort.

"Come on!" His free hand was at her elbow, forcing her to walk in step with him across the icy blacktop. She had to be calm. She had to do whatever he ordered.

"Up here." He forced her up the glazed stairs, his fingers biting into her arm. As they approached two large doors, he released her arm and fumbled in his pocket for something. He pulled out a key. It clicked as he forced it in the lock and turned. "In here."

She stepped into the darkness of the medical school and the door slammed shut behind them, sending a reverberating bang through the empty halls. It was dark inside except for the green exit lights and red fire alarms. The smell of disinfectant permeated the ethereal glow of the building.

Should she try to take him on in the darkness? No. She couldn't take the chance, not with his finger on the trigger and her hands tied behind her back. It was a crazy, desperate thought. She'd have to plan her moves carefully.

"Keep moving."

They were going down the hall when he pushed her to the right. "Down there."

He was forcing her to move down the stairs to the basement. They reached the bottom level and he pushed her to the left. "Down this way." His voice was a forced, rasping whisper. She could tell he had a deep voice. He couldn't hide that.

They made their way down a sloping ramp. Her shoes clicked against the hard cement floor. Water trickled nearby. They went past an area of thick pipes and shafts and stopped. She heard a click as a small lightbulb illuminated the hall and revealed two thick doors. He fumbled in his pocket again and pulled out the clanking keys. Another grating sound, and the handle turned. He pushed the door open.

"Move in there."

She stepped into the dim room. The click of the light switch behind her made her jump. The dusty overhead fluorescent lights blinked on, bathing the room in a greenish glow. Shelves lined the wall filled with oversized jars of human organs. He ripped the tape from her mouth and pulled out the gauze. "You can scream all you want now. No one will hear you down here, but if you do scream, I'll shoot you."

"Where are we?" Van asked, her voice taking on an echo in the dungeon-like room.

He thrust her to the floor. "What's wrong? Don't you like dead bodies?" he asked.

She felt a pain in her hip. "What do you want with me?"

He hovered over her, his gun pointing down at her. "You might be worth one lousy laptop if we play our cards right."

He grabbed her legs and forced them together, then bound them tightly and tied her to a large pipe rising from the cement floor to the ceiling. He retrieved some new gauze, stuffed it in her mouth, and again taped it. He headed for the door.

* * *

Conrad threw himself into the seat of his Honda and, barely giving the engine time to catch, put his foot on the gas. He had to get to campus; it was almost time to meet Brad. His stomach had been upset since Brad called, and now he tried not to think of the danger that possibly lurked on campus.

The windshield was fogging up. He tried to wipe it with his glove-covered hand, but he smeared it, making it worse. He pulled off his gloves one at a time with his teeth and smeared his hand across the windshield. It didn't help. Headlights glared at him and a horn honked. He swerved. Was he over the line? He couldn't tell. The roads were a sheet of ice.

He approached an intersection with a stop sign and saw headlights coming from the other direction. He put his foot on the brake and the Honda slid through the intersection. The other car blared its horn and slid, almost hitting him. The car swerved back and forth on the ice before sliding away. His heart was pounding. He felt beads of perspiration forming on the palms of his hands. His stomach was in knots.

He had to get there. He had to find out what was in the laptop. He had to help Brad. He felt a sense of urgency. It was like a dark cloud loomed over him, threatening to break any minute.

* * *

The cab let Brad off west of campus, and he was walking up a slick sidewalk when his cell phone rang. He looked at the caller ID, but didn't recognize the number. It looked like someone was using a prepaid phone card.

"Hello?"

He heard a voice so muffled, so low, he had to strain to hear it.

"If you ever want to see Detective Chandler alive again, you will do what I say. I want the laptop. Do you understand what I'm saying? Detective Chandler for the laptop. In one hour, I want you to bring the laptop to a bench by the family monument courtyard."

"Wait a minute," Brad said. "How do I know you really have the detective? If you do have her, how do I know she's still alive? I want proof."

"Proof? What kind of proof?" The whisper was angry now.

"Let me talk to her."

"You idiot. She's not here."

"I have to talk with her, or you won't get the laptop."

"Maybe I'll just kill her."

Brad swallowed hard, absolute dryness in his mouth. "That's a chance I'll have to take. What makes you think I care what happens to her anyway?"

"I know you care. I know you wouldn't want anyone to die because you were too selfish to help them."

Brad felt a chill go up his spine. He remembered the promise he had made at the mall. He had promised to stop thinking only of himself and to start serving others. Now here was a test. He was being asked to sacrifice something for someone else. He gulped hard. He had to buy some time.

"If I don't hear her voice saying something that makes it very clear to me that you really have her, I will not give you the laptop."

The receiver on the other end was slammed down. Had he just cost Detective Chandler her life? Did this person really have her? He moved quickly across campus toward the dorms, feet crunching into thick, powdery snow. It was good snow for skiing. He had planned on going skiing over the holiday break, but that was before his world turned upside down. He often went with his parents to their cabin in the mountains on the day after Christmas. He imagined the roaring fire in the cabin fireplace, lounging on the rugged leather furniture, roasting marshmallows in the fire with Mom and Dad. Tears stung his eyes and rolled down his cheeks.

Death. It was all around him now. The man—the voice on the phone—who had taken his parents now perhaps had Detective Chandler. What was to stop the man from killing her after he got the laptop? He'd killed others. He had set Brad up, made it look like he'd killed his parents. A foreboding of danger coursed through his system. His gaze moved restlessly around the campus. No one was in sight. Icy perspiration chilled his body.

He rounded the corner, and the dorms were in full view. They seemed strangely bleak as they loomed against the dark backdrop. The snow slapped against the dorm windows mercilessly. Had it only been a week since he and Jess had left the dorms that unforgettable morning when his whole life changed? A sense of awareness washed over him. There was something he had missed. He tried to grasp it in his mind, but it got lost in the muddle. What was eluding him? His mouth went dry, and he could hear the pounding of his heart.

As he approached the dorms, he thought of the last time he had been there. That morning when he was rushing to take Jess to the airport, that awful morning. As he imagined Jess rushing about to get ready, a thought came to him. It was that man, the man who was talking to Thornton outside Amy Saunders' office that day at the police station. Saunders was asking about the shape of the head. What was it that Thornton said to that man?

He could hear the voice in his head: *"You should have seen Chandler. Jones and me, we tore the dorm apart. Chandler was running around like a mother hen, putting things back in place. I mean she put all the clothes back in the closets, remade the beds, picked up the trash we had dumped on the floor. She wanted to leave the place neat like we found it."*

The gears in Brad's head began to spin . . . remade the beds . . . remade the beds . . . remade the beds.

He could picture Jess running around the dorm room, tidying up like he always did. He hated a mess; everything had its place. But there hadn't been time to make the beds or tidy up. "Come on, Jess, you don't have time for that. Let's see how fast I can get you to the airport." They had left a mess.

What did it mean? He found his legs moving faster, crunching harder into the snow. He must be wrong. He must have heard wrong.

Brad dashed through the snow toward the dorm's side door. The snow pelted his face, and the wind pulled at his coat. As he rounded the side of the building, he saw Conrad standing by the door.

"Boy, am I glad to see you. It's freezing out here."

"Sorry." Brad fumbled in his pocket for his keys. He forced the pass key into the steel lock and turned it, then pulled the door open and stepped into the narrow stairwell. Conrad followed. Brad brushed sleet from his coat and wiped his face with his hand. They made their way up.

As they left the dimly lighted stairwell, they entered the third floor's dark hall. Brad felt a chill shiver up his back. The wind was howling outside with a harsh, mournful sound. They made their way down to room 310.

Brad's breath was coming in deep, rasping gasps. He felt his heart pounding. He couldn't breathe, and his lungs and throat hurt from running in the cold, wet wind. His numbed fingers fumbled with the key. He felt the lock turn and pushed open the door.

The room was dark. He couldn't see. He groped for the light switch, and, finding it, flipped the lights on. The room was perfectly neat, organized in a way only Jess could appreciate. Everything was in its place, and the beds were made with military precision.

He thought back to that fateful Friday morning. They had overslept. Jess never overslept. Jess was always punctual, no matter how late he stayed up. Jess was especially punctual when he had something important to do, something like getting to the airport on time. Maybe he hadn't overslept. Maybe he wasn't late getting up at all. Maybe he was late getting back from a murder. Perhaps he had turned the alarm clocks off after he got back later than he had expected. He unplugged the clocks to explain why the alarms didn't go off.

No! What am I thinking? Jess is family—and my friend. He wouldn't do this. He wouldn't hurt Mom and Dad. He'd have no reason to. I must be going crazy even to think such a thing.

Then Brad remembered the afternoon before that morning. Brad had been packing his duffel bag. Jess, who had been trying to study, watched him pack. Most importantly of all, Jess saw him put the gun in his duffel bag. Jess was the only other person who knew Brad's gun was in that duffel bag. Why would a killer stop to dig through a duffel bag for a gun unless he knew the gun was there in the first place? There was only one person who knew that gun was there. Jess was also the only person who had access to Brad's security fob to turn the system on and off.

Jess had called several times. He called the hospital on Wednesday night. Brad told Jess about Dad's yearbooks. That was the night someone tried to attack Conrad when he went to retrieve the yearbooks. That was the night Von Hauser was killed. Jess was the man in the ski mask. Jess was the one who kept breaking into the house. Why? He was looking for the laptop. The answer had to be in the laptop. Brad felt sick with the realization that his own cousin had killed his parents. Why? Why would he do this?

"Jess," Brad said.

"What's that?" Conrad asked.

"It's Jess. He murdered Mom and Dad."

CHAPTER 21

Van's clothes were wet and clammy. She had been trying to work her hands loose from the harsh rope that cut into her wrists. She could feel the warm, sticky blood, running, crusting. She felt the cords weakening, but her face was moist with perspiration, her hands sticky with blood, her body aching with pain. She was weakening too. She couldn't keep this up much longer.

And then she heard the sound—something thudding against the door. Was he coming back? Had all her work been for nothing? Would he be angry? Would he kill her? She stared at the door. It was opening. The light switch clicked.

In the dusty light, she saw him, rigid and angry. What had happened? What was wrong? He walked in, and started searching through drawers. He pulled something out, then marched over to her with it, gun in hand. "You've been busy. I thought you might. That's why I have some more rope over here. Too bad it's so jagged. Your arms don't look like they can take much more. I don't think you'll be trying to get away again."

He ripped the tape and gauze from her mouth. "You're going to make a recording for Bradley now."

"What kind of recording? Why?"

"Cool it! Okay?"

She could hear the anger in his voice. Things weren't going as he'd planned. He wanted a laptop, obviously Allen Armstrong's laptop. What was so important about it? She looked at the gun. He was going to kill her once he got the laptop. She was sure of that. She could see it in those eyes, peering out at her from those tiny slits in his black mask. He was a killer. He was cunning, too, but there was something very unstable about him. How could she trick him?

She then noticed the item he had brought over. It was a recorder. He pushed it to her mouth, knocking her lips against her teeth. She gasped.

"No tricks, Detective."

"What do you want me to do?"

"I want you to talk into this recorder. I want you to tell Bradley something that only the two of you would know. And remember, it had better be something that I like or you'll be in big trouble."

"I need to think a minute," she said nervously.

There was silence for a couple of minutes. "Your time to think is up." His finger was poised over the record button. "When I push this down, start talking."

He pushed the button. She cleared her throat. "Brad, I—I want you to know I understand what you were telling me about how you don't want to go to medical school. I understand how you hate death and dying, but I think you should stick it out and go."

The recorder stopped. "That's enough, Detective. That was nice of you to encourage your friend."

He rewound the cassette and played it back. She could see a smile in the mouth hole of his mask. "Very well done."

He untied her aching wrists and retied them with new rope. The rough rope sent stings of pain through her lower arms. "I don't think your wrists are up to any more games. You stay still, you hear?"

"Yes."

Once again, he covered her mouth with gauze and tape before leaving, slamming the door behind him. She could hear the clatter of the key in the lock. She bit her lip against the pain in her wrists. There was no way out. When he returned with the laptop, he would kill her.

* * *

Conrad sat studying the laptop. He'd already failed several times to break the security device. His hands and forehead were sweating. He wiped his forehead with his sleeve and began punching keys again. He was having trouble concentrating. He was too keyed up. The whole world seemed to be falling in around him. His head was throbbing.

Concentrate, he told himself. He needed to focus. Please let me get in, he prayed silently. I need to get in. But his mind kept thinking about everything Brad had just told him about Jess. What was in this stupid box that could have been worth murder to Jess?

Brad's cell phone rang, and Conrad jumped.

Brad grabbed the phone and glanced at the Caller ID. Again, it looked like someone was using a prepaid calling card. "Hello?"

"Brad, I—I want you to know I understand what you were telling me about how you don't want to go to medical school. I understand how you hate death and dying, but I think you should stick it out and go."

It was Detective Chandler's voice, but not Detective Chandler's voice. It wasn't the confident voice he admired. There was fear in there somewhere. What had he done to her? What had Jess done to her?

"There's your evidence." It was the deep whisper again. It didn't sound like Jess. "Bring the laptop to the bench by the family monument courtyard in thirty minutes. If I even sense a cop, I'll kill her." The phone went dead.

Somewhere in the past few minutes, the fear and pain had retreated from Brad. Overwhelming numbness had taken over and cemented his determination to see this thing through. He was standing back, looking at things from outside himself. He was in shock of course, but he still had a job to do. He had to save Detective Chandler.

* * *

Van tried rubbing her wrists against the cinder block wall, but the cords were too tight and they bit into her wrists. She couldn't get them in contact with the wall. She tried to think. Her only hope was to try and overpower him somehow.

What would he do with her when he got the laptop? She shuddered, then stopped and listened. She thought she heard something. Was he coming back already? She struggled back into her former position. She heard the key in the lock. The door flew open. He switched on the fluorescent lights and grunted in satisfaction. She was as he had left her. Van lifted her head. He hurried over to her and tore the tape and gauze away.

"Are you afraid, Detective?"

"No."

"Good. It won't help your situation."

"Won't you please let me go to the bathroom?"

His eyes narrowed in the holes of his mask. "Well, you've probably been waiting a long time."

He cut the rope from the pole and pulled her to her feet. He cut the ropes on her ankles. "You're lucky. We happen to have a bathroom right here."

He pushed her toward the back of the room. He opened the door, snapped on the light, and grabbed her arm, pushing her into the small bathroom. "I'll close the door," he said, "but don't try anything."

The cords bit through her wrists and she winced with pain. "What about the rope? Can you untie my hands?"

He took the knife and pressed its sharp blade against her throat. "You wouldn't try anything, would you?"

"I just want to go to the bathroom."

He laughed and backed away, pulling the knife from her throat. He grabbed her arm and pulled her around. Pain shot through her wrists. With one soundless swipe, he cut the cords from her wrists.

Her muscles ached. She stretched, flexed her fingers, and rubbed her wrists. Why had he cut her hands loose? Was he planning to kill her when she came from the bathroom or was he getting careless? Perhaps he was overconfident, having subdued her so many times. She entered the musty bathroom and closed the door.

"Make it fast," he yelled from the outer room.

She looked around: a toilet and a sink with a cabinet under it. She knelt down before the sink and pulled the cabinet door open. In the darkness inside the small compartment, she could see a wrench and a broken piece of pipe with a jagged edge.

"Hurry up!" His voice was edgy.

Don't worry, I will, she thought as she grabbed the pipe, waited an appropriate amount of time, and flushed the toilet.

"Come out of there!"

She opened the door, holding the pipe to her side. He came over to her with his knife held down by his side. With extraordinary strength, she raised the pipe in her right hand and lunged at him. Shocked, he backed away, but there was no way he could avoid the inevitable jab. He slumped to the floor under the steel blow to his side and the knife fell from his hand.

With the pipe still in her hand, she swung it toward his head, but he threw himself around her legs. They fell together, clumsily and heavily. She felt his teeth bite into her side. The pain was blinding. She screamed, and her grip on the pipe relaxed for a moment. He grabbed the pipe, jerking it from her hand and tossing it across the room. It hit the far wall with an incredible crack.

She reached up and grabbed the ski mask, yanking it from his head. She gasped. "Jess!"

She reached up to scratch his face, but he grabbed her arms, and, with great force, pushed them to the floor. He was on top of her now, holding her arms against the hard cement floor. His face was in her face, his breath blowing down on her. His eyes were black narrow pits spewing rage.

"I'm going to kill you, lady. There's no way around it now."

Gulping air, she turned her head away. She couldn't stand to look at him.

* * *

The pain. It was so hard to think with the pain shooting through his head. If he could only get into the stupid database file, it would relieve some of the pain. The phone call hadn't helped matters. It had only made him more nervous and less able to concentrate. *Concentrate, Conrad. Concentrate.* He was going to be too late. He knew he was going to be too late.

CHAPTER 22

Thornton poured himself a strong drink. He was alone in his apartment, and he wanted to get drunk, wanted to forget his loneliness. It had been a tough week. Maybe alcohol could wash thoughts of Van out of his mind.

And there was that stupid kid. It was such a simple case. The kid resented his parents but loved their money. He felt trapped. He wanted freedom and a big wallet. He slipped in on them and shot them to death. Kids like that thought they owned the world, thought they could do anything they wanted and get away with it.

But, behind all his surety, something was bothering Thornton. He pressed his finger on his throbbing cheekbone. Though he tried to ignore it, there was something funny about the whole case. He had to admit there were still holes, unanswered questions. Why did the kid leave his gun where it could be found so easily? Who was the masked man who broke into the Armstrong home? Who was trying to kill Brad? What was so important about that laptop? And to top it all off, Jensen had just located a woman from Arizona with a yellow Volkswagen who was visiting relatives in Salt Lake City. She confirmed that she had gone off the road the previous Friday morning and had been helped by a young man meeting Brad's description, although she wasn't certain of the exact time.

* * *

"I've got it!" Conrad yelled. "I got it!"
Brad and Conrad huddled around the laptop. Brad began to read:

"Long-term test results of Armstrong Pharmaceuticals' weight-loss drug, Tenuis, on test subjects Albert Richards, Mark Wilson, Tongata Uloa, Otto Von Hauser, Peter Andrews. All middle-aged men with mild-to-moderate weight-gain problems. Two subjects show signs of anxiety, insomnia, and dizziness. All subjects experienced addiction and psychiatric disturbances. Three subjects have developed malignant tumors. Drug must be taken off the market and all users notified of dangers."

Brad let his mind run back to the Friday night when Von Hauser came to his see Dad. What was it he had said? *"This isn't enough. I need more. You got me into this, now you're going to get me out."*

Had Von Hauser become addicted? Was he demanding more Tenuis? Was Dad refusing to renew his prescription because he'd become addicted? Why didn't Von Hauser just get a prescription from someone else? Obviously he couldn't afford it. He was getting the drug free from Dad.

Was this what it was all about—a stupid drug? Was Uncle Gordon involved in this? Would he have his son kill his own brother over a stupid drug? Surely this can't be why Jess killed Mom and Dad. There had to be more to it.

"Now what?" Conrad asked.

Brad tried to recall Detective Chandler's words: *"Brad, I—I want you to know I understand what you were telling me about how you don't want to go to medical school. I understand how you hate death and dying, but I think you should stick it out and go."*

"The medical school!" Brad said.

"What?"

"It's a message, Conrad. Detective Chandler was telling me to go to the medical school. It makes sense. Jess has been hanging out at campus, the only part of Salt Lake he knows. He has keys to two places on campus—the dorm room and the pathology lab. That's why Detective Chandler is referring to death and dying."

"Let's call the police, Brad."

Brad glanced at the clock. It was almost time to meet Jess with the laptop. "You call the police, Conrad. Tell them to go to the pathology lab at the medical school."

"What are you going to do?"

"It's time to meet Jess. If I'm not there, he'll kill Detective Chandler."

"You're not going to meet him?"

"No."

Brad dashed down the hall to the back exit stairs. He stumbled down the metal stairs and dashed out into the cold night where heavy snowflakes stung his face. Glancing around, he made sure no one was in sight and disappeared down the snow-covered hillside into a grove of trees. The snow crunched under his feet as he headed toward the medical school.

* * *

Jess had tied Van up again and thrown her in a corner like an old sack of potatoes. He was at the sink, splashing his face, trying to calm himself. Fearfully, she watched as he mended his wounds. He'd been about to kill her. What stopped him? Maybe he was afraid he'd still need her. He didn't have the laptop yet.

She bit her lip against the pain. There was no way out, no way. When he got the laptop, he'd kill her. And Brad would go to jail, possibly die for a crime he didn't commit. She was the only one who knew the truth now. Jess had killed Allen and Peggy Armstrong.

Jess pulled the ski mask over his head. "Well, our time together is almost up. I'm going to go get the laptop."

* * *

Thornton's thoughts were disturbed by his phone ringing. He grabbed it.

"Yeah?"

"Thornton. This is Carmichael. Conrad Henderson just called and said that Brad is at the University of Utah Medical School and that something's going down."

Thornton jumped up from the couch. "Meet me up there, Carmichael. And get Scarface." He slammed the phone down and bolted for the door.

* * *

The sound of breaking glass seemed to resound throughout the whole campus. Brad looked around. The area was deserted. He returned his focus to the basement window he had just smashed with a rock. He sat down on the wet, cold ground and kicked in all the jagged edges. He climbed through the window, landing on his knees in someone's office. He went to the door and opened it. He stuck his head out into the dim hall lit only by a few lights at each stairwell.

He carefully made his way into the hall. The squeaking of his wet shoes annoyed him but couldn't be helped. He made his way down the hall, noticing the sterile scent of the linoleum floors.

He rounded the corner and before him stood two big doors. How was he going to get into the pathology lab? Was Detective Chandler even in there? He glanced at his watch. Jess should be at the meeting place by now. It would take him a few minutes to realize that Brad was not going to show and make his way back here.

He went up to the big doors and knocked. "Detective Chandler? Are you in there?"

He heard a low groan. Her mouth was covered, but she was there. "Don't worry. Stay still. Stay quiet. I'm going to get you out."

* * *

Leaning on her right elbow, Van dragged herself up. She squirmed up against the wall. Raw pain wailed through her arms and legs. She tried rubbing the tape on her face against the wall to wear it off. She had to warn Brad that Jess would be back any minute. Brad would get himself killed.

It was no use. She couldn't get the tape loose. Her face was aching from being rubbed against the cinder block wall. There was no hope for either of them now.

And then she heard it: something thudding against the door. Was Brad coming for her? Was Jess back? Had he killed Brad? Her eyes were fixed on the door. It was opening. She closed her eyes. The light switch clicked on. She blinked at the brightness. Jess was framed in the door, his eyes staring at her through the holes of his mask. He approached with his gun pointing steadily at her.

* * *

As soon as Jess had passed, Brad waited impatiently for the click of the lock and the squeak of the door opening. Assured that Jess was in the room, he stepped out in the hall and cautiously made his way to the steel doors. The door was cracked open, blue fluorescent light spilling into the hall in front of the doors.

Brad peered in the opening. His brain absorbed the nightmarish scene: Detective Chandler half-lying, half-sitting against a cinder block wall, her face and legs bloody, trying to pull away from the figure bent over her.

Brad felt a tremendous surge of power, a terrible burst of energy as he burst through the door and threw himself on Jess, butting his head into Jess's back. Jess sprawled forward, and his gun clanked against the cement floor.

Jess rolled over onto Brad. Brad pushed himself up and rolled over onto Jess. He put his hands around Jess's throat and squeezed. With great force, Jess butted his head into Brad's face, splitting Brad's lip. Brad loosened his grip on Jess's throat and fell back. He could hear frantic, unintelligible sounds coming from Detective Chandler.

Jess was on top of him, his gloved hands wrapped around Brad's throat, choking out air. He was sinking into unconsciousness when the hands loosened their pressure. Brad choked—great gurgling sounds—then opened his eyes. Detective Chandler had worked her way over and was kicking Jess in the side with her tied feet. Jess pushed her back against the wall. She fell back.

With superhuman strength, Brad howled and threw Jess from his body. Jess flew through the air, landing hard against a lab table. Brad scrambled across the floor, grabbed the gun, stood, and pointed it at Jess's head.

"Hold it, Jess, or I'll shoot."

He heard the padding of shoes in the hall. Thornton ran into the room, his gun drawn. Jones, Carmichael, and others hurried in after him.

"Get the guy in the mask," Thornton said.

Some officers ran and grabbed Jess. Brad set down the gun and reached to help Detective Chandler as Thornton cut her ropes. Brad's gaze fell on Thornton's face. What was it he saw there? Shame? Embarrassment? Maybe anger?

* * *

Tuesday, December 23

Again Brad found himself sitting in one of the interview rooms at the Salt Lake City Police Department. His lawyer, Victor Kline, was sitting next to him at a long table. Detective Chandler walked into the room with a middle-aged woman whose salt-and-pepper hair swept back in a bun gave her a certain air of sophistication. The two women sat across the table from them.

"Brad," Detective Chandler said, "this is Pamela Duvall, a counselor who has been working with Jess. I brought her along today because I thought she would be able to answer some of your questions better than I could. Your uncle has waived patient-counselor privilege on Jess's behalf for this purpose."

"Hello," Pamela said and grasped Brad's hand. She then shook Victor Kline's hand.

"Where would you like to begin?" Detective Chandler asked Brad.

"Why? That's all I want to know is why."

Pamela smiled faintly. "I'm afraid you've started with the most difficult question, but I'll try to give you my take on things. For three days now Jess has been talking. I call this purging. It happens often after a killer has been caught. He's been carrying a great weight around, and he's happy to finally unload it on someone who's willing to listen. In an odd sort of way, he is as relieved as the victims and the police that the ordeal is finally over. He's been out of control, unable to rein in his impulses, and, to a degree, grateful to the police for stopping him. Perhaps it will be best if Detective Chandler fills you in on the day-to-day details while I tell you what I think may have been going through Jess's mind at the time. Is that okay, Detective Chandler?"

"Yes," Detective Chandler said. "Let's start with Thursday, December 11, the day before Jess was to leave for Christmas break. He watched you pack that day, Brad. He saw you put the .22 in your duffel bag. He wasn't that interested in what you were doing. It would be later when he recalled that you had packed the gun. Jess got a phone call from his father. His father was very upset and was breathing heavily. He told Jess that he was having chest pains. Gordon and Allen had just argued over the phone. It was all about a drug that Armstrong Pharmaceuticals had marketed, a weight-loss drug. It was FDA approved, and Allen had tested it before it went on the market, but he felt that longer-term testing was needed. However, Gordon had been in a hurry to get it on the market because his competitors were coming out with a similar drug. Gordon went ahead and put the drug on the market, but Allen continued his studies by retaining five test subjects out of the many who had been used in testing the drug. Unlike most of the other subjects, these particular individuals continued to have weight problems, which is why they agreed to continue the testing. That and the money, no doubt. When three of these subjects developed malignant tumors, Allen asked Gordon to pull the drug from the market and do further testing. He also wanted Gordon to make a public statement about the possibility that the drug could cause cancer."

"At this point," Pamela said, "Jess went into some sort of panic mode. He was scared that his father was going to have a heart attack. Gordon added to Jess's stress by making a difficult request. He asked Jess to go to your father's house to talk with him, to reason with him. He had a compromise to offer. Gordon would agree to quietly take the drug off the market as soon as he could replace it with another drug, which he would claim was better. There would be no public statement, and the test subjects would be compensated. This request was especially unusual because Gordon rarely, if ever, asked for help from anyone. He was a very independent individual. Jess took this request to heart. The fact that his father was even asking it told him that his father was desperate. Jess knew that a public statement could open the door for anyone who had ever taken the drug to sue the company. Stocks would obviously drop. There would be a scandal, and the media would be all over this. With Gordon's delicate heart condition, Jess saw this as a threat to his father's life. In Jess's mind, Gordon's request was a cry by Gordon for Jess to save his life. This was compounded with the guilt Jess still feels over the death of his mother. He began to recall his carelessness in driving and his futile efforts to save his mother's life. In his mind, going to his Uncle Allen on behalf of his father was like diving to save his mother. It was a heroic effort to save a parent."

Brad felt tears streaming down his face. He wasn't sure why he was crying. Perhaps it was for Mom and Dad; perhaps it was for Jess and Uncle Gordon; but most likely it was caused by the unfolding background to a senseless act.

"Jess went to talk with your father while you were taking your final exam," Detective Chandler said. "Allen was upset that Gordon had involved Jess. He apparently felt that it was an unfair move on Gordon's part, and he told Jess that. He told Jess that Gordon was greedy, that he didn't care about people, that he was using Jess in his plan to place money before human life. Allen told Jess that Gordon's health problems were a result of his own greed, and that Gordon needed to accept the fact that he had made a bad business decision that was going to cost the company some money. Allen told Jess that he thought Gordon was exaggerating the damage this would do to the company. After all, Allen was a large stockholder in the company, and he was confident that the company could weather the storm."

"The thoughts that were going through Jess's mind at this time were, no doubt, complex," Pamela said. "Jess felt a lot of anger because Allen had hit a nerve when he said that Gordon was using Jess. This implied that perhaps Gordon didn't really love Jess, a fear that Jess had harbored for a very long time, particularly after his mother's death. Apparently, Gordon did blame Jess for the accident and had directed some of his anger toward Jess. Instead of working through their feelings at that time, the two of them suppressed their true feelings and pretended that everything was all right. In Jess's mind, taking care of this problem for his father could put him on the road to redemption. It was an opportunity to regain his father's love by saving his life. Failure was not an option for him. When he left his uncle's house that afternoon, rather than face the actual problem the company was facing head-on, he simplified the problem, turning his uncle into the problem. All he knew was that he had to eliminate the problem, and as he put it, 'one thought led to another thought and another and another.'"

"Jess waited for you to go to sleep that night," Detective Chandler interjected. "He then turned off your alarm clocks and went to your dad's office. His plan was to destroy anything he could that related to Allen's testing of the drug Tenuis. Jess had gone with you a few times to your dad's office; he knew the lock code and where your dad kept his passwords. He also knew from things you had said that your father kept work-related files on his home computer. His clumsy plan was to kill your parents with your gun and let you take the rap for it. He was planning on leaving the next morning for California. Knowing that his father was angry with your father, he thought that his father would be pleased with what he had done. However, at the airport, you mentioned your dad's laptop. Jess had forgotten about the laptop. He knew there could be incriminating evidence in there concerning the drug testing. He got rid of you as quickly as possible at the airport and doubled back. Our mistake was that we failed to check the airport records concerning Jess's flight. We just weren't focused on Jess."

"It's at this point that Jess begins to follow the pattern of a spree killer," Pamela said. "The first act of killing was impulsive, irrational, perhaps insane, but when things are not working out, the killer reacts to every perceived threat with the same solution—murder."

"Jess went back to the dorms," Detective Chandler said. "All of the dorms except one were being closed for the holidays. With no one in your dorm and very few people still on campus, Jess would hang out in your dorm room and in the pathology lab. He almost got caught when we arrived to search the place on Saturday morning but managed to hide in a bathroom down the hall. He called his father Friday morning. Gordon was furious, but because he really did love Jess, he wanted to protect him. He demanded that Jess come home immediately where the two of them could figure out what to do. At that point, Jess hadn't explained everything to Gordon. He didn't tell him that he had framed you, Brad."

The door opening interrupted Detective Chandler's explanation. Detective Thornton walked into the room, closing the door behind him. "Sorry I'm late. I was in the captain's office." He glanced at Brad and then looked away. He grabbed a chair from the corner and sat beside Detective Chandler. Brad felt none of the anger that used to come with Thornton's presence. He felt a little sorry for Thornton. This had no doubt been a humiliating experience for him. He was apparently humbled by it, and Brad was somehow satisfied with that. Knowing now what had happened somehow calmed his emotions and at the same time filled him with profound sorrow.

"His father's anger was perceived as rejection," Pamela said. "Jess still wanted to prove himself to his father. He desperately wanted his father's love. In his bewilderment over Jess's actions, Gordon tried to explain to Jess that what he had done had not helped their situation one bit. There were still five long-term test subjects out there, and Allen had possibly told them about the drug already. They were all living proof to the drug's possible side effects."

"What Gordon unwittingly did," Detective Chandler said, "was suggest to Jess that he needed to get rid of these five men as well. Jess told his father he would get home as soon as he safely could. However, he planned to come home with the news that he had taken care of the threat posed by the five test subjects. He killed two of them that very night after tracking them down using information he had gained from Allen's files. He also broke into your house that night to look for the laptop. He was on an adrenaline high, which is why he was able to get hit and jump through windows without serious injury. He almost got caught in the dorms again the night we went there looking for you. He once again hid without being detected, but he heard Thornton mention that you might be in your dad's office. He watched from behind some trees as the police went in looking for you. After they left, he waited and saw you come out of the building. He followed you down to the Rio Grande area. He waited all night for you. He followed you the next day. When he saw you come out of Amazing Computers with the laptop, he panicked once again."

"It's all so stupid," said Brad. "Jess is a smart guy. This doesn't sound like him at all. He had to know the more bodies that started showing up, the more likely he would be caught."

"You're assuming that Jess was using logic," Pamela said. "Jess was being motivated by his emotions, which he had lost control of. Of course, emotions are linked to thoughts, and Jess wasn't thinking right. Somewhere along the line, Jess snapped. We don't know exactly why or how it happens, but it does happen. We can see the tragic stories of such cases on the news on any given night."

"There is also evidence of rational thought, though," Thornton said. "Jess admits that he killed both Wilson and Richards in the Rio Grande area, but he dumped Richards' body in the Jordan River so police wouldn't connect the two deaths. He also hit them over the head to avoid the gunshot sounds, but he managed to get Uloa in his stolen car, which is why he was able to shoot him in a remote area. Von Hauser had to be hit too because someone in the building could have heard the shots."

"You no doubt want to make sure he doesn't get off using the insanity plea," Kline said.

"You got it," Thornton said.

"The human psyche is quite complex," Pamela said. "The insanity defense absolves from punishment an individual who knows what he is doing yet is driven to kill by delusions, fears, or compulsions. The idea is that the mind can be impaired in numerous ways that we don't really fully understand."

"I believe it rests on the notion that a killer knows what is right and wrong and still acts wrongly," Thornton said.

"Obviously Jess was thinking impulsively, not thinking things through," Detective Chandler said. "Look at his plan to kidnap me. He wanted the laptop. That was his focus. It didn't occur to him that Brad could download any information in the laptop."

"Of course he planned on killing Brad once he got the laptop anyway," Thornton said. "He was going to make it look like a suicide. He still thought he could pin the whole thing on Brad."

"What about Uncle Gordon?" Brad asked.

"He will be charged as an accessory," Thornton said.

"His plan seems to have been to get Jess home to California and to get you acquitted for your parents' murders," Detective Chandler said. "However, he couldn't control Jess's actions any more than Jess could. Jess ditched him at the airport after the funeral. Gordon blames himself for Jess's actions. He was, after all, angry when he called Jess on Thursday afternoon. However, no one could have guessed that the things he said would have led to murder."

"Like I said," Pamela added, "the human mind is a complex thing. The antecedent that pushed Jess to murder could go as far back as his early childhood. Who can understand how a complex set of thought patterns and incidents converge in such a way that a mind goes haywire?"

"Do you have any other questions, Brad?" Detective Chandler asked.

"Just one. What happened to the fifth test subject?"

"He's still alive," Detective Chandler said. "Jess was having a hard time getting to him. We know he was still planning on killing him before he left for California."

"I don't think I want to hear any more today," Brad said.

Detective Chandler stood up. "You can call us anytime"

Thornton stood up. "Brad, I want to apologize. It was a tough case. We . . . I . . . made some mistakes." Thornton held out his hand.

Brad smiled and then grasped Thornton's hand. "It's okay. We all made some mistakes, and it worked itself out in the end."

Brad and Kline stood and walked toward the door. Pamela followed. Thornton turned to Detective Chandler. "I owe you an apology too, Detective Chandler. I said some things I had no right to and didn't really mean. I want you to know that I respect you as a detective and think you have a lot to offer our department."

Detective Chandler held her hand out to Thornton. "It's okay, Detective Thornton. Like Brad said, we all made our share of mistakes. I said some things I shouldn't have as well. It did work out in the end."

Thornton grasped her hand. "I suppose it made for a lousy weekend."

"Actually, it was one of the best weekends I've had in a long time. I called my mom and dad and talked with them for a long time. I might even go visit them this summer."

"Really," Thornton said. "That's good news."

EPILOGUE

Six Months Later

Brad sat nervously on the stand as Bishop Henderson spoke to the congregation.

"Brothers and sisters, as you know this is a special day for my family. We have had the honor of adding a new family member to our home this year. Bradley Armstrong has lived with us while completing his first year at the University of Utah. As most of you know, Brad is majoring in journalism at the U. While Darlene and I know we can never replace his remarkable parents, we do want Bradley to know that we think of him as a second son."

Bishop Henderson turned and smiled at Brad. Brad returned the smile. The bishop continued: "When I think of Brad, I think of obedience in the face of adversity. When I look at Brad, I am reminded on a daily basis that the Lord provides trials and afflictions for those that He loves. I thank the Lord daily that Brad has prepared himself to go on a mission. I will now ask Brad to address us, and then I will have a few closing remarks."

Brad stood and walked to the podium. He looked out on the smiling faces of the congregation. They had become like family as they supported him in his struggles after the loss of his parents. Brad looked down at Conrad, who would be leaving on a mission himself next month, then over at Darlene, who was wiping her running makeup as she cried. He glanced to the back of the room where he saw Detective Chandler with her new boyfriend, Matthew. When Brad had called Detective Chandler to invite her to hear him speak, they had both laughed when she told him she was dating a lawyer.

Brad cleared his throat. "When the bishop asked me to speak on any topic that I felt inspired to speak on today, my mind reviewed the events of the last six months, and I tried to determine what I have learned from everything that has happened to me. Eventually three words came to mind—*justice, judgment,* and *freedom.*

"I would like to start with justice. A reporter asked me if I was satisfied that justice was served in the case against those involved with my parents' deaths. I thought I knew what he meant by that word, *justice.* He meant revenge, exacting the last pound of flesh for the wrong done to me. In that sense, the answer is no. And I don't believe justice, in the gospel meaning of the term, is ever being served if our motive is revenge. Vengeance is not justice. It is only ruthlessness. It does not bring peace. Believe me, I know. It only brings anger and vindictiveness. Instead of happiness, it brings despair.

"I don't believe a mortal remedy exists for every wrong committed against us on this earth, nor do I believe in earthly compensation for every worldly loss. However, I think we are compensated in a spiritual sense for these things. Our goal in this life is to become like Christ— not to act like Christ, but to actually become like Christ. This means we have to have a change of heart, a conversion. Such a transformation often comes about more readily through suffering and adversity than by comfort and tranquility. The Lord has promised us that He will consecrate our afflictions for our gain. This is real justice, real compensation—perhaps the only compensation we should expect from life.

"We can expect to be tried in the furnace of afflictions in this life. Some of you have already experienced this. Some of you have suffered the death of a loved one. Perhaps for some of you this loss seemed unjust, which only adds to the trial's intensity. Some of you suffer from debilitating illnesses. Some of you have suffered abuse of one kind or another. Some of you struggle with feelings of rejection, inadequacy, or depression. In such cases where your suffering is not plainly apparent, you often find yourself suffering alone.

"In too many cases, we may mistakenly think the Lord is trying to teach us to act in certain ways. Like rats that feel an electric shock, we no longer take that path of the maze. I don't think that's what the Lord has in mind for us. He's not so concerned with how we act as He is with what we become.

"The reason charity never fails is that it is not an act but a condition of being. Charity is something one becomes. This leads me to my next topic—judgment. I believe the final judgment is not going to be a summation of good and evil acts. I don't believe it's going to be about what we have done. I believe it is going to be about what we have become. The question won't be: 'What did you do on the earth?' The question may very well be, 'Have you become like Christ?' Being like Christ means that we love our neighbors and our enemies and are very careful in the manner in which we judge them.

"Too often we judge others by what they do and how they act and not by what they are or what they can become. Too often we judge people by what they wear and what they say. We judge them by the type of house they live in or the kind of car they drive. We even judge them by where they live and whom they know. Christ was able to look through all of this to see the heart. We should pray for the gift of discernment. What a great gift to be able to discern the heart of an individual without being swayed by the earthly trappings of appearance.

"As mortals, we have a very difficult time judging the heart. We don't know why people do what they do. We don't know everything that a person has experienced in life. We don't know all their pains or their heartaches and sadness. As the hymn says, 'In the quiet heart is hidden sorrow that the eye can't see.' I believe this is why the Lord has told us to judge not that we be not judged. The chances are too great that we will misjudge. When and if we make it to the celestial kingdom, we might be very surprised at who we find there.

"Instead of being judgmental of others, let's concentrate on loving others. If we must err, let's err on the side of mercy and love. Harsh judgment, I believe, leads to despair. Love and mercy fills our lives with hope and encouragement.

"I would like to conclude by talking about freedom. It's something I've been thinking a lot about over the past several months. It's something that has come to mean a lot to me. I believe that true freedom, no matter what our circumstances in life, can only come through the Atonement of Jesus Christ. Jesus said, 'And ye shall know the truth, and the truth shall make you free (John 8:32).' I believe that with all my heart.

"At this point in my life, I plan on putting the past behind me. It's done and over with, and there's nothing I can do about it. I, of course, understand that the past is a part of me, and experiences, wonderful experiences that I had with my parents, are a part of who I am, what I have become. In this sense, my parents will always be with me. I don't expect I'll dwell too much on the future, either. I suppose I could fear it if I dwelt on it enough, but I don't know what that will bring me other than fear. None of us know what it's going to bring, so perhaps we should concentrate on living in the present and concerning ourselves with what we are becoming today. In the next two years, I am going to concentrate on being the best person I can be each day. I'm going to concentrate on what I'm doing to others more than on what they are doing to me. I'm going to try to be like Christ. Hopefully, when you see me in two years, I will have become someone better, someone more like Him."

ABOUT THE AUTHOR

J. Michael Hunter was born and raised in the Blue Ridge Mountains of Virginia. He received a B.A. in history and a master's degree in Library and Information Science from Brigham Young University. He received a second master's degree in humanities with an emphasis in history from California State University, Dominguez Hills.

Michael has worked as a reference librarian in the Church Historical Department, Salt Lake City, and was the American, British, and Mormon History librarian at the Harold B. Lee Library at Brigham Young University for three years. Currently, he is the Mormon Studies Librarian and head of the Religion and Family History section at the Lee Library.

Michael has also published over twenty articles about the history of Utah and the Latter-day Saints.

He resides in Lehi, Utah, with his wife LeAnn and their three children: Victoria, Elizabeth, and Cody.